VIA Folios 145

The End of Aphrodite

The End of Aphrodite

Laurette Folk

BORDIGHERA PRESS

Library of Congress Control Number: 2019943038

Printed in the United States.

Published by
BORDIGHERA PRESS
John D. Calandra Italian American Institute
25 West 43rd Street, 17th Floor
New York, NY 10036

VIA Folios 145
ISBN 978-1-59954-150-1

CONTENTS

For Lauretta

It came to me one night as I was falling asleep
that I had finished with those amorous adventures
to which I had long been a slave. Finished with love?
my heart murmured. To which I responded that many profound
    discoveries
awaited us . . .

LOUISE GLÜCK

Part I

MERMAID
Samantha, 1986

Etta was the silhouette truckers had on the flaps over their tires. Her hair turned blue in the sun. She had eyes the color of the rocks after the tide went out. She terrified me. She thrilled me. The summer she lived with us, I defied my father and his warnings of the treacherous riptide and followed Etta to Salt Island during a full or new moon—only then does the sea part enough to expose a path through the water to the rocky shoals. Etta dove into the water crisscrossing over the sandbar and swam its length. When she came up her hair was a long fin. We rummaged through the brush and found fire pits with beer tabs and, like primitive people, squatted on our haunches, sifting through the ash and shards of glass to find usable relics. She showed me how to take beer can tabs and curl the tab part over the handle part, connecting them to one another in strands for necklaces and bracelets. I thought maybe we could build a hut and buy a rowboat and marry sailors, giving birth to babes as slick as seal pups, birthing them in tidal pools, where they slipped into the foaming waves, lost.

I went with my mother to see Etta in her new home in February, around Valentine's Day. I was anxious to see her and embarrassed by my sentimental feelings. I had hardly spoken a word to her since my fifteenth birthday in November. It was the funk I was in; lethargy was a viscous liquid, pouring heavy on me and turning into pounds as I occupied my days with soap operas, fattening snacks, and stale fantasies. Now it was winter. Even the morning sun seemed to be a frozen pink orb sitting on the icebergs off Good Harbor, ready to crack in half if you blew your warm life breath on it.

We drove up the long sloping driveway, wet from melting ice, and parked next to Patrick's yellow Volkswagen Bug with a Vietnam Vet plate. The Bug sat in front of a dilapidated shed that had a sagging roof and peeling white paint. Behind us the entire house was peeling white paint, a grander version of the shed. It was an old farmhouse built in 1874, as the plaque near the front door stated. Etta appeared at a side door in a gray button-down sweater, something an old spinster might wear. Her dark eyes were void of that black coal eyeliner, her trademark.

She was more reserved, and I thought of the Portuguese Virgin Mary statue downtown when I looked at her. "The Blessed Mama is preggers there," my friend Noline told me once when we were cutting across the lawn of the church last summer.

My mother went to her sister, perfunctorily hugged her and kissed her on the cheek. My emotional energy dissipated watching them greet each other; I didn't want to look like a fool and get all crazy with tears and such, so I kissed hello, stoically, just like my mother did.

I asked for the bathroom, a refuge to be alone for a moment to compose myself. I checked behind the shower curtain to view the tub, brown with age around the basin. There were bottles of shampoo and an old back-scrubbing brush hanging from the showerhead. I could see myself in the fixtures, a Samantha with a distorted head. Etta had cleaned this bathroom before we came. I opened the cabinet behind the mirror and spied razors, a bottle of aspirin, hemorrhoid cream, Scope mouthwash, and cotton balls. Typical bathroom toiletries. Much to my disappointment, my aunt and her lover appeared to be as normal as everyone else.

Next to the bathroom was a door to a separate room. I peered inside to find a mountain of junk, dressers, box springs, a white birdcage, oval framed pictures of people long dead, the television set with rabbit ears. On a dresser next to the door, resting atop a crocheted doily, was a Polaroid picture of a woman with cat eye glasses and white hair, wearing a lavender housedress. She looked like the Grateful Dead skeleton with skin draped over it. It must have been Patrick's mother; someone had stuffed what was left of her in this room. I closed the door and went to the kitchen where my mother and Etta were having a casual conversation about the house. Etta called Patrick's mother "the old lady," and was bemoaning the effort it took to put the house back in order. "The tub was full of dishes; there was so much shit on the floor you couldn't walk from one room to the next." She lowered her voice and said, "The neighbor found the old lady lying in the living room with maggots in her eye sockets."

"That's horrible," my mother said. "Where was Patrick?"

"Living and working in Boston at the time. He came up on weekends sometimes."

"How old was she?"

"Oh you know, eighties. She was a tough old coot," Etta replied. "Didn't like to let people in her house."

Etta said they put in the French doors to the dining room, called an exterminator, kicked out the raccoons in the fireplace. "Could you imagine?" My mother shook her head. Etta said she stripped the furniture, bought new curtains. She loved the place because it had charm, despite the water stains on the ceiling and the crumbling horse-hair plaster walls.

"I had to repaint the cabinets," Etta continued.

"You did a nice job," my mother said, examining her sister's work.

"Thanks," Etta said and smiled warmly. Both women simultaneously looked my way for a moment to invite me in to the conversation, and I noticed that they had the same pair of eyes. I had not seen it so pronounced before, this resemblance between them.

"Is it haunted?" I asked.

"Not that I know of," said my aunt.

"So," my mother said, "what are your plans?"

"Plans?"

"Yeah."

"What do you mean."

"Are you going to make this official?"

"This? You mean, shall I get a stamped piece of paper? I don't think it's necessary," Etta said.

"OK," my mother said. And that was that. She was calm, her face was not contorted in frustration, her mouth was not tightly shut, her eyebrows were not elevated in anger. I waited for something from Etta, but she turned away, went to the refrigerator and bent over to retrieve a Pepperidge Farm icebox cake. Etta sat down, pulled the cake from the box and cut into that delectable chocolate frosting with a butter knife. I nearly started to shiver with anticipation. That's when my mother said, "Not too big. She's got to watch it."

"What do you mean I have to watch it?" I asked.

"You've got to watch how much you eat. You're becoming voluptuous."

Me, watch it? I still had the image of my girl body, thin legs and arms, bony knees and elbows. My image of myself was distorted, as it was the time I was six and I thought I could fall through the slits on the boardwalk down by St. Peter's Marina during Fiesta. My father had to put me up over his shoulders to keep me from becoming hysterical. It was the same ridiculous, childish thought—the thought that I could fall through a slit and the thought that I could fit into some of the pants you find on the rack at The Limited and Express.

"I'm getting fat," I said to Etta. "Voluptuous is another word for fat."

"That's not what I said. You're exaggerating," my mother interjected.

"She's becoming a woman," Etta said. "This is what happens. Women become . . . soft."

The truth is, my body was transforming into my mother's body. My knees were becoming her knees, big knees with little fat dimples around them. My spare tire belly, hers too. Etta, though rounder, did not have the patches of fat around the knees.

I had taken a few bites of the cake and pushed it aside. I would stop stuffing myself right then and there. I would start running.

"Oh just eat it for cryin' out loud," Etta said.

"No."

"OK, fine." Etta stabbed it with her fork and stuffed half of it in her face.

After we had our cake, we went to the nursery where Etta had just painted the walls a lime green. There were framed pictures of cartoon bunnies and duckies, a nest of eggs over the crib. All of the furniture was freshly painted white. A baby's quilt with knitted rattles and bears was draped over the crib. Somehow it all seemed right. My mother fingered the fabric. "Lovely," she said. Then we climbed the narrow staircase to Patrick's studio where there were holes and strips of torn wallpaper. Patrick was standing at an easel with his John Lennon glasses hanging at the tip of his nose. He seemed less arthritically stiff, and I noticed then how the extra scruff of his unshaven face had made him seem more male, as did the flannel shirt with a small patch of hair sneaking up over the top button. In that moment I could see how Etta found Patrick attractive.

"My, you have quite a view from up here," my mother said.

"Yes," he said. "I find it peaceful."

The pink was settling to gray outside and it was colder; the melting snow was starting to crystallize into winter again. Patrick's studio was drafty but equipped with a heater that smelled like electricity, the coils inside blazing a neon fire. There was a boom box playing Chopin, canvases of all shapes and sizes with horrid blotches of paint. Coffee cans of brushes, crowded wooden benches, piles of pictures of men dressed in camouflage, goofing around with their helmets resting on their machine guns, or looking bored, smoking. On the wood floor were splotches of paint framed with masking tape. I noticed one of the framings was reproduced on a canvas resting on an easel. Patrick informed me these painting were his "gravity" series. "It was serendipitous," he said. "I got the idea when I looked down at the paint that dripped onto the floor and liked the design there better than the one on the canvas. Your mind can't help but play with it, you know, like a Rorschach test."

"So in actuality, the viewer is the artist," Etta said.

"Interesting," my mother said, bored.

"What do you see here?" Patrick asked us, holding up the canvas of scarlet red blotches.

"Paint," my mother said.

"I see red climbing roses, like the ones on the side of the house last summer," Etta offered.

"What do you see, Samantha?" Patrick asked.

"I see a head wound."

"Hmmm. Yes," Patrick said. "Exactly."

I wandered around the room, until I found a painting of Etta in the nude. Oh here we go, I thought. Upon a closer look, it was indeed lovely, not in a Botticelli kind of way, but an Egon Schiele kind of way: less ethereal goddess, more visceral human. Patrick had given Etta's body his complete attention, every stroke, a rendering of truth.

"Huh," my mother said, viewing the painting.

"This is how we met. Patrick asked me if I would model."

"She's my muse." Patrick regarded Etta with a countenance of pure love. "Here, there are more," he said, and hobbled over to the wall, pointing to a few canvases on the floor. I wondered then, as I watched him move without his cane, if there was shrapnel in his legs.

The paintings revealed how Etta's body changed with her pregnancy, how the hips rounded, the belly and the breasts bloomed. It was a manifestation of Etta's personal celebration, the burgeoning body, the lowered eyelids, the smile of subtle joy.

"Well Etta, thank God Pop is dead because if he weren't, this would surely kill him," my mother said.

Etta rolled her eyes at my mother. "But what do you think?"

My mother went closer to the paintings. She stepped back, tilted her head some more. "What do I think? What do you want me to say?"

"One word," Etta said. "Give me one word."

My mother didn't answer. She went to Etta and put her hand on her belly and rested it there. Etta put her hand over my mother's. I felt the need to hide when I looked at them.

"Why don't you two stay for dinner? We have plenty," Etta asked.

"Oh no," my mother said, withdrawing her hand. "There's nothing in the house. I was going to stop off at the market on the way home. Sam can stay."

"I have homework."

"It's Friday night. And you don't have any plans. You never do."

"In that case, you can sleep over," Etta said. "Patrick is going to make *paella*."

"Wow," my mother said. "A man who cooks and paints his girlfriend in the nude. What more could a woman ask for?"

Etta draped a white cloth over the dining room table and lit slender white candles while Patrick hummed to the soft jazz record on the stereo as he shucked and chopped. He placed the meal in an exotic clay pot and baked it in the oven. Etta poured me some red wine in a long-stemmed glass and melted Brie to swipe with crackers. They moved in and out of each other's space without touching, and I wondered whether they were just being polite, squelching any tendencies toward affection for my sake. And I felt like a guest, not a kid. They asked me questions, and I told them my thoughts. They considered my thoughts. We talked about art—Patrick was studying Pollock and Etta was reading Whitman. It was comfortable and congenial being in their house of sin, as my mother often referred to it, and I opted to stay for the night instead of hightailing it home. Plus, the wine made me unbearably sleepy, as did the heat hissing and clanging from the radiators in the dining room.

It was cold in the bedroom, and I immediately sobered up. I could see into the neighboring house perfectly from Patrick's old bedroom; someone was watching the television show *Barnaby Jones*. I waited to see the person who'd found the old coot with her eye sockets full of maggots, but he must have been sitting out of my view, asleep on the couch or engaged in some task. I made sure the shades were pulled down so the person couldn't see how, when I removed my bra, my breasts hung down like eggplants. I looked at myself in the mirror and the cold aroused me. I became strange, perverted, in Patrick's old bedroom.

There was still a masculine feel to the room, despite Etta's attempt at neutralizing it with feminine attributes—a mauve quilt with eyelet pillow shams and valence curtains. The room with its dark colonial furniture reminded me of the inside of a ship. Above the bed hung, most appropriately, a painting of a vessel in a storm (obviously done in an earlier period). There was a dusty bottle of Brut on the dresser, and adhered to the old, colonial desk was a sticker of the Grateful Dead skeleton, wearing a wig and holding a red rose in its bony hand. Patrick's senior picture rested on the desk, and I picked it up to look at it more closely. He had calm eyes, blond hair brushing his shoulders, cheeks with a slight dimple in the smile. I thought of pressing the cool glass to my bare chest.

My aunt had given me one of her nightgowns, a long black satin gown with spaghetti straps and lace at the bust and hem. I looked as if I were ready for a tryst. There was a knock at the door then, and my aunt peeked her head in.

"Look at you," she said. I crossed my arms over my chest in response. Etta waltzed in. "Do you need a robe? Here, let me go and get you a robe. It can get drafty in this house." She went to fetch the robe and I pulled back the covers and burrowed into the bed. I was chilled to the bone. Etta came back in and draped her blue robe across the mauve quilt. "There are some blankets in the hall closet if you need them. I just changed the sheets on this bed, so they are clean. Anything else?" she asked.

"Nothing I can think of."

"OK then," Etta said, her lips forming a cryptic smile. "You know, I thought of you the other day. A woman was shaping a mermaid in the sand down at the beach. When she left I went up to it, and I saw your face."

"Is she still there?" I asked.

"She slipped under the water when the tide came in. It reminded me of the sailor story Daniel used to tell of a young girl who was sold as a wife to an old man. She tried to kill herself by diving off a cliff into the ocean, but instead of dying, she was transformed when she hit the water."

"Into what?" I asked.

"A Selkie, a mermaid, some type of sea creature."

The floorboards in the hallway creaked. Etta's face registered someone there; she murmured something to Patrick as he passed her.

"You seem happy here. Happier than when you lived with Daniel."

"It's a borrowed house, Samantha."

"Patrick doesn't own it?"

"I don't own it. Night night," she said, and switched off the light.

I turned to the window to see if my friend Barnaby was awake, but the television and the lights were shut off, and I could see nothing but darkness and a figure swimming through it. "There is no man," I told her and pulled the shade.

§

She had come to us after the separation, after Daniel had left to go live on his boat. We had seen him once on Salt Island when we were on the rocks; like us, he was looking for a hideout. Etta acknowledged him with a raised eyebrow and turned her back. He waited for her to turn around, looked at me; his face was scrawnier then, unshaven. Young. I couldn't speak, and it seemed wrong because I called him Uncle and he sat at our table and told us sailor stories and jokes; he fixed his motorcycle with my father's tools. I remember how his goodbye kiss smelled of beer and cloves. He ceded the place to us; we left shortly after, when others made their way through the brush, lovers looking for a place to be alone.

My aunt Etta kept her clothes in an opened suitcase in the corner of the room; silk underwear, tank tops, baby doll negligees, faded jeans, black bras, heaped in a pile. Sometimes, when she wasn't home, I wore the negligees, fit the hoops in my ears and modeled for the mirror. I closed the door, peeled off my panties, heard the waves swish across the sand, the sea pull at her slips, claiming the shoreline again and again. Our crooked house creaked. It felt like sin, that loose lace.

On Saturday nights I fell asleep waiting for her to come home. At three in the morning when the moon was high, she stumbled her way to the suitcase, fumbling through silks and cotton, bending her arms like folded wings to unstrap her bra in the blue white moonlight, then, groping for the end of the bed, finding the top sheet, pulling it back, pausing, waiting to hear me breathe. She laid down her hips; I smelled whiskey. Sunday mornings meant the early Mass and a pancake breakfast afterward. Etta stayed behind and slept through both. I would come home with a newly purified soul and tread lightly around my aunt, the sinner, trading a paisley skirt for my well-worn blue jeans. Etta descended when the breakfast table was abandoned, save the syrup-stained dishes and my mother, reading the Sunday paper, her reading glasses balanced precariously on the tip of her nose. Etta, dressed in a powdered blue robe missing its tie, a knot in the back of her head from her thrashing, sat across from her sister, cupping her black coffee and staring at a small hole in the tablecloth. To sit between them would be to interfere with the thought waves they had bouncing off one another; this is how they communicated at times, silently, below any frequency the rest of us could understand.

My mother flipped the page of the newspaper, pretending to be nonchalant. She played it cool with her sister and tolerated her lifestyle as she would a rash, something you had to wait out until it ran its course.

"There's pancake batter in the fridge," my mother said.

"I'm not much of a breakfast eater," Etta said.

Etta outstretched a leg, sipped from her coffee cup. She waited, continued to stare at the hole.

"You going back to the house?" my mother asked.

"It's not my house."

"It was your house," my mother retorted, under her breath. Somebody's got to give it a good cleaning before the realtor shows up."

"I'm not dealing with that *bullshit.*"

"*Someone* has to deal with the bullshit," my mother said. "And what about all of Mom and Dad's furniture? We need to bring it all back here. Put it in the basement. Again."

Other words were exchanged, and I waited for my mother to break, to be kind, to say something soothing to her sister, but she didn't. Couldn't.

Etta waited a while for the request to settle in and gnaw at her, then she rose from her chair, went to the sink, dumped her coffee and shuffled back upstairs to her lair, cursing my mother under her breath.

My mother, the elder, more responsible sister, went to the house where Etta and Daniel lived to retrieve some of the heirlooms, specifically, the Venetian glass goblets my grandparents bought on a trip to Italy, my grandmother's china and her wedding dress. She came in with a big garbage bag with the wedding dress in it and handed it to me to put in the cedar closet downstairs. I hid there, took off my clothes and fit myself inside the regality of tulle and satin, of virgin white. I looked down at the gaping satin bustier and my girl breasts; they were small birds. I danced and thought of Etta dancing with Daniel on their wedding night, how they left the surface of the earth and took long strides in the evening sky.

I eventually abandoned the dress for the veil and would return several times that summer, surreptitiously, to undress and pull the tulle tightly around my skin, wrapping my entire naked body up like a cocoon. I thought of the monarch butterfly we kept in a cooler in the back of Mr. Padfield's fourth grade class; as it matured you could see more and more of its wings: a thing serene and folded. Waiting.

I confided in Etta about my heart's affections. This was not an easy thing to do; merely saying the name of my beloved could result in an outbreak of hives. I sought Etta's advice because it was obvious men liked *her*, but she hardly took me seriously. "Just be yourself," she would say. "What are you worried about?" She didn't understand my predicament, the urgency intermixed with terror. She didn't understand what it was to be shy.

I had liked Scott Sorrensen since the fourth grade. Back in elementary school, there was no question he liked me. He used to place me before him in the softball and kickball lineups. Once he locked me in the janitor's closet and another time he taped my hair to the desk. I made note of his forearms, out of the corner of my eye, the thick veins pushed to the surface by firm muscle. I wasn't particularly certain of the color of his eyes because I could not hold his gaze for any longer than a millisecond. I knew his body, however, his square shoulders, his broad chest, that tight butt in his Levis.

I looked for Mrs. Sorrensen's green station wagon with the faux wood paneling everywhere I went, at the mall, at the supermarket, at stoplights, on the highway. I told myself it was only a matter of time before I saw it in the right place at the right time. I fantasized about what would occur, how Scott would find me in the cereal aisle in the supermarket. He would look incredulous. Then he would smile. *It's you*, he would say.

My friend Noline tried to convince me Scott was a flying asshole. We were in Noline's kitchen at the time, baking honey cookies because Noline's mother was a health freak and believed honey was healthier than sugar. (This caused Noline to eat all the sugar-filled things we had at my house: cookies, ice cream, you name it.) She asked me why I liked Scott and my reply was that he was cute and had a nice body.

"But you never talk to him, Sam. Ever. You never know, he could be a flying asshole."

Flying asshole was the brainchild of Noline and her Catholic school friends. At her birthday party, they sat around laughing, drawing butt cheeks with wings coming out of them. I thought it very weird that girls who went to a Jesus school had such devil mouths. *I* never used the word asshole. I never swore; if I wanted to give my brother the middle finger, I gave him the ring finger instead. I was afraid of sinning. I was afraid of making Yahweh mad, because if Yahweh got mad, bad things happened; cities were burned to ashes or drowned by floods, people turned to salt. It was better to stay on his good side.

It was painfully obvious I was a romantic when I attended my first school dance. I wore a white shirt with pearl buttons and a rose petal skirt with silk stockings. I went with my friend Evelyn who wore a yellow skirt with white sandals and her long blond hair in a bun secured with a daisy flower barrette. My mother took a picture of us in front of the lamppost on the front lawn just before the sun went down; with our bright clothing we appeared holy in the darkening grass. Evelyn and I spoke anxiously in the backseat of my mother's car of who would go, what music would be played. I pictured tables with ironed linens, votive candles, slender vases with single red roses. The boys would be dressed in button down shirts with ties and black-laced shoes. Evelyn thought the gym would have streamers and possibly punch in a crystal bowl, but

I told her no, ficus trees with lights and maybe an arbor, and yes, the punch bowl. There would be slow dancing. She said boys would press their hands to our backs and whisper how lovely we looked in our ears. I went with fervent hope that Scott would be there.

We arrived late, the only ones walking down the semi-lit hallway, toward the throbbing beat in the gym. It was dark and colored lights from a strobe were ricocheting off the walls; from what I could see there were no ficus trees. Everyone was dressed in jeans and concert t-shirts. Boys and girls gathered in clumps with some girls scurrying as messengers from one boy clump back to a girl clump. Evelyn and I moved along the back wall, away from the speakers that blasted "Centerfold" by the J. Geils Band. We hid in the corner and stayed there for most of the night, unsure of what to do. I continuously glanced at the doors to the gym, to see if Scott would appear, but he didn't. An hour later, I was exhausted by my own allegiance to him. Then a boy, Bobby Marino, approached us wearing a Kiss concert t-shirt and cutoffs; his hair was parted down the middle and impeccably feathered. Both the boys and girls in each clump were now staring at us, whispering.

Bobby Marino was a burnout. He was liked among the burnout girls who smoked and did drugs and got drunk. But in that moment that Bobby was walking toward me, a scene flashed in my mind of Bobby and me lying on a blanket in the grass; he had his head in my lap and I was stroking his feathered hair. I could make concessions, I decided.

Bobby Marino leaned over and shouted in my ear. "Do you want to see something?"

He produced a baggie from his pocket. From what I could see there was something small in it, like a turd. He put the bag in my hand. "Do you know what this is?" he asked. I felt the thing through the bag and peered closely to observe what appeared to be shredded leaves and stems; I knew what it was, but I opted to play dumb, to be the idiot he thought I was, because it was easier that way.

"Tea?"

He laughed and the strobe flashed off his braces.

"I can get you high, little girl. Do you want to get high?" he asked.

"No," I immediately replied.

"I didn't think so," he said laughing. Then he walked away toward the boy clump and shouted in their ears. They all started laughing. I bit my lip. Evelyn asked me what happened. "Nothing," I said and went to the pay phone in the hallway to call my mother to come and fetch me.

It was that night that Etta gave me the notebook and set me on my path.

She was perched up in bed with her reading glasses on, engrossed in a book. "Home so soon?"

"It was ridiculous," I said, tossing my sandals in the closet. "I'm ridiculous."

"Why are you ridiculous?"

"Because I am naïve."

"Why are you naïve?"

"There was no dancing. People just stood around in jeans and t-shirts shouting over the music. I thought it would be different. I thought there would be red roses in vases on white linen table cloths."

"Of course you did," my aunt said.

"So you think I am naïve too," I said. I took off my clothes and put on my nightgown; then I pulled the covers over my head. My aunt tugged them off of me. "I think you are imaginative," she said. "And I think you are perceptive." She reached down by the side of the bed. "I have something for you." She handed me a thin, flexible thing wrapped gingerly with a pink bow and purple tissue paper. "I was going to give it to you tomorrow, but you seem to need it now."

I accepted it, perplexed; there was no occasion. I was uncomfortable when someone gave me something and there was no occasion. "Why are you giving me this?"

"Because no one ever gave it to me and I know better."

I unwrapped the gift carefully, making sure not to tear the tissue so that I could save it. On the cover were the title *A Woman's Notebook* and a subtitle that said "a blank book with quotes by women." I turned the pages, each with a quote and a sketch of a lotus, a rose, or some other delicate flower. I read the first quote, "The purpose of life, after all is to live it, to taste experience to the utmost, to reach out eagerly and without fear for newer and richer experience. Eleanor Roosevelt, 1884-1962, American Stateswoman."

"I thought you might find the quotes inspiring," Etta said.

I savored the pages of the journal between my fingers. The word "papyrus" from social studies class emerged in my mind. I thought of Anne Frank, the girl writer who was famous.

Etta picked up her book again. "Here you can work on your naivete."

§

It took me a while to fall asleep because I was cold and terrified the ghost of the old coot would hover over me in the night, or sit on my chest and sniff at my soul, like a cat. I shifted, pulled the sheets from the mattress, lay awake listening to the wind, to the house settling further into its bones. I got up, wrapped the robe around me, went out to the hall closet to get the blanket. I turned on the light and expected to see the old lady standing at the far end of the hall, but there was no one. When I was warm enough to fall asleep, I dreamt of Patrick's studio, only there were no paintings in it, just mannequins he was fitting together for a front window at Filene's. But he was putting the legs where the arms should be and the arms where the legs should be, and the people looked like crabs. I was telling him this was something he shouldn't do; we were going to get in trouble with the manager. It was in this state of anxiety that I awoke to someone fumbling with the doorknob to my room.

The door slowly creaked open wide enough for me to see a figure. I could feel my heart beat clear through to my throat, and I nearly puked from fright. The figure hobbled into the room, and I immediately knew it was Patrick and not the old coot. He stood above me for a moment, and I became aware of the hair on his skinny legs, the too-short shirt that exposed a glimpse of tighty-whities. I slid to the side of the bed against the wall while he groped for the covers and then, in one motion, twisted and fell flat on his back. He started to snore. I was paralyzed and lay crunched next to the wall thinking of what to do next. Then I heard footsteps outside in the hall; someone had pulled the door shut. What the f is going on here, I thought. What kind of place is this?

When Patrick stopped snoring, I stared at him long and hard, and he turned to face me. He opened his eyes, and I could see the spark of blue in the little bit of light in the room. I was thinking, Can he see me? I felt his warmth reach my skin. Then he placed his hand under my robe and slid it down my hip. He hoisted me up, and I saw then the flex of a secret muscle in his arm, a strength he did not have during waking life. I lay atop him; he cupped my chin, pulled me toward him. He slid the nightgown down and put his mouth to my skin, and I folded in the heat, collapsing into him. I relented, went toward his mouth, kissed, gave in. It was a transformative heat, a melding into the soft and hard parts of him amidst the ebb and flow of breath. After a while, my legs tingled and then went numb. Then, quite suddenly, the epicenter of me split and quaked. I fell back, aside him, slid down to the floor, entangled in the sheet. I couldn't move my legs. He started to snore and I recoiled, breathless but aware. I carefully shimmied away and untangled myself from the sheet like a fish from a net and sat there listening to him snoring and breathing while my body throbbed in pleasant aftershocks. When it was over, I went to my aunt's room and found her propped up in bed, a silhouette.

"Aunt Etta," I whispered.

"Samantha."

I cleared my throat. "He wanted his bed back," I said.

"He was sleepwalking?"

"Yes, I think so."

"He does that sometimes. Come under with me."

The bed was warm from her body, and I immediately felt heavy under it. I slid under the weighted covers and turned to see the profile of her face, highlighted by the moonlight coming from the window.

"I shut the door. He was in there, and I shut the door on you," she said. I held my breath. Was this a confession? "I came back and saw that he wasn't here," my aunt continued. She drew in a breath and let it out. Her voice was slurred, soft. "I couldn't move. Everything got so heavy, and I couldn't move."

"Oh," I said, stupidly.

It was all so surreal and strange, like everyone in the house was an altered self, the self that's slowed and blurred, as if it were under water.

I lay there staring at the ceiling, waiting. A clock ticked softly near her end of the bed. Etta turned toward the wall, indicating that she wanted to sleep, but just when I thought she had nodded off, she spoke. "Sometimes I think I can hear it, from way up here," she said.

"What?"

"The drone of a boat."

"A boat?"

"He's searching for me out there."

"Who?"

She sniffed, stirred in the bed. I heard it then—a small cry.

"Aunt Etta?"

After a few moments, her breath became a constant rolling rhythm. The clock ticked, a rhythm under a rhythm. There was something familiar about that rhythm under a rhythm that put me at ease, but I kept one eye peeled until dawn, more awake than I had been all winter.

EDEN
Etta, 1968

Kissing Crazy Anthony was like kissing a brother, despite his new man body, despite his sensual heat. When Anthony rolled on top of Etta and pressed her hard into the hollow part of the couch in his grandmother's basement, her fingers slipped through the cracks and fumbled with dimes, pennies, flakes of cannoli shells. A satellite moth peppered around the light of the lonely bulb above them; she heard its small body batting itself against the glass and wondered if it was drawn to the heat or the light, whether it wanted to feel the flame on its wings or drown itself in a white radiance.

Etta had known Anthony for years; his father delivered the milk bottles and he used to take the ride with him on the way to school. Lately, he'd come over to see Pop and they talked about Thunderbirds and bookies and Jerry Vale. (Pop liked him because he drank his wine, that drivel he concocted in the basement and kept in the garage in old milk bottles.) One early evening in May, a week before graduation, Etta saw Anthony in the graveyard, slipping under the earth. She went to the sinkhole, fenced off by yellow tape, barricaded by a backhoe and called down to him. He stuck his face out, under the roots and overhanging dirt. "Don't say nothin'," he said. She scrambled down below, took one look at the coffins split open like flowers, at a skull cap and a femur bone floating in shards of dark cloth. It was unbearably damp. Something said, *Rise Up. Get out.* She did.

His grandmother's house had been vacant since she died and the furniture in the rooms was covered in sheets. Anthony regarded it as a sacrilege to make love to Etta in the main rooms of the house, so he took her down to the basement. He switched on the light, a single bulb above an old plaid green couch with a tear across its belly revealing its padded viscera. The basement had a black ceramic tile with speckled white that reminded Etta of outer space; old pool balls were scattered about a standard size table, as if someone just took a shot. Years ago, Anthony's grandfather held tournaments in the basement where the neighborhood old-timers made bets on who would beat whom. Pop, who used to win tournaments in the army, never went, though they begged him. He didn't think it right to take their money.

Anthony patted the cushion and watched Etta as she walked about the room to a sagging aluminum folding table with Geppeto's bakery boxes on it. She picked one up and opened it, thinking she'd find a stale piece of something, but everything was devoured.

"They still smell sweet, don't they?" Anthony said. "I keep them to smell when there's nothing else, to bring back the memory of eating the goodies." He got up from the couch, grabbed her wrists and sat back down. Then he smelled her, gently sticking his nose in her hair. "You smell like bread," he said. "Yeast."

But Etta wasn't listening to a word Anthony said. She was thinking about the gypsies, hippie kids who played guitar and read poems to one another sitting on the hood of Patsy's Pinto under the light of a street lamp in Bohack's parking lot. Etta met Patsy in Home Economics class; she liked Patsy's easygoing ways, the way her eyelids were always at half mast, as if she were perpetually dreaming. One night Patsy's brother Hank read a long, crazy poem called "Howl." Hank smelled of patchouli and leather and had dirt under his fingernails. He had hair the color of wheat, the same as his sister, and just as long and wild. Hank read the poem standing on the hood of the Pinto and the light shown down on him as if he were reciting a soliloquy. Who makes words like that? Etta wondered. Something about windows of skulls, hydrogen jukeboxes, a soul's illuminated hair. Who contemplates the hair of a soul? The words were reckless, limitless, and brave. Who contemplates the hair of a soul? The gypsies, that's who; they don't worry when they're going to get their next meal of escarole and beans like most of the people in the neighborhood.

Somewhere water was dripping. Anthony had Etta naked in the palms of his hands. She melded to his heat as the moth flitted and pinged at the light bulb. When ecstasy ruptured then pooled and all thoughts were eradicated, she noticed the moth had landed on the arm of the couch. Anthony crushed it with his thumb, this erratic bead of life, and it fell down dead onto the cold ceramic floor.

The last time Etta saw Anthony, he sat on the plaid, green couch with a meal made by his mother, the tomato-stained Tupperware placed on the floor next to him. Before him was a plate of spaghetti, a saucer of olive oil for dipping bread, a sliced loaf, a slab of butter, silverware and a white cloth napkin, a bottle of Schlitz beer. He wore a white t-shirt that showed off his biceps and was barefoot.

"A little bird told me," he said, swirling some spaghetti around his fork. "A little bird told me he saw you with those long hairs in Bohack's parking lot. No girlfriend of mine is going to associate herself with that kind of *filth*."

"Who said I was your girlfriend?" Etta asked.

"Well if you're not my girlfriend, then what are you?" he asked

He had been asking her to go steady; he told her he wanted to go to her house and eat dinner with her folks because *la famiglia* was important to him. Anthony sat up straight in front of the aluminum folding table that supported his meal. There was fury in his eyes. He tucked the napkin into his t-shirt, and started swirling the spaghetti with his fork, its capture ensured with a spoon guiding the macaroni around until it reached critical mass.

"So are you going to tell me what you are or do I need to guess?"

"You're a pig."

Anthony picked up a pool ball and hurled it at the window; it made a clean hole through the glass. Etta scrambled out, running away as fast as she could with the wings in her chest beating hard, her throat burning from the rush of air.

A week later she received a bouquet of flowers with a card neatly tucked between the leaves. Etta opened the card; on the front were irises with "Thinking of You" in perfect Hallmark script. Inside, "Thoughts of you have a special place in my heart." On the opposite page was Anthony's dilapidated handwriting that read: "You're in my guts."

It wasn't long afterward she packed up and left with the gypsies for California.

She asked herself, would my father ever throw a pool ball at my mother?

Never.

Hank told Etta and Patsy they were going to California by way of Vermont to pick up a friend. "Vincent can be our personal tour guide, man. The dude knows every nook and cranny between here and Sausalito. Done the trip seven or eight times," he said, wrestling with a map in the driver's seat of Patsy's Pinto. Patsy tapped at the dashboard singing to the Rolling Stones as the old Pinto, with its rusted door edges and crack across the windshield, pulled out of the driveway. Etta looked up at the living room picture window and saw her father looming. She had seen him this way many times before—the silhouette of a watcher. At night when she would return from her carousing, he would be still sitting and smoking in the living room, waiting, thinking, as the arabesques of smoke wafted above his head. Would he wait for her as he did before? When her father was in shadow, smoking and listening to his old world operas, he took on a curious mystique, different from his everyday self that tolerated the drudgery they both knew. She pressed her hand to the glass of the passenger window as Hank drove away.

Hours later the car rumbled over a dirt road to an opening in the woods of Vermont, to hanging lanterns and amateur guitar, the smell of citronella and pot. "O Captain! My Captain!" Hank said to a long-haired man with a beer in one hand and a spatula in another cooking up corn and trout over an open flame. Vincent put his beer down and shook Hank's hand.

"Etta, come here, babe. Meet the Captain."

Etta extended her hand as people danced around her, wild-haired, hip-less people who cooed and swayed, who wore amulets and braided leather headbands and big-buckled belts. Vincent had hair the length of Hank's and Patsy's but pulled back in a band; he was only slightly taller than Etta and wore camel-colored cords with yellow star patches and faded moons. Vincent nodded his head to Etta, and in the glow of the fire, she could see his eyes, a sort of black that pulled at her.

Patsy's older sister Lauren approached them, a sultry goddess with flowing white cotton sleeves and pink purple-heart sunglasses, her sticky-fingered children in tow. The children, in ratty clothes and dirty feet, clasped lollipops that swirled in a vortex of pink and yellow, and pulled at Lauren's limbs. Etta thought of the cellar gatherings in the North End where she and her sister each took a leg of her mother's and hid behind it until a family member pried them loose to go play with the other kids outside. Parties always made her nervous.

"Estes Park is a disaster. Too many tourists. You don't really get a sense of wilderness when everybody's Grandma is wheeled up to watch the caribou and there's a little kid poking it with a stick," Vincent said to Hank.

The two men stopped talking when Etta sat down. She smiled awkwardly. Vincent put two cobs and half a fish in a bowl and slid it to her. He smiled back. "Thank you," she said.

"Big Bend was an amazing park, man," Vincent continued. He looked at Etta out of the corner of his eye. "There is *nobody* down there, man. It's a four-hour drive from the nearest town. Ten hours from Houston. We camped down by the Rio Grande, paid a ferryman to take us across the river to Boquillas, Me-hico. It cost fifty cents for the little guy to row us there and back. *And* he made us dinner. Can't beat that! His wife and daughter fed us like we were generals, man. It was mad shit."

What corner of the world has a ferryman with a wife who cooks you dinner, she wondered. Etta ate her corn; it tasted sweet and fresh. A dwindling sun sparkled through the deep woods as birdsong filled the trees. Vincent continued to talk to Hank, but he randomly glanced at Etta, almost shyly. Vincent stopped talking and bit into his corn. He stared at Etta and she noticed that he had corn bits in his hair and on his face. He stared at her with a look of lust and a face full of corn bits. Etta wanted to laugh out loud; men were so foolish at times.

At twilight they sat around nude on bamboo mats, smoking and drinking cheap bottles of wine. Lauren was the first to remove her goddess garb and dance in a circle with her arms out wide and her face up to the twilight sky. The crowd giggled and yahooed until moments later, they were all stripping themselves, dancing. With the hush of water in the distance, the warm breezes through the trees, the fire highlighting the sun-kissed skin of the hippies, Etta let her guard down and noticed the bodies in the waning sun, their odd shapes as they rolled in the coming darkness. Etta stared across the fire at Vincent, at the naked men lounging on mats running their hands down the curves of the women, smoothing them with oils, at their penises tucked like turtles inside dark spaces, then expanding, stretching their necks under the stars. Vincent saw Etta staring at him, passed his mandolin to the man next to him and made his way over to her.

"Come," he said.

She followed his moon white ass through soft grasses in the waning twilight to an opening in the woods. The grass was pressed down in wide patches from the bodies of deer, and Vincent lay his mat and a lantern down in one of the imprints. He sat in half lotus position and asked her to sit with her back to him, also in half lotus. They sat there for a while in silence feeling how their bodies breathed. Etta felt trapped in the moment; Vincent was trying to bring mind into it, and Etta did not know how to deal with mind. She looked up at the darkening trees and felt fear; this was something she did not consider, that freedom would include fear. She tried a thought—her father laughing in the night to Johnny Carson—it eased her a bit. She thought of his black comb in the bathroom with the hair gel on it.

Vincent took a breath. She smelled him, the peculiar aroma of some herbal oil.

"Why do you want to go to Cali?" he asked.

"Why not?"

Vincent slapped at himself, at the hovering mosquitoes. "*Kaahlee*," he said, playing with the word. "Black petal of night. The goddess who swallows the sun in the West and gives birth to it in the East."

Etta had no idea what Vincent was talking about and thought he might be drunk.

"You sort of look like Joan Baez," he said. "I've always had a thing for Joan Baez."

It was not desire that made Etta rise up to her knees and press herself against Vincent; it was anxiety. Her long black hair flowed into his, as Vincent sat there, calm, with his thumbs and index fingers touching. For a moment she thought she had made a mistake until he cocked his head back and pulled her to him. She slid to the front of him, wrapping her legs around his back. When she looked down at him, he had become smaller. He shuddered slightly and his eyes, in the pale light of the early evening were those of a boy, excited, apprehensive and wide. Vincent was changing with the intimacy; Etta could feel the ebb of the Captain's power and the rise of her own.

§

Vincent lay in front of her, propped on an elbow. In the light from the lantern, Etta traced the hair on his chest up to his neck where the strands of a hemp choker were tied. The pendant attached to it was a slippery black thing, a figure with multiple arms. Etta took it between her fingers.

"Kali," he said. "The godd-*ess*."

She thought of her mother's miniature Pieta on the sill in the living room, how Christ was draped across Mary's lap like a curtain. She used to touch the Christ with her fingers, feeling his nose, his feet and fingers, his crown of thorns. She traced her finger down Mary's veiled head. These were the deities she knew.

Vincent moved his hand down the small of Etta's back and pushed her to him. He was getting hard again. "I wear her out of sheer reverence," he stated, "because of what she did to me."

Etta almost laughed. "What did she do to you?"

He twirled a strand of Etta's hair between his fingers. "She broke my neck."

Vincent drove a Volkswagen bus with a Day-Glo pink dragon blowing hearts and a dancing fish draped in blue pearls. He kept a Rand McNally atlas with all the main roads in America highlighted in crayon green under the front passenger seat. He told Etta of his old life as a physics student at Berkeley and how after he broke his neck by diving into a shallow river, he dropped out. The doctor said he escaped paralysis by an eighth of an inch; his recovery took several months and it was his friend Charles who took care of him here in Vermont. Vincent claimed that Kali laid waste to his old life and from the ashes sprouted a new one, a life of meditation and yoga. He told Etta he sat for days in meditation and had several breakthroughs about the mind; in stillness, one becomes acutely aware of the rhythms of the natural world and the importance of these rhythms. He believed in these rhythms; if only people could find the proper time to eat and harmonize it with their digestive tracts they'd do away with cancer, heart disease, nervous breakdowns, all the major illnesses.

Vincent ate roots and berries and alfalfa and was unbelievably flatulent. He was eccentric and amusing, sensual and compassionate and in just a few days, he told Etta he was falling for her and she him. When Patsy and Hank left for California, Vincent told them he and Etta would meet them there in a few weeks. They stayed in a cottage at the Birch Forest Inn where Vincent worked the grounds. It was appropriate, Vincent claimed, for a man and woman to be isolated to get to know one another. Most days Etta had contact with one other person, Vincent's friend Charles who owned the inn; he was a bachelor in his early fifties, a balding, thin man who had a taste for fine art, antiques and gardening. Charles was quirky but cultured; he had a talent for the art of conversation, cooking, was well traveled and despite his being periphery, Etta found him interesting.

Vincent bought Etta a pair of hiking boots and took her into the Green Mountains. They decided to hike Mount Mansfield, the highest peak in Vermont. When she felt the gravity of the mountain pull at her bones, she thought about turning back and letting Vincent have his mountain to himself; she was nearly heaving with lack of breath and the backs of her heels were blistering. Vincent stood on an outcropping of rock and pulled his canteen. "Take smaller steps," he said. "You'll be less tired." He raised the canteen and took a drink. "Don't drink too much," he said, handing it to her. She sipped the cool water and it tasted like a delicacy.

Etta bent to loosen her boots and smooth her heels with her fingers. Vincent rustled through the pack for a Band-Aid. While he bent to ooze an ointment over the frayed skin and patched up her feet, she smelled the musk of his male sweat and thought of how Christ bent to wash the feet of his apostles. The moment was tender, as were the small birds flitting through the pines, the silent wind bending the tops of the trees. She noticed the way the light filtered through the needles and onto Vincent's bearded face. With his wetted tendrils of hair falling over his eyes, he looked sanctified.

When she finally broke open with sweat, she began to find her rhythm and concentrated on her footing. They continued up the rocky trail silently for hours, until they reached tree line where the pines gave way to shrubbery, lichen and rock. They perched at an outlook where they ate bologna and mustard sandwiches and observed the blue haze rim of earth. Etta felt a keen sense of elation in the drastic heights of virgin wilderness, the silver fingers of lake water, the pinnacle of reflected light tracing the movement of a car along the mountain road thousands of feet below. She had a vision of her mother in Watertown, earthbound, her fingers pulling at clothespins that hung towels, sheets, and her father's pale yellow shirts.

In the mornings, Etta took a walk along the backroads near the inn. Vincent taught her to be mindful as she walked, to notice her breath, the way her feet felt when pressed to the earth. He told her mindfulness would eliminate her anxiety, but Etta knew it was Vincent who eliminated her anxiety. Their life at the inn, near a blossoming garden and a river running through the tall pines was idyllic; Vincent's confidence, his knowledge of the world and its mechanisms, his sensuality; all of these things eased her. She walked until beads of sweat collected on her brow and between her breasts. She picked yellow and orange flowers that grew from the bank of earth amidst wet crab grass.

When Etta returned to the cottage, the shadow of the gnomon on Vincent's sundial was half way between Roman numeral eight and nine. She could see it there, a thin, dagger. Vincent sat in lotus against the wall; he did not open his eyes and look at her when she walked in. She pulled the roots off the flowers and stuck the bottoms in the glass of water Vincent kept by his side of the bed. She lay on the bed when Vincent rose and went to her. He was honing in on the exact rhythm for making love to her; now it happened quicker and with heightened intensity. Afterward, he grinned, as if he was proud of himself and Etta could see his shiny pink lips in there, under the hair of his face which left abrasions when they kissed. She could feel the tender place on the skin, the sting on her chin when she touched it.

In the evening the wild flowers folded their petals like they had died. She filled the cup with more water and then traced the small hairs that grew along the stem with her finger. The next day, Etta woke to the wildflowers with open faces, bursting with bloom as if they were just born for the morning. Would she have noticed this subtlety before, living her old life? She was more aware now, more alive herself, and therefore could see it in other things. This is what Vincent said would happen.

Several weeks later, Etta was fitting a sheet to the corners of the mattress in Room 2 when Charles popped his head in the room. "Have you seen Vincent? There's a call for him," he said.

"In the garden," Etta said. "I'll get him."

She went out to the garden where Vincent was positioning a sundial on its post. He had been making the pedestal for a week now, digging out the foundation, placing the forms level, pouring the concrete, planing it when it dried. Etta came forward when Vincent was positioning the gnomon with his compass. "Charles says the phone's for you." Vincent looked up at her and put his compass in his pocket. He squeezed her shoulder and trotted up to the inn. She waited for a moment and then followed him in and heard his wild laugh, excited by Hank's voice on the other side. Vincent moved into the pantry when Etta came in and continued the conversation in there. She left him and went to the room to continue making the beds. When she heard the screen door slam, she went back out to the garden.

Vincent, prostrate at the gnomon, looked up at her when she stood next to him. "The gnomon casts the shadow on the hour," Vincent said. "See here," he pointed, showing her the dial like it was a creature he found in the forest, "this thing is the gnomon. You point it in the direction of Polaris, the North Star. The sun revolves around Polaris in almost a perfect circle, so if you can find good ol' Polaris, you point this baby right at it and you can observe the rhythm of the sun." Vincent shielded the sun with his hand and peered up at Etta. He examined the expression on her face. "What's wrong?" he asked.

"That was Hank," she said.

"Yes. He's wondering what the hell we're doing."

"Do you want to leave?" she asked.

"Yes," he said. "You know I do. That is not the question. The question is, do *you* want to leave?"

She sat down on a bench and looked out at the garden at the many different forms of flower life. It was now late August and the heads of the sunflowers hung heavy with seed; the corn stalks were nearly as tall with hefty husks. There were sensually shaped zucchini, foxgloves and hollyhocks and pink roses coaxed over a wire trellis. There was not a weed, nor a stray blade of grass in the dirt; even the slate slabs of the walkway were swept. It was Charles's work, this meticulous caretaking; this beauty called to life.

"Of course I do," Etta said. "I told you I'd go anywhere with you. I want to be with you."

Vincent placed the level on the face of the sundial. He watched as the bubbles settled just inside the lines. Then he stood up and took off his t-shirt. His beard was full now and it seemed grossly out of place in the heat. "Think about what you are saying," he said.

"What do you mean?"

"I have a life out there, Etta. You wouldn't understand."

"You don't want me to go."

"I never said that," he said, picking up the level and placing it north south. He eyeballed the bubbles again and this time they were slightly outside the black lines. "Shit," he said and took the dial off the pedestal. He squatted on his haunches and looked up at Etta. "This little Eden here, this is your home. It would be any woman's home. But me, I can't sit still for too long. I got to keep moving, man. You must have read Kerouac? You know about him don't you? We got the same soul."

He had exhausted her; he had loved her in every room in the inn and was now done with her. With every room, it was easier for him to detach from her. He got dressed, washed his face, put on his shoes, and went back to work while Etta lay in the bed feeling emotional and abandoned.

Vincent conveniently dismissed himself from the conversation and went to the shed. Etta felt a pang in her gut. She thought of Charles, how he must have had an artistic interest in the world. You could see it in the way he decorated the rooms and the beauty of the garden. Was it this that replaced love? Etta did not come from a family where artistic talent was a consideration. If a glimmer of it showed up somewhere, it was ignored; there simply were no resources to cultivate it. Perhaps if she were born in Vermont, she might have taken up pottery, the most tactile of the arts, and sculpted her own bowls and vessels. She could stand outside the door of a room in the inn and feel OK.

§

In her dreams it was not Vincent she was going to California with, but her father. She glanced over at his face in the sideview mirror, his black hair slicked back, the golden lines curling around his eyes, the smile that held a cigar tightly in his teeth. He had his elbow propped on the door and the wind in the Cadillac tossed the arias around in the back seat. They were going to wine country, Napa Valley, where the grapes grow in luscious vines row after row in the gilded countryside. Etta waked in a state of bliss.

Vincent did not speak of California again and spent whole days meditating facing the south wall of the cottage. After the first full day of meditation, she started to leave food at his side—a sliced garden tomato and red onion on a bed of alfalfa with a glass of water—but he took nothing. He had grown thinner and hardly spoke to her or Charles; he seemed to be retreating inside himself. She had no idea what to say to him or how to behave around him. Etta waited patiently for him to return to himself, lying awake next to him hearing him breathe deeply and soundly.

She had written several letters to her parents, telling them the truth of her whereabouts. It was mid-September when Etta finally called home and found out that her father was dead. She took a bus from Montpelier to Boston and then a train to Watertown. Her mother was down on her knees, scrubbing the floor in the foyer when she arrived, her hair done up in an array of fat curls styled nearly perfectly on the top of her head. "Be careful, it's wet," Philomena said, motioning to the floor around her. She looked up at her daughter, "Help me up." Etta held strong as her mother put her weight into her hand, balancing her girth to get one foot then the other flat on the ground again. Philomena wore black stockings that had a slight sheen to them and her old ratty slippers that were permanently molded to the shapes of her feet.

"I just wanted to get this floor cleaned for tomorrow."

"Ma, why don't you sit down," Etta said.

"I can't. There's too much to do before we have a house full of people." She looked up at her daughter. "Don't they feed you in Vermont? Look how skinny you are. What's the matter with a woman having some meat on her bones? A man likes something to grab onto. Your father, now he liked a good behind."

With the mention of her father, Etta bit her lower lip. She looked around her and focused on the cigar in the ashtray on the coffee table. Her mother saw her do this and she exhaled. Philomena walked toward her and put her hands up to her daughter's face. Etta collapsed into her, burying her head in her mother's hair, feeling the hairspray sting the inside of her nostrils.

"It's OK, girl. He went fast. It was a good death. No suffering," she said, as she patted her daughter's back. Etta pulled herself away and looked at her mother's face. She was not crying. This was just like Philomena to be strong now; she was never the type to cry in front of others, but probably spent the morning weeping through the rosary. "Go wash up. The viewing starts at eight."

There was no evidence that her father had died. His toiletries were still in the cabinet, his electric razor, plugged in above the sink, his cup of black combs beside the mirror. He was still there in the hair oil smell of the comb, in the stray hairs in the razor. Etta lifted up the shade to look at the backyard. It was gray and the night was coming, yet she could still see the silhouettes of the fig trees on the lawn, the tangle of grapevines over the trellis, the Virgin set back by the fence with the last of the mums dying around her. There was something wrong about the view. It took her a moment to realize what it was; the younger figs had no jackets. This is what her father called the twine and burlap he used to cover the trees from the ice and snow. He had died before he could cover his trees.

Etta left the bathroom and went down into the garage, flicked on the light and saw the bulb's reflection off the windshield of the Caddy. The garage had that same smell of oil-saturated cloths and fertilizer. Wine jugs were behind the door, rose, burgundy and a white wine that had no visible label; his tools, the rakes, shears, electric trimmer, shovels all hung from the side wall. Etta took the shears, rummaged through the metal cabinet where her father kept smaller items and pulled out a ball of twine. There was no burlap that she could see, and this was disheartening; a trip to the hardware store would make this endeavor too big to complete in the little time she had available before the wake. Then an image appeared; it was the trunk of her father's car. She fetched the keys, popped the trunk, and beheld the burlap rolls.

Etta swathed the baby trees in the burlap and tied the twine around the slender trunks. She turned to go back inside to get herself ready when she instinctively glanced up at the kitchen window to see her mother, looking down upon her, crying.

Etta felt it was her duty to stay with Philomena for a few weeks to make sure she was OK. Philomena prepared her usual delectable dinners for Etta as she did her husband. She had no cookbook, no box of recipes, only what she had remembered from her mother's unwritten library of meals consisting mainly of Calabrese peasant dishes like pasta and broccoli with garlic, pasta fagioli, and ciambotta. Etta was not used to eating so heavily. She and Vincent often had a bowl of cereal or a salad for dinner while sitting on her bed watching the evening news.

While Philomena loaded Etta's plate, she filled her in on all the shortcomings of Pop's family, how Rita sent a house plant and not flowers to the wake because she was a cheapskate, how none of his sisters had called her since the funeral, how Henrietta's daughter's husband was addicted to pills. Etta listened and asked questions at first, but soon Philomena was repeating her stories and Etta was exhausted by them. Etta was also exhausted chauffeuring Philomena to the store or to the bank or to the beauty parlor to have her hair done. Living with her mother had degraded into drudgery only after a few weeks.

She was waiting for Vincent to call, for him to snap out of the trance he was in. But Vincent did not call. Etta had taken on a restlessness, a deep-rooted anxiety that would not let her be. When she slept, she dreamt of waves, walls of treacherous water welling up off shore. People in the waves were like debris, knocked about and pummeled to the sand. In the dreams, Etta always observed the waves from afar, how they crashed over sea walls and sprawled over asphalt roads. She was mesmerized by the waves, the height of the water, the power they were capable of.

One night Philomena called Etta down to dinner and Etta told her she wasn't hungry. She could not bear another evening of discussing people she could not relate to, nor the food heaped in a pile on her plate. But Philomena was insistent. "I cooked a nice meal here and you're not going to eat it?"

"I'm just not hungry right now," Etta shouted down to the kitchen. "I will eat something later."

"But later it will be cold and then you will have to reheat it. That's a waste of gas."

Philomena had become frugal since Pop died, constantly flicking off lights. She hand-washed clothes in the basement sink and drank coffee from the morning pot. Etta went to the doorway to look at her mother who was leaning on the railing at the bottom of the stairs with her foot on the first step. She knew her mother needed her to come and sit down at the table, as Pop would have done. Philomena examined her daughter from below, and Etta waited for her to say something, but she didn't; she saw to it that Etta left the room and descended the stairs before she went back to the kitchen.

As Etta sat down to eat, she observed the dull yellow appliances she had known for years, the coffee pot with a frayed chord, the spotless floor Philomena swept clear of hard spaghetti bits, stray lentils, Cheerios, and coffee grinds. Philomena bent to pick up a garlic skin that had escaped the counter, bending over so Etta could see her behind gleam in blue polyester pants. She looked at the slab of steak in front of her and Etta felt a wave swell. Philomena sat down as Etta cut her steak pizzaiola into pieces and raised one to her mouth. The wave had gathered height and mass; it walled off everything. Etta chewed, but she could not swallow. She gagged and spit out the chewed meat onto the plate.

"What's the matter with you? That's a good piece of meat."

"It's not the meat," Etta said. She put her hands to her face to block her mother out.

"You're an anorexic, aren't you," Philomena said. "I knew it. Let me tell you something girlie, Rosy can walk around with her daughter looking like someone from a concentration camp, but I won't."

Etta's cousin Theresa had always been a very delicate girl, thin, tall with a voice barely audible while her aunt Rosy, Pop's sister, had a strident voice, wore long flowery summer dresses and wrapped up her cushions, mattresses, upholstery in a hard plastic covering that made everyone uncomfortable. But Rosy was a goodhearted person who insisted you not stay at a hotel while you were visiting Florida. She would cook for you, preparing feasts while circling the table and prodding you to eat more. This was most disconcerting to all who came, to gorge oneself silly while Theresa, so thin you could see the outlines of her bones, crept about the kitchen toasting her half of low-fat frozen bagel.

"You need to see Dr. Deltoro," Philomena said.

"Why? I am *not* an anorexic."

"You're not right Etta. I can tell."

Etta felt defeated, helpless. Maybe she did need to see a doctor. Perhaps she should go to Deltoro, to get something to calm her nerves.

Deltoro hadn't changed much since she last saw him, except for his sideburns turning white; he had the same bulbous nose, big warm hand that took hers and swallowed it up.

"Did you mother get the flowers I sent? I was out of town for the funeral."

Etta nodded her head.

"He was a good man, your father," Deltoro said. He moved his cold stethoscope around Etta's body. Etta breathed. He peered into her eyes with a sharp white light, into her ears, into her nostrils. Then he stood back about two feet and just looked at her. Etta could not look at him, so she looked at his watch, a Timex with gold Roman numerals.

"What sort of thoughts have you been having? Do you think of hurting yourself?"

"No," she said. "Not directly . . ."

"What do you mean 'not directly'?"

"I can't explain it."

Etta took a breath and let it out. She managed to look at Deltoro, who took a step closer. She had Vincent's face in her mind, or she *thought* she had Vincent's face in her mind; she could still locate some of his features, but his memory was starting to fade. Her body responded to the thought with a queer spasm, and she started to gag, as if she were going to vomit, but nothing came out. She stepped down off the examining table shaking. Deltoro put his hands on her to steady her. He pulled her closer to him and she put her head on his chest, trying to breathe. He held her until she stopped gagging and could breathe again.

"You're a bundle of nerves, Etta," he said.

The drug Dr. Deltoro gave Etta numbed her enough so that she felt somewhat relaxed and could eat. The pill was like a wash of warmth oozing into her limbs, slowing her movements and thoughts, numbing her so that she could function without feeling the need to hide. In the late afternoon when it was still light, Etta took Pop's Cadillac down to the banks of the Charles River, a place the two of them went when Etta was a child to feed the ducks and search for coins in the parking lot. Here they walked along the river observing the picnickers, the college kids in crew boats, the couples in the grass. Often they found enough change to go and get an ice cream in Harvard Square where they both sat on stools looking out the window to the passersby, eating pistachio ice cream. This was one of Pop's favorite things to do, watch people as they go about their business. "Where are they all going?" he used to ask Etta. She would tell him she didn't know. "Me neither," he would say. "Where does anyone really go?"

It was Charles who called and offered her a job. He told her he would even drive to Massachusetts, but Etta declined and told him she would take the bus back. The night Charles called, Etta did not dream of waves. Her dream was about the inn and her passing through a closet door to find a new room. It had a tub full of goldfish with a waterfall in the middle of it, water lilies, old antique furniture, and a bay window that overlooked the garden. She was so convinced this new room existed that she found herself thinking about it when she woke up, going over each of the rooms in the inn to figure out if it was one of these. But it wasn't, it was something different and new coming from inside her.

When Etta returned, Charles was like a little boy, and Vincent was like a ghost. Charles greeted Etta at the bus terminal, carried her bag, talked feverishly about the banal things that had happened since she left.

When she saw Vincent, he was sickly thin and ashen. He hardly said two words to her. Etta set to unpacking her things. She pulled out the novel *Dharma Bums* she started before she left for her father's funeral and laid it by the bed she shared with Vincent in the cottage. Tucked inside it, was a newspaper article of Vincent hitchhiking from Yellowstone to Yosemite written by a reporter who picked him up in northern California. He was *On the Road*. Vincent wasn't wearing a shirt in the picture; he had his pack and mandolin on his back and he was laughing, as if he just made a snide remark to the reporter and found himself amusing.

Charles paid Etta for the housekeeping of the rooms, as well as shopping and cooking breakfast for the guests for room and board and fifty dollars a week. The foliage season was nearing its end, being almost November, and there were very few guests, so Etta could relax. She enjoyed being out at dusk feeling the air get cold once again and watching the sky blush; she often sat with Charles by the fire, drinking a glass of wine and watching Montpelier's evening news. In the serenity of the evening, Charles smoked his corncob pipe. He was changing his appearance by growing a beard and visually becoming less the Charles she knew; he started to form a different identity.

Charles and Etta began to have dinner together, without Vincent because Vincent stopped eating. Etta asked Charles what he thought was going on with Vincent, and he just dismissed the whole thing as sulking because he really didn't know what to do with his life. He convinced Etta it was just a phase, he had seen it before, and it would pass. Etta was reassured by Charles' insight and content to be with someone who seemed as if he knew what he wanted out of life. While they did the dishes, she noticed his arms. The hairs on his arms clung together, his man hairs were wet and Etta found herself wanting him to put the wet hands on her. The transformation in Charles, the extra hair on his face, the close proximity day in and day out was doing something to her. He glanced at her, wiped his wet hands and Etta thought of a doctor wiping his hands after delivering a baby; there was power in those wet hands. Charles put the towel down and moved into Etta's space, bending down to kiss her and Etta allowed herself to be kissed. It was a good kiss, warm and neat. She wished Vincent had seen it. He led her across the hall to a vacant room and laid her on the bed. When Charles sat above her and took off his shirt, Etta realized just how long his arms were and how the dark hair on his back rounded his shoulders. She was suddenly repulsed, and although something inside her was screaming *abort, abandon ship*, she shut her eyes and let Charles remove her shirt and pants while she lay somewhere in the vacuous space between body and heart. Was it mind? Charles traced his finger around her body, as if he were following a road on a map. Etta's rising image was that of a beach after a storm with pieces of a ship washed ashore, and bottles and tree limbs and trunks, strewn across the sand and she wanted to cry for all the broken things.

"You're thinking of Vincent," Charles said. "I'm not asking to take his place. I'm just wondering if there's room for me, too."

Etta sat up and looked at Charles. He was fifteen years older than her and the sadness in his eyes brought out the wrinkles in his face. She dressed herself and went back to the cottage.

Vincent was there, in the bed, reading her book. Etta suddenly felt a wash of hope; he was doing something normal. But when she came in, he barely looked at her. He shut the book. She looked at his chest, the outline of muscles in his arms. His was the type of male beauty she appreciated and needed. Etta started to undress for bed, hoping he would reach for her.

"He isn't who you think he is," Vincent said. She looked at him, and he nodded toward the inn. "Him."

Outside the wind started to whistle around the eaves of the cottage.

The next day, Charles bought Etta a jade necklace, placed it in a gold box with a red bow and left it on the breakfast table with a note beside it. "Etta, for you. Saw them in an antique shop and thought they would show off your eyes." When she picked up the necklace, there were tissue paper folded neatly around two tickets to Bizet's *Carmen*. A night out on the town might get Charles hopeful of a romance but to miss her father's *Carmen*? When Charles came in for some coffee, Etta confronted him.

"I just wanted to thank you for the gifts. But I feel strange accepting them."

"Why?" he asked. "You are my friend. Besides, I just thought they would look good on you. Have you tried them on?"

"Not yet," Etta said.

"You have a nice neckline. I thought, well, your eyes—"

"Yes," Etta said. "And the opera—"

"You are going, I hope?"

The way Charles said this, he seemed detached from the response. This eased Etta's mind. "Yes, I am going," she said.

The theatre was an old opera house in the town of Claremont, New Hampshire, approximately one hour southeast of the inn. Charles saw a date on the pedestal of a column on the way in, and told Etta it was built in 1926, but must have been rehabilitated within the last ten years, given the newly pointed bricks on the exterior. "The mural on the ceiling was repainted also, wait till you see it," he said. Etta strained her neck to view the mural of the woman donning shield, spear and golden helmet.

"Who is she supposed to be?"

"I believe she is Minerva. Patroness of all art and skill. The ancients believed she taught women to sew and men to use the wheel. She was born from her father's head, you know. Cracked it open like a coconut."

"I think every woman is born from her father's head," Etta said.

There were mostly older people in the crowd, silver-haired men and women who seemed to know each other; they congregated in the aisles, kissed one another's soft, stretched, translucent, rice paper-like skin, and held on to one another to keep balance. Etta's father's skin was thick and brown; this is how she remembered it, a young skin, alive and healthy from the fresh air. Etta thought how Pop would not have handled aging well; this is why he had to die. She can't imagine him dealing with failing bones and organs, with needing to lean on someone else.

The music of the opera opened like a dream. She closed her eyes and curled over to the farthest part of her seat, away from Charles. She thought of the living room with her father sitting in his chair, his left ankle on his right knee, humming the melody as the smoke from the cigar danced its arabesques above his head. Etta saw him in the chair, but knew he was elsewhere, somewhere the opera and the wine took him to. Etta wept now and watched as the songs now accompanied characters; voices now had bodies.

Ahh, that Carmen is a floozy, her mother would say.

Charles offered a white handkerchief and she took it, staining the pristine cloth with blush and mascara. She folded the handkerchief and put it in her purse. She would wash it for him: it was the least she could do.

The trees loomed in the beams of the headlights.

"Have a nightcap with me," Charles asked as they walked to the door.

"No thanks, I am so tired."

He frowned. "Just one."

Etta obliged him. They went to the den and Charles poured Etta a scotch and soda and then one for himself. He lit his corncob pipe and puffed at it. Etta regarded the silhouette of his head, that hard circular line. Everything was wrong.

They sat silently, drinking. Charles spoke. "Could you do me a favor, Etta? Could you please go to the window, just as you are, and look out? The way the moonlight is coming in—I promise to not touch you."

"Why?"

"I like to look at you, that's why."

Etta got up and walked to the window; the chill in the room made her more tense. Etta touched the cold pane with her fingertips. Her breath made a flat cloud on the glass. There was nothing moving on the land, no deer, no coyote, no rustle in the trees, just stillness, darkness. It was Charles who knew the winter would come to an end. It was Charles who knew how to bring the ground back to life. She wrapped her arms about herself and rested her head on the cold pane of the window. Charles got up and walked toward her. He stood silently behind her looking out on the darkened land.

"Don't you understand a woman like you should be cherished?" he said.

Etta went back to the cottage and to bed. In a dream, her father sat in a dressing room in the back of the stage smoking a cigar while people powdered his face. When he rose, she followed him not to the stage, but to the audience where seats reclined all the way down like stretchers. Pop went to the old people, holding their hands, their elbows, helping them to lie down on the stretchers to die. Etta followed suit, positioning them in place so they were comfortable, laying their delicate white heads down on the cushion of the reclined chairs. The cigar smoke descended like a fog onto the crowd. It was so intense Etta became nauseous, her stomach unbearably sour and she woke up to see Vincent, away from her, huddled against the wall.

Etta shared some of her pills with Vincent, and he finished the rest of the bottle in two days. Vincent and Etta had resumed their intimacy, although there was something different about it, less tender. Theirs became a hard and faceless kind of sex that had her up against the headboard. When Etta communicated her discomfort, Vincent listened and thanked her for speaking her mind. "This is the sign of a healthy relationship," he said. "Good communication."

Vincent went back to his chores and keeping the grounds. He chopped and hauled wood, painted the trim in the den, raked leaves. He organized a potluck and invited his friends.

The night of the autumn potluck the hippies in their Nehru jackets and wraparound skirts gathered around Vincent and laughed at his jokes between songs. The tribal sounding music seemed to get louder now, competing with the laughter and conversation. Lauren's boyfriend Marshal sat on the couch popping grapes, waiting patiently for Vincent to finish; he had an axe to grind about Sirhan Sirhan firing blanks. "Those fed pigs took him under cover and did some fed pig magic on the bastard, some psycho-manipulation. They have psycho-hypnotic tricks up their sleeves, too, man. You know what I'm talking about . . . Nam. Farm boys, fresh outs, post-pubescent newbies, man. They find that primordial-blood-lusting-ass-kicker and they rouse him from the shadows of the id, give 'em an about face toward the call of Uncle Sam. That's why you have the My Lai massacre. Shit like that."

"Kennedy was a Zionist," Vincent replied. "You know how that goes."

"Of course I know how that goes."

Marshal had a stash of LSD lemonade in the fridge. Etta knew virtually nothing about the drug and a woman named Lambda surmised this, feeling it was her place to educate the newbie on *inter-being-ness*, and the "dissolution of our discrete vessels." "Listen," Lamba said with bejeweled, twisting, Hindu arms, "Just think of what it could be like to not be bound by conventional modes of communication." She smiled, a fake flash interjected into the conversation, and Etta noted how her teeth were small, almost like a child's teeth. Etta was uncomfortable with *inter-being-ness* and becoming one with the hippies. When Lauren came out with a tray of Dixie Cups filled with lemonade, Etta surreptitiously dumped hers behind the couch.

"Just lie still," Vincent advised, sitting on the end of the couch with his left knee jostling up and down.

Lauren lit votive candles in precarious places and dimmed the lights. The hippies slowed their movements and waited. Someone said the rug was turning into water. "I see a tail," Marshal said. He kneeled prostrate on the rug. Bored with the anxiety of LSD, Etta decided to help Charles clean up; she tossed plates of deviled eggs and Mandarin orange gelatin salad into the trash in the kitchen where there was a bright unwavering light. Charles sat down at the kitchen table with a slice of apple pie.

"Decided not to partake?"

"I'm not sure if it's my thing," Etta replied.

"Jibberish of the mind. I'd rather not meet up again with my father the saber-toothed watermelon."

Charles finished his pie and headed off to bed. "Just make sure they don't light the place on fire."

Etta sat for a while taking stabs at a pecan pie and debated with herself about the door to the sublime, about Vincent, about fear. But it wasn't any one of these thoughts that inspired her to pull open the refrigerator door; it was the feeling of being disregarded. The pitcher of lemonade had a few ounces left; she gulped it down and walked back in.

Etta sat on the edge of the couch opposite Vincent and watched Marshal now supine on the rug with his head propped up by a couch pillow. "You're all crocodiles now," he said. "Wading in the water with lipstick mouths." Hands slapped at the pulled skin of a drum in simple rhythm, the flute played a scale. Marshal gasped and fell backward, laughing. "There's a cherry beating between its teeth." He straightened up, ran his fingers through his hair, anxiously. "It beats like a heart."

"Jesus, I don't see any of that," Lauren said.

"Now it's unraveling."

"What?"

"The heart. Into a million seeds. Like flies filling the room." Marshal's face widened with elation. Etta imagined seeing his face break from the perspective of the ceiling, as if she were a perched bird. Lauren began to examine the charms on her bracelet and lay down her head in Marshal's lap.

After a short while, Etta watched the different features of the room begin to fall away; a dark bog appeared with a landscape of decaying forms and intermittent shining eyes. The eyes dimmed and wobbled, separated, coalesced. She looked for Vincent, but he was gone.

The full moon lit up the world. Earth appeared blue in the full moon's reflected light; time was exempt from being neither day nor night, but a bizarre counterpart of the two. The aura and the milky blue light affected Etta; there was something divine about them, but this particular divinity was not holy, was not compassionate. The divine aura and the divine light were more portentous than anything, intimating something rising in the night from the dead stalks of the garden, something walking across the cold wet grass, passing into rooms by way of drafts from windows and open doors.

She followed the slate stone path, went inside and turned on the light. Vincent was not in the bedroom. A drum began to beat from the epicenter of the inn and vibrated the windows of the cottage. Etta heard something in the bathroom, banging in rhythm against the wall, then a rush of water from the shower. Her heart beat wildly as she cracked open the bathroom door and saw the floor covered in urine and towels, the sink filled with hair. The shower curtain rustled. She pulled back the curtain and saw them, a body standing with legs crossed—yellow eyes glowing, tendrils like snakes. Behind it stood Charles, his body hair wet with tiny tributaries of water, his hands blue—blue was everywhere, on the walls, curling about the drain. Vincent teetered and smiled stupidly; his eyes went pale and deadened. Etta suddenly awoke then, as if the night and all that happened beforehand were a dream.

HUMANS
Samantha, 1986

The sun had just set and the sky was a soft rose when my dog Casper and I went for our late afternoon walk. We went along the path, watching gray clouds usurp the day's blue. It was cold and the trail was icy, so I had to be careful. We reached an overlook where you could see the curve of the Cape Ann coast and the beacons at Twin Lights. Casper must have not caught her scent, but I saw her. I looked up and at first I thought she was a deer watching me; then she ducked her head to catch a scent from the ground and dropped her bottom jaw to pant, giving me a doggy smile of acknowledgement. Fuzz, Joan's skinny lady German shepherd, had succeeded in stealthily following us through the woods. I got up and went toward her, wanting to greet her with a pat, and that's when Casper's attention was piqued. He trotted up to her, his golden fur standing up along his spine, his tail regally curled in a perfect circle. Fuzz let him smell her and then lick her underbelly. I tried to push them along; it was getting dark. But Casper had his own agenda. He started pawing at Fuzz, trying to pull her to him, wanting to mount her. Fuzz wanted nothing of it; she turned around and screeched at him, a high-pitched primordial bark that sent a shiver down my spine. I had never heard Fuzz bark before and this startled both Casper and me. He backed away, his ears flat against his head. Then Fuzz stole through the bushes, deeper into the labyrinth.

There was something about that dog Fuzz. There was something about our neighbor Joan. At times I thought they were one and the same, as if Joan could possess her dog's body and run wild in the woods whenever she pleased. In my bed, I thought of Joan roaming the woods at night, trotting down our well-tread trail, waiting for the moon to rise.

We started back home and Fuzz appeared behind us when we reached the end of the trail. I caught her by the collar and after I dropped off Casper, delivered her safely to Joan because I feared she might get hit by a car, running free like that.

Joan's house was filled with interesting items: an abandoned bird's nest sealed in a bell jar, a puppet with an Asian goatee and silky red garb, a basket of a dozen egg shells perfectly composed save two holes for blowing out the yoke. Joan had once placed a weightless, delicate egg in my hand, showed me the holes where she chipped away at the shell with a needle and blew in through one while the yoke slipped through the other. This seemed magical to me, squeezing a yoke through a tiny hole. Also, there was always a low-pitched hum, as if the house were alive.

Upon delivering Fuzz, I nearly forced myself through the door. By the look on Joan's face, she didn't want company, but I needed a confidant. The first thing I noticed was a small wooden chest placed on a weathered lobster trap that served as a coffee table in the living room. I leaned in to look closely at the carvings of grain and vines, an hourglass, a full moon, and the sun. I touched the clasp; outside the wind blew steely ripples in the ocean. The room noticeably darkened. Above me loomed Joan.

I pulled away. "I'm sorry. I shouldn't be touching your things."

Joan stroked the engravings, tentatively. She had slender fingers with nails cut down to the quick, the tops of her fingers noticeably rounded for optimum tactility. She was soft-spoken and kept her graying hair long, but pinned back, a few stray gray swirls cascaded down her temples.

"Oh. Oh no that's all right. This was one of Nathan's projects," she said. "He is a carpenter by trade, but his love is woodcarving."

"It looks like it contains something important."

"An urn. We had a dog many years ago. Jake. After he passed we had him cremated. Nathan made the chest. I was doing some cleaning and found it."

I thought of the dog's dust, sinking my hand into it, if it felt like sand or soot, if there were chips of bone, things that didn't burn. I thought of Nathan's hands, how the fingers bent at the knuckles, how the thumb curled around a carving tool. Nathan's fingers were deft too, perhaps dry, slightly at the tips, like my father's, wider than Joan's, and swift, clean when plucking at a guitar or peeling a shirt off a woman's shoulder. I met him once when he came to visit his mother. I remember he sat out on the deck and played guitar, showed me how to make a fairy's house out of sticks and moss. After he left, I thought about him for weeks.

"Do you think a dog has a soul?" I asked Joan.

"You need only to look into a dog's eyes to know the answer to that."

"Catholics aren't supposed to be cremated," I offered.

"I'm not sure if that's true anymore," Joan added. "They can't keep the ashes. They must be buried in consecrated ground."

"Were you ever Catholic?"

"No."

"Are you Methodist?"

"No, I'm Joan. Just Joan."

Next to the chest was a picture of a woman. The woman was dressed in a black turtleneck with her hair pulled back in a ponytail. She was looking straight at the camera and her face was serious. She was not particularly pretty, but she was vivid, compared to the blurred world in the background. What registered in my mind were her glassy eyes. The face was familiar, but I couldn't place it that night, how she was the girl who disappeared. *Evil*, my mother said to my grandmother on the phone at night in the dark as they discussed current events. *There are evil forces at work in this world.*

"This is my daughter, Elise," Joan said, sliding a nubby finger over the face.

"She's pretty," I said, even though I wasn't sure if that were true. "Where does she live?"

Joan paused a moment. "Far away."

"Does she visit?"

"Yes. In the spring."

"I met your son, but not your daughter."

"She doesn't stay long," Joan said. "She never stays long."

Why had I not remembered the face? We were still living in Watertown at the time, when my brother and I shared a room. My bed was closest to the door that was always left slightly ajar to let in the light from the hall because we were afraid of the dark. I heard the phone conversations, the evening news reports. I said a rosary for her each night she was missing.

"She had long hair when she was a girl. Down past her bum," Joan said. "She never wanted it cut. I called it Magdalene hair and used to brush it every night to manage it."

"After Mary Magdalene. She was known to have beautiful long hair, so long she could wear it as a cloak."

"Right."

"She was the prostitute who loved Jesus. That's what they told us in CCD. He cast seven demons out of her."

"I suppose they told you Eve was to blame for your periods too."

"Well, yes . . ."

Joan regarded me intently. Her wiry grays were especially wild, as if the wind were blowing inside the house without me knowing it. I wondered if she owned a brush.

"Would you like some tea? Here let me take your coat," Joan asked and went into the kitchen. I followed and handed her my coat. "I have chamomile and Earl Grey."

"Nothing special," I said. "We don't drink fancy tea at my house."

"I'll give you the chamomile then. By the way, how's your aunt? I know your mother is concerned about her."

I thought about the baby out of wedlock, my own shenanigans with Patrick. These were sins.

"She's living in sin," I said.

"Sin?"

Sin. The word made me think of Lent, that gray time of year when everything is still dead, how we were given a black nail one Good Friday and the priest shut the lights off in the church while we were still in it. I thought of how I fasted that day, to see if I could do it, go without food and water for twenty-four hours. It was the least I could do. I could have told Joan that I may have been on to something—that after a while, the starving body feels light and holy. Spirit is approachable. I ate breakfast on Saturday, however, because the approach of spirit terrified me.

"She's not married. It's a sin."

"Maybe she's just living her life. That's all any of us can do."

"Some sins are worse than others," I said.

"And what about the log in your own eye?"

"I barely sin. I'm afraid of God's wrath."

Joan scoffed. "God's wrath. This isn't the Middle Ages."

"I believe in evolution too, you know," I said. "We're learning about it in biology class and it makes sense."

"Of course it makes sense." She poured the tea and passed me a carafe of milk and a bowl of sugar. I wanted to show her I had other thoughts. I told her about the beak variations in finches in the Galapagos Islands. I thought then of Ms. White, my teacher, who showed us jars of baby pigs floating in formaldehyde.

There elapsed a silence between us then while we drank our tea.

That's when I thought of that word *divorce*—a word that always seemed to precede the word shame in my family. It was a word that lay in the middle of a sentence like a dead bird or a rotten fish. Etta was getting divorced; Joan was divorced.

The house hummed and the wind howled outside. Fuzz came in then, from the darkness of the living room. "Did you have a good walk, Fuzzy?" Joan asked her. Fuzz stretched her front legs, lowering her bones to the floor, then raising up and stretching her back legs, giving each a little kick.

Joan spoke first. "It's OK you know," she said.

"What's OK?"

Outside there was a light on the deck highlighting dead things in pots. The wind blew hard then and rattled the panes of the glass.

"To be human."

I drank my tea and left Joan and walked the path back to my house in the dark night.

The next day, in art class, I had a lack of ideas in my head. Everyone else was making jars, bowls and other vessels, contentedly. I wanted to make a statue but I didn't know what I was doing. I molded, sculpted, in vain; I was missing crucial information. I pounded the clay down again in frustration. Time was running out, the figure needed to be done by the end of the period so that Miss Rita could fire it up with the others.

"Samantha," she said, "what are you trying to do?"

Miss Rita was one of the cool teachers who had a funky hairdo; one side was cut short, the other was long. I found it somewhat disconcerting, opting for symmetry myself, but I liked her nonetheless.

"I don't know. Something," I said. "I want a figure. A female figure."

"Well, that can be complicated. There's only ten minutes left until the end of the period. We have to clean up in five."

"Geez Samantha, why do you have to be so difficult? Just make a stupid bowl," Mickey Distasio said. Mickey had pointed ears like Spock and small squinty eyes. He was the comedian in the class. "My bowl looks like a scrotum," he said.

Steve Simpson, who sat next to Mickey, snickered. Steve was Mickey's sidekick, the only other male in the class and the one who laughed at everything Mickey said. Steve was cute, had blue eyes with flat brown hair he tried to keep feathered, but always fell into his eyes; he was too much of a flirt to ever consider. At times he was downright annoying, trying to touch me or brush up against me.

"I have to impose my manhood in this class full of ladies," Mickey said.

Miss Rita gave him the evil eye and then turned to me. "Why don't you make some sketches of what you are trying to achieve," she said.

"Can I come back after school?" I asked her.

"I'll be firing at three, so know what you want to do."

I looked at Mickey. He had clay everywhere, smeared on his hands, his face, shirt. "I'm going to stick a love potion in my scrotum," he said. "It's going to knock you out."

"You're wacked," I said.

"You're just jealous you don't have a scrotum."

"I don't give a crap about your damn scrotum."

"Test-eeee," he said. "Get it, teste, testes, scrotum. Do you get it?"

"I get it."

"Let's see. What else can I put in my scrotum . . ."

"Condominiums," Steve replied.

In library study hall, the quiet tickled my brain. I picked out a book on Rodin, the sculptor, and flipped through it. There were pictures of sculptures, mostly nude women and men in various positions, legs spread to more adequately display genitals, people making love, men and women crouched or folded over rocks. These bodies were not clothed in veils and dresses and robes as I had known statues to be; they were just humble human bodies doing what bodies do. This is what Rodin seemed to be saying with his creations. And in that humility I started to recognize *that* different beauty. A human beauty. I thought of Joan. I made a sketch and took it to Miss Rita after school.

Miss Rita sat alone at her desk marking in her grade book. Kids walked by outside, I could hear their voices soften with distance. I took out my sketch. I smoothed my hands on my thighs, preparing to begin. The torso emerged in my hands, breasts, a belly, hips; I stroked the small of her back, fingering her spine, remembering what Etta's spine looked like as she sat in the sunlight on the rocks, molding the blades into her shoulders, rounding the curve of the back, down, down. The clay was cool, soft, and smelled like dirt in spring. It dried and caked in the creases of my hands and underneath my fingernails.

This was my answer to Mickey's scrotum.

Miss Rita came over. "How am I supposed to fire that!"

"You're firing the scrotum."

"Yes. The scrotum. I don't think it's all that recognizable. But this, well. It's lovely, really. The way it . . . slopes and the intimation . . . well, the roundness. It's well, yes. OK. I may have some showcase material I can drape over it."

I left feeling as if I had dispelled something, a hidden need. I felt euphoric.

Miss Rita fired up both the scrotum and my piece and all the other nondescript bowls and vessels. We painted them (I had a hell of a time keeping Steve and Mickey from touching the breasts) and when they were dry, she placed the torso and the scrotum in her showcase, just like she always did with the work that exhibits the most talent. She draped a white cloth over the breasts and tucked the scrotum in the back. I was proud of my work when I saw it in the showcase Monday morning before homeroom. By third period, however, the cloth fell and she was fully exposed. By fifth, she was missing. Someone removed her from the showcase and brought her who knows where.

THE PRESS FOR NORMALCY
Joan

In the spring when Elise returns she will appear behind the sheer curtain at Joan's bedroom window. It will be early, the first light of dawn, when Joan will see the curtain become illuminated from a source within the room. She will wake to this illumination and wait for her eyes to adjust and fully assimilate her daughter's ghost. Sometimes Elise is hesitant, veiled by the curtain for what seems like hours. Joan can only see the side of her face as she peers out the window at the ocean breaking into surf. "Come from behind the curtain, Elise," she will tell her daughter and Elise will fade. Once she whispered softly, "Are you sad, Elise?" Elise turned her back and ascended to the ceiling and up through the light fixture.

Tonight, there was the question of dinner. Joan opened up the refrigerator door and looked at the contents inside: a carton of eggs, an onion, the usual condiments, a bag of carrots, a stick of butter, a jar of strawberry preserves, and a bottle of white wine. She wasn't one to do a big shopping and keep the refrigerator stocked, now that she lived alone. Oftentimes, a simple meal like rice and beans with cumin and olive oil sufficed. Tomorrow she'll go, fill her basket with the essential items, check out in the express lane and be done with it. Joan grabbed the bottle of chardonnay and closed the refrigerator door. She poured herself a glass. Overhead there was the sound of geese in flight. She moved to the window to glimpse the slender black bodies, but it was too dark to see anything. As she leaned over, she felt tension in her throat and her back. She closed her eyes, sipped the wine, and it went down her throat cold.

After Samantha left, Joan brought the chest to the kitchen table, fetched a cloth, opened the latch and removed the urn made of gold mother of pearl. What was she thinking letting Samantha in when the chest was out? Did she want it to be found? She took the white candle from the cabinet, lit it, and watched as the reflection glowed like a hologram in the glass of the sliding doors. It looked like a moth, pattering the pane. She shined the urn, removing all fingerprints and set it on the table. Joan sat down and fetched the book of poems in the cabinet drawer. Sometimes she read the poems to herself after she ate dinner, sometimes before. The book was composed of quality parchment Elise bought at an art store; the poems were handwritten in calligraphy, the pages were tied together with twine. There were doodles of ravens and birch trees on the cover. Joan opened to the first poem:

Here in the world of partial faces
                        and figments
the workings of algebra do not apply
            nor do falling apples
                        or the apogees and perigees
of ellipses.

Here we do not eat or drink but
                        subsist by memory
alone—
            wait for slow moving vessels, their cargo

once vagrant spirits and lovers
            who descend weary and wary,
perplexed by phantom limbs
                        and eyes and ears.

I
allow the newly initiated
            their wanderings
                        their reunion with other shades
in hallowed places
            upon entering their names
                        in a papyrus ledger.

Here they call me queen
            but I am more the interloper
                        the partially abducted,
staid, until the grain above is green
            by my mother's hand.

I heed when She rises
            from mournful slumber
strolling amongst orchards
            swollen with scent,

the ecstasy of her faith
              poised like a kiss.

Fuzz came into the kitchen and had a drink from her water bowl; the dog's soft lapping put Joan at ease and the black depression slid back a little. Her old dog moaning when her bones hit the floor, the soft snoring through her big wet black nose, the rise and fall of her dog belly; these things were soothing. If it weren't for her familiar, what would she do? Fuzz got her out of bed in the morning, gave her a purpose—to care for another being—and carried the momentum of the day.

Joan made herself a small dinner of a poached egg and toast. She sat in front of the empty dish and watched the candle burn. There was a whiteness to the light that resembled the light of the surf on a summer morning, the light of her daughter's face by the window. From a young age, Elise seemed to always be working things in her mind, assessing the world around her, as if she didn't trust it. This was the face she saw illuminated—the anxious face, the distrustful face. Joan had often chastised herself for not breastfeeding her as she did Nathan; maybe if she did her daughter would have felt more secure. Was it the fact that her father traveled the world and was hardly ever home? At night the girl would nervously twirl her long Magdalene hair and rock in her bed as Joan sat at her side, reassuring her of her father's whereabouts and when he would return. It became crucial; Joan had started to notice small patches of scalp developing under the child's ears upon combing her hair, and deduced the girl was pulling it out, surreptitiously, due to her anxiety.

They were living in Colorado at the time. Roger and Joan had moved there when they were first married so Roger could learn how to fly. The masculinity of the environs of Colorado, the rugged Rockies, the endless sky and sun seemed to rouse Roger's own virility. He traded his Irish knit sweaters for a hunting jacket and contemplated buying a gun. He began reading Hemingway faithfully. This was a different man than the grad student she had met, one of those English literature brains who had an ambitiously broad vocabulary, smoked a pipe, dressed like a gentleman, and spoke as if he were giving a commencement speech. Joan observed the great ravines, the dense firs, the winding highway, the landscape of tweed, and felt no affinity for the land. She missed New England terribly; it was in her bones. Her family could be traced back to the first Puritans who came ashore in Salem; she was a descendent of women who knew nature intimately and passed down the recipes of herbal remedies. Here the plant life was an enigma, and there were no telltale signs of the seasons; they seemed to subtly meld into one another. It was disconcerting to her to not see the harbingers of fall or spring, to not witness the first red leaf on the driveway in August, or the first crocus in March, to not find a single plump tomato in the supermarket, or fresh clams for chowder.

Joan had taken a job at the high school where the students were well-mannered, well-dressed and well-liked, where she was given a list of books to teach and not to teach. When Betty Friedan's article was published in *Good Housekeeping*, the women in her neighborhood insisted they were fine with being *Mrs. Peter F. Albright, Jr.* because housework was not so terrible, especially with the invention of modern appliances. Where else could they go where they were the bosses of their own domain? Although the voice in the article resonated with her very being, Joan could not admit to herself she was no different in her intentions to catch her man and keep him.

She left her job in June of 1960 and gave birth to Elise in December of that same year. A year later, she had Nathan. Like the women around her, she was engulfed in the world of rearing two small children. While her children were young, she had just begun to experience the ennui, the "dissatisfied groping" and "yearning" and longed to be back at school studying and writing, being alive in her mind. This was all suspended, however, due to Elise's anxieties.

Joan taught Elise to sew. She bought quality cotton fabrics with flower prints and the two spent hours following the tissue paper patterns, measuring, cutting and manipulating the workings of Joan's Singer sewing machine. The process of sewing their own clothes just as they preferred them was for Joan a striving toward self in the midst of all that was not self, and for Elise, an activity she did with someone else. While there were times she would play with her brother and his Cub Scout friends—boys with their blond hair buzz-cut who brought knowledge of tent building, compasses and campfires—she had no girlfriends and this bothered Joan immensely. More often, Elise kept herself company with a book or the paint-by-numbers set Roger bought her (Joan winced at the cover, how it claimed "to make every man a Rembrandt"). Elise spent hours crafting her pictures and seemed content.

If Elise was such a sensitive child, she must've known on some level that things weren't right. That day, that God-awful day was evidence of it— the day Roger told her the truth and Elise did something unfathomable, something so bizarre, it seemed the stuff of myth. Surely it was the tenuousness of her parents' marriage that was the reason why Elise was always anxious; that was the real anxiety.

Sitting in front of the flickering light of the candle, Joan thought of the times in school when she and Roger walked Commonwealth Avenue flanked by elegant brownstones with romantic window box arrangements of ivy and impatiens and talked about Tolstoy or Kafka. Joan savored talking to a man who actually had a clue about the sorrows and ecstasies of life, even if these were only through literature. She tolerated his brooding over other women because she thought he was attractive with his unruly hair falling in his eyes, fine jaw, and self-deprecating sense of humor. She was a plain girl herself, less attractive for her sex than he was for his, with no striking features that were emblematic of a particular beauty. But intellectually she could keep up with him. They had a good rapport and liked spending time with each other.

Roger had virtually no male friends; Joan's roommate claimed he had no competitive spirit to assert himself in the face of an adversary, and he was unbearably moody, like a woman. *You* would be good for him, she had told Joan, because you are a woman of conviction; Roger needs someone like you.

And she was good to him. Some nights after class, she would bring him dinner, her grandmother's shepherd's pie, ratatouille, fried chicken. He was always appreciative and told her she would make someone a fine wife. When she did not come, he would call her and invite her over to listen to a new jazz record or read the latest chapter of his novel. He did not like to be alone.

Just before graduation, Joan visited Roger in his apartment and he didn't seem himself. He stared blankly out the window watching the students walking to their evening classes under the verdant canopy that muffled the sounds of cars on Commonwealth Avenue one street over. On the table was a bottle of scotch and an empty rocks glass. Dishes were growing mold in the sink. Roger did not look at Joan as she let herself in and sat down next to him. He mumbled to himself, bemoaned not applying for his master's; he had procrastinated with the applications and missed the due dates. His novel wasn't going anywhere. Having no interest in teaching or his father's business, he dreaded what he would do without the bosom of academia to nestle in. After a period of silence, he said, "I need to tell someone this. I am quite certain I am losing my mind."

He reached into his sweater pocket for his parcel of tobacco and pipe. He lit a match, cupped the pipe, and Joan could see that his hands were shaking. He put down the unlit pipe and Joan took his hands in hers. He did not look at her. She tucked a curl behind his ear. Joan felt then that this was an opportunity.

"Thank you for touching me," he said. "I need to be touched."

He told her that while he was walking along the Charles River he felt a peculiar angst come over him; it oozed up out of the muck of the river and like an acid, ate through any decent thought. The people around him continued to be blissfully engaged in their lives, but he was suddenly strikingly aware of how alienated he was from everyone around him. He thought of Sartre and Camus, the plight of the alienated individual in a meaningless life. He started to sweat; his heart started to pound. He looked up at the sky over the river and became so entangled in its vastness, he became dizzy and short of breath. It was not a rational thought—how the vastness of the sky could drive him mad—but he believed it. He cowered, started to run; it was imperative he find a safe, familiar place. He told Joan that he was certain these were the thoughts of a madman.

"I should have listened to my mother and became a priest. I should have thrown myself at religion. I should have learned how to pray."

Roger grabbed the scotch bottle and Joan took it out of his hands.

"This might make things worse. I will make some tea."

She found some Earl Grey in the cabinet and put the flame under the kettle on the stove. Roger continued to look out the window. "I am afraid of going outside. I am afraid of those feelings. I am going to die a madman in this apartment with you taking care of me."

Joan smirked. She set two cups of tea on the table.

"I am going to tell you what we are going to do. I am going to pour this tea and we are going to drink it."

"Do you think I am crazy?"

"I think you are afraid of going out into the world. I think you had an anxiety attack."

"I think I need analysis. Most of my professors are in analysis. It comes with the hopelessness of literature."

"I think you should drink your tea after I pour it. Then I think you should get in bed. I will read to you to calm you down. *Aesop's Fables*. I saw it around here somewhere. You need some life lessons."

Roger did what Joan told him to do. She told him to lie down in his bed and she pulled up a chair and read several stories to him and he closed his eyes. Joan's voice was soothing to him.

"You're too good to me, Joanie," he said.

She closed the book and when he opened his eyes, she no longer saw the blank terror that was there initially.

"Would you be willing to lie next to me?" he asked.

Joan moved into the bed besides Roger and he kissed her. It was the first time he kissed her, and it was tender and innocent. Joan felt herself sink into Roger's embrace with complete abandon. She kissed him back passionately, and her passion gave him the assurance he needed to retire his mind and its whims for the sensuality of the body.

The next day Joan walked along the Charles with Roger, holding his hand. He seemed apprehensive, but able to manage. "I thought I had an idea about what the existentialists meant by angst. I realize now it was all cerebral. Now I can feel it with my gut."

For Roger's graduation present, Joan took him, blindfolded, to an airstrip just outside Newburyport. "We're going to indulge in the vastness of the sky," she told him when she took his blindfold off. Roger sat in the copilot's seat and surveyed the instruments, asking the pilot—a young man not much older than himself—what each of them was used for.

The plane was a small craft, sat only three people, and as it sped down the runway, Roger distinctly felt the ecstasy of liftoff and dropped Joan's hand. The plane climbed higher and higher and the land seemed to swirl downward, as if it were water down a drain. Upon reaching altitude, there was a padded silence and a placid feeling as if they were floating in a dream. Outside, the clouds waltzed slowing around the plane and the kingdom of fear seemed to be a very far away place. When the young pilot asked Roger to take the controls, he didn't balk.

Afterward, Roger told Joan that he knew how to conquer his angst. He needed to make a decision, expel the ambiguity of his life. He was going to enlist in the Air Force.

There were nights when Joan played Duke Ellington low on the phonograph, lit candles around the living room and they would make love on the floor. Joan never stopped longing for Roger's body, his plum and powdered male smell, his lean build and muscular thighs, the scramble of light brown hair across his chest. Afterward, they would stare at the ceiling; "You're too good to me Joanie," Roger would say.

Sitting before the light of the candle, before the urn of her daughter's ashes, she thought about Roger's proposal, how he brought her red roses and came to her mother's house in Magnolia. Roger told Joan that she made him feel safe, that, perhaps, he loved her. "What else could this attachment be?" he asked.

She was three months pregnant. After they eloped and moved to Colorado, she miscarried.

The marriage officially fell apart around Elise's tenth birthday. Joan decided to throw her a party; she wanted her to have girlfriends. They would have cake and make friendship bracelets. Elise protested. She didn't want any girls to come to her house. She thought the girls in her class were dumb. But Joan was adamant and got a list of names from her teacher. Although twelve invitations were sent, three girls attended. The mothers came to the door with their girls promptly at two in the afternoon as specified on the invitation. They were dressed in A-line party dresses with ribbons in their hair that matched the same ribbon around each elegantly wrapped present. Their mothers wore similar A-line dresses with pocketbooks dangling from their gloved wrists.

Once the mothers left, the girls huddled together like ducks. They talked only to one another and not to Elise, who sat quietly working on a bracelet. Then, at one point, Joan distinctly remembered that Elise disappeared. She called for her outside in the yard, down the basement and upstairs. She fetched her son and had him call for her. The pretty little girls stared at her with wondrous eyes and Joan felt the blood pump hard out of her heart. "Are we playing hide and seek? Is Elise hiding?" they asked. The impeccably dressed girls rushed out the door and dispersed into the red dirt of the hills after Joan's son Nathan. They rambled about until Joan succeeded in rounding them up by tempting them with cake.

"Why would we have cake without Elise? It's *her* birthday," one of them said.

"She must be in the house. We checked everywhere out here."

"Maybe she's hiding upstairs!"

They raced into the house. Joan followed them pleading as they went from room to room, opening closets, pulling up bedspreads. "Got her!" The girl was on her knees peering under Joan's bed, pulling back the bed cover as if she were coaxing out a cat. The others dropped to their knees and started giggling.

"Quick! Grab her foot!"

"Ow, she just kicked me!"

Joan heard a muffled howl from the bottom of the bed as the girls scrambled about poking and pulling her daughter's hair. "Stop!" she yelled. Then one of them shrieked and the others immediately scurried away from the bed.

"She bit me! That animal bit me!"

Joan rushed to the girl to inspect her hand, now imprinted with white teeth marks that broke the skin. The girls stood up and escorted the wounded out of the bedroom, stroking her hair. Joan got down on her knees and looked under the bed where her daughter was curled, her long hair shielding her face.

"What am I supposed to say to the mother? Good God, Elise, what the hell am I supposed to say to *that* mother?"

Elise started to sob, "This is all your fault! Can't you see that they hate me? Can't you see that I hate them? Why would you do this to me?"

Joan froze with guilt. She was exhausted and frazzled. Elise was right; it was a terrible idea. When the mothers came; Joan stood before them and like a prisoner bearing lashings, took the brunt of the women's collective insults regarding how Elise was feral and needed a cage, how Joan was a hippie with no morals or sense of decorum, how the family should just pack up and go somewhere else, because they weren't liked in the community.

"Get out of my house," Joan said, and tossed each of the gifts onto the lawn after them.

Joan anticipated Elise giving her a fight when she told her to put out her school clothes for the morning and she was right. Elise didn't want to go to school. Joan didn't budge; if she let Elise have her way and stay home it would be twice as hard to go the next day. She began to sob and this pained Joan. She told her daughter that Daddy would take her to school tomorrow. This seemed to not only appease Elise; it appeased Joan as well. She realized then she was happy to relinquish some of the burden of the child.

Joan took a hot bath, styled her hair, made up her face, and slipped into the black polyester catsuit she had made for Roger's return. She perfumed her wrists and neck. She had every intention of forgetting the events of the day.

Joan lit the votive candles and put them around the house. She put on the Duke Ellington record, covered the dining room table with a white tablecloth and fetched ivory colored tapered candles. At ten past nine, the front door opened. Joan dimmed the lights and went to the kitchen to pour the wine; she waited for her husband to say something about the candles and the tablecloth. He didn't. She heard him ascend the stairs to the bedroom. After a short while, he appeared in the kitchen in his undershirt and uniform pants. He leaned himself up against the wall and looked at the floor. He appeared as if he was going to cry.

"Joanie," he said. He sighed, a long, loose breath. "You look very pretty."

He ran his finger down her arm, tenderly, almost forlornly.

Joan had the two wine glasses in her hands. She sipped from one and put it down. Suddenly her muscles became taut.

"What's wrong?" she asked.

Roger did not answer.

"Look at me Roger. What's wrong?"

Roger went and sat at the dining room table. He ran his fingers through his hair. Joan thought perhaps someone was dead. His mother had a weak heart and she was old. Or perhaps she had fallen. Suddenly Joan was chilled; she went and grabbed a throw blanket from the couch, wrapped it around her and sat across from him at the dining room table. Outside a car drove by, its headlights illuminating the street in front of it.

Roger moved in his chair, put up his hands to his face. She heard him sigh. She looked down at the woolen threads of the throw around her, how they were unraveling.

"You've put up with me all these years, Joanie. You've always been so good to me," he said finally.

"Why do you say that. Stop saying that."

She stood up and moved away from the table into the living room where the sounds of "Take the A Train" played low.

"It was wrong, Joan," Roger said, becoming more composed, more confident. He told her how infidelity was a sign of something terribly amiss in a marriage, that he had fallen in love, deeply in love, for the first time in his life. Roger's face seemed different when he said this; it was as if some great burden had lifted. Despite her immediate anger, Joan believed him when he said he was happy. She felt that it was right. It was something that was bound to happen—his falling in love—an event that always lived inside her.

Joan shut off the record player. She thought of the girls looking under the bed, pulling on her daughter's hair. She thought of New England in the spring when the lilacs bloomed and the rain soaked the earth. Outside the red lights of a car stopped at the end of the street.

"We need to talk about this," Roger said. He rubbed his eyes with his hands. "At some point we're going to have to talk about this," he said. "About arrangements."

"Arrangements?" she asked. "You make the fucking arrangements."

Joan went upstairs to the bedroom and slammed the door. She locked
it from the inside and pulled the bed covers around her, shaking with
cold. Roger came upstairs and shook the door. She would go to her
mother's house in Magnolia. She would leave him everything, the house,
the furniture, the cars, but she would take her children. She needed
to clear her head and make her own arrangements. The era of magical
thinking was over.

In the morning, the sun pronounced itself in narrow sheets beneath the
opaque curtains of her bedroom, trying to get in. Joan rose, still dressed
in the catsuit, opened her bedroom door and heard her husband snoring
on the couch in the living room. What would she tell the children? Her
insides were vacuous and her stomach churned. She needed her children
to be strong as she would be strong; she needed to continue to press
for normalcy. She would do this first by getting them to school. Joan
opened the door to Nathan's room where her son was swaddled in his
bed sheet like a big yellow grub. She put her hand on his shoulder and
nudged him.

"It's morning honey, come on, you have to get up."

Nathan unwrapped himself and blinked his eyes. It was one of Roger's
expressions, the way his tired face crinkled. "Five more minutes," he said.

"No, Nathan, now."

Outside she heard the far away sounds of cars and magpies. Nathan
pulled open a drawer and it screeched, just as it would any other morning.
Joan went to Elise's room and saw that her daughter was already sitting
up in bed. But it wasn't Elise; it was someone else. Joan squinted and
moved slowly toward the figure that regarded her suspiciously; it took
Joan a moment to comprehend exactly who or what she was looking
at. She gasped, recoiled from her daughter whose bare scalp was now
prominent and mottled with patches of purple. Her hair lay on the
rumpled bedspread in front of her, a tangled creature, lifeless.

§

Her face, my winter mother
With few diamonds in her gown
This evening
Heaven's pearl and pull of water

She is white light
And my bath tonight

My mistress spirit and wife
You speak lovely words
Beneath my life

Joan read the poem aloud just to hear a voice in the room. Then
she sat silently in front of the mother of pearl urn and the dinner plate
with its stain of yolk, while the flame danced and Fuzz whimpered in her
sleep. The night was silent save the soft whistling of the wind through the
eaves. She closed her eyes and an image flashed before her mind. It was
that of a painting of sunflowers, the one Elise painted in the Garden of
the Gods. Joan thought a picnic might help take her mind of things and
settle Elise. She packed a lunch and the children brought their respective
items to busy themselves: Elise her paint by numbers and Nathan a tent
to pitch. They set down on the outskirts of the sunflower field. Nathan
began to assemble his tent for shade. Elise set up her paints. Joan spread
the sheet flat on the grass and stretched out her legs in the sun.

The Garden of the Gods, with its ubiquitous red dirt, upright
riverbeds and backdrop of Pikes Peak seemed like an alternate world
to Joan. It was a place more for prodigious reptiles and mammals, a
primitive landscape. Even the birds were bigger, the magpies and the
scrub jays were the size of cats. Above was the great blue vault of sky;
the trees shied from it, keeping close to the ground. Joan felt exposed;
there was always some agitation regarding this alternate place, but she
stayed hopeful. There were the columbines, fairy-like flowers that she
delighted in. There were the sunflowers, how the slender bodies followed
the wind and she wished she could relax enough to doze as she did on the
beach where the sea lapped at the shore and sailboats glided across the
rim of the water on Cape Ann in Massachusetts where her mother lived.

That day, Elise had a creative breakthrough; she abandoned the
numbers and the lines and was instead painting the agile stalks of the

sunflowers. Joan nearly gasped, but said nothing to interrupt her. She attempted to read a book—*The Awakening* by Kate Chopin—and read the same sentence four or five times before she put the book down; she was preoccupied with the emergence of Elise's fragile, nascent flowers. Nathan asked for some potato salad and she made him a dish and poured three cups of lemonade. She placed a dish of eggs and potato salad next to Elise and made a plate for herself. They ate while the wind carried a man's voice over the hills. Joan could not make out the words, only the intonations, as if the man were gently instructing a child. At times she felt the man was close, coming down the trail behind her, but when she turned her head, no one was there. Joan went back to reading her sentence. She thought of what she might make for dinner. She closed her eyes and saw her mother then, hunched over strawberry bushes. She thought of the mushrooms she and her mother gathered in the woods, the soft humus of the earth, the taste of the mushrooms in butter, seasoned with sage and thyme. She thought of the strawberries at Connor Farm, the green baskets they used for collecting and how the berries would burst and the red juice would stain the green of the basket. The humid air. The locust trees. These thoughts trickled in and out as if her mind was a sieve and could hold nothing.

Elise handed Joan the finished painting. "Here. This is for you, Mommy."

The manner in which the flowers were painted, delicately, almost impressionistic, had displayed an acute awareness of the essence of the subject. Elise put her head on her mother's lap. Joan stroked her daughter's hair. "This is lovely . . . this is . . ." She stopped. She noticed a silhouette of a man in the upper right hand corner. Was it just the way the watercolor had formed? It was subtle, entangled in the flowers. There was clearly a head, shoulders, a distinct body, a dark body.

"Who is this?" Joan asked, showing her daughter the figure.

"That's the man," Elise said.

"What man?" Joan asked.

Elise shrugged her shoulders.

Joan thought of the disembodied voice. "Did you hear him talking?"

Elise nodded her head yes.

Did Elise know back then that a man would come for her? Did

she know like Anna Karenina knew that she would be hit by that train?
Tolstoy was a genius; he realized that somewhere inside ourselves we
carry around glimpses of our own death.

Joan looked at the way the shadows flickered on the wall and felt the
nameless hollowness of grief. She had failed her daughter; she could not
deny that. Joan thought about the knives in the drawer, the pills in the
cabinet. She thought about the dark cold water. She stared at the food
on her plate, the wine glass, touched the flame with her finger and felt
the prick of pain. She dared herself to hold her finger inside the flame
just above the blue. The flame circled her finger like a ring; it was almost
enjoyable to feel the flame burning her hand. She snatched it back then
snuffed out the candle and the kitchen was silent and dark.

NOVELTY FADES

Elise, 1976

When Elise couldn't sleep, she carefully navigated her grandmother's floorboards, keeping in mind which one creaked the most as if she were traversing a minefield. She slipped a winter coat over her nightgown and went walking under the sky of spilled stars. Here, engulfed in darkness, her internal darkness retreated; her mood lifted with the raw beauty of night. At the beach, the ocean was an invisible thing and treacherous without the moon but audible in its tumbling surf. The lobster boats droned offshore; it was comforting to know there were others out there. Elise sat in the cool sand and smoked, waiting for the harbinger of day, that blurred eye of God to rise tentatively in the East. Later, during study period, she would fall asleep at the brink of a dream, only to be wrenched back into wakefulness by the scrape of chairs preceding the second period bell.

She had not written one number, not one variable in her notebook and was already failing Mrs. Kanter's Pre-Calculus class after three weeks of school. Instead, she doodled, and wrote lines that came to her head, inspired somewhat remotely by the classroom. The elfish teacher circulated the room to check on the progress of the other students, especially diligent in following the antics of parabolas. When Mrs. Kanter approached Elise, she noticed the doodles and the four-line poem:

> Letters are squiggly
> On black slate
> Privilege to write there
> Where the grown up lives
>
> Our writing always looks
> Too small
> Slanted, going down
> Like a fly

Mrs. Kanter inspected Elise's notebook, read the poem and told her to go to the office— this class was for students who wanted to learn, not write drivel and daydream out the window. Elise unabashedly picked up her things, her books, her leather fringed purse and went out the door. She faced the long hall toward the principal's office when she registered how the stairwell doors, freshly painted, were propped open some ten feet away. She went surreptitiously down the stairs and out a side door into the glorious October morning.

Elise walked nonchalantly down Ferncroft Road, passed the officer perched at the mouth of the school driveway, also daydreaming, and toward Willow Street, the route that would take her out of town. She kept her head down, noting pieces of chrome, the crunch of sandal on pebbles on asphalt, the sound of whirring cars, a dead hawk with its pure white breast ripped apart and wings frayed every which way. She had hitchhiked before with her friend Temesia; once they were picked up by a man with a wooden arm. He drove them from Magnolia to Gloucester in a pea green Mustang and Temesia cajoled him into telling the story about how he lost his arm by getting tangled up in his gear while fishing in the Georges Bank. Temesia was good that way, acting sweet and innocent and sometimes downright stupid to get what she wanted. From that day on she and Temesia hitchhiked nearly every day to Crane Beach or Rockport or Singing Beach. Familiar roads had become adventurous windings in the backseat of a stranger's car.

Elise had known Temesia since they were both in the fourth grade. Her mother would find the girls dressing up Nana's dogs and singing in Elise's room or out in the yard with aster wreathes in their hair. At night, her mother would hear about the Old Sirs and the Lady Bells, stately firs and miniature mushrooms the girls had found and used in the stories of fairies they created. Elise liked Temesia because she was imaginative. As a young girl, Temesia believed in shy fairies that lived under rocks; you had to sit very still in order to see one out of the corner of your eye. She gave names to mushrooms, trees, and rocks and had a pet raccoon she nursed with a bottle when it was young. Temesia could climb a tree to the top and often had sap clumped in her hair. Once she had the idea of eating milk with a spoon and Elise could swear that the milk tasted like ice cream.

Now, Temesia had a boyfriend who was obsessed with her. His name was Rick Beaulieu, son of Richard Beaulieu, an insurance agent who had his office in the town, his name written on the glass window in gilded lettering. Elise loathed Rick. She loathed his lettered jacket, his tall lean frame, the slight gap between his front teeth when he laughed at something stupid, how he only adored Elise because she was Temesia's best friend. She loathed the way Rick was always touching Temesia, stroking her hair, holding her hand, her elbow, her hip. But Rick wasn't the only one Elise loathed. She loathed Mrs. Granger, Temesia's mother who had always regarded Elise with what Nana referred to as a "hairy eyeball." She too had become overly concerned with her daughter, the way she sat in chairs, how her hair looked, if there was dirt under her fingernails, because according to Mrs. Granger, Temesia was a lady now and needed to present herself accordingly, to secure a husband.

Elise knew it bothered her mother that she didn't have a boyfriend of her own. Her mother often made comments about the boys in town, how Derek Coombs was making eyes at Elise at Crosby's Market. Elise scoffed. "Oh, OK. He's not cool. You want a cool person," her mother would say. Sometimes she would plead with her daughter, "Isn't there anyone, Elise?" Her mother's worried eyes made her feel as if she were doomed.

There was someone, Mr. Sullivan, her poetry teacher, Hippie Sullivan is what the kids called him. Elise thought of him when her mother asked about boys, but it wasn't that she was infatuated with him or attracted to him; she sensed that perhaps she could talk to him, that he might have a clue about the undercurrents, the mechanisms, the agendas that made people act in certain ways. Hippie Sullivan had blond hair down past his ears, wore thick leather belts, bell-bottom jeans, and Jesus sandals. He brought in a braided rug and a lamp to cozy up his classroom and the students would laze on fat pillows reading Langston Hughes, Frost, Sexton. Elise wondered about Hippie Sullivan's body, his lovers, was enchanted by the way he looked up at the ceiling tiles and recited Yeats. She could see him with the poets themselves listening to jazz in someone's basement, jugs of wine on the table, mystifying clouds of smoke, pillars of old tomes, faces torn up in laughter or tears. "The poet," he said, "has a certain intimacy with life itself."

§

Elise lived in the same house her grandfather built on ten acres of farmland, most of it grown in by deciduous trees and marked by boundaries permanently set in place by rock walls. The house itself was quite large with nineteen rooms, each with a portrait of some distant ancestor dressed in the dark clothing and ethereal lace of the Puritan era. Nana would tell her the stories of the ancestors, light a candle, and open the window so that its flame elongated like a finger, pointing above Elise's head to the portrait of Annabelle Bradstreet, a woman who lived alone in a root cellar in the woods and kept company with a pack of dogs. Elise was enamored by Nana's stories of Annabelle, how she tore out her own hair to make poppets of her enemies, vexing them with unmentionable ailments. "Normal is boring," Nana said. "Consider yourself lucky to have such genes."

Elise's grandmother, the renowned Margaret Bradstreet, was a statuesque, robust woman with shoulder length white hair secured off her face with gold bobby pins. She wore her dead husband's flannel shirts because she couldn't see giving them away if they kept her warm and fit her almost perfectly. When Elise and her brother arrived in Magnolia after their parents' divorce, people went out of their way to say hello to Margaret Bradstreet's grandchildren and make them feel welcome. Nana believed an idle mind was the devil's workshop; she taught the children how to swim and sail, how to navigate the trails in the woods, grow a garden of herbs, play the piano. Life had a joyous rhythm when Nana was sane.

Junior year Elise changed her appearance. This was coincidental to the police arresting Nana for breaking into the Second Congregational Church at three in the morning one Sunday night. When Nana was admitted into the nursing home, Elise stopped wearing skirts and button down shirts and started wearing halter tops and jeans she sewed herself. She strung beads in her hair and wore braids. Often she was sent home for the derogatory words she had written on the patches of her jeans, words from Janis Joplin songs, Allen Ginsberg poems, words like *mouth-wracked and battered bleak of brain, cocksman and Adonis of Denver*. Elise had no political agenda; she was not out to offend anyone. She just liked the words and wanted to decorate herself with them. Temesia told her she was brave, an artist. Others, Rick, Mrs. Granger, teachers, classmates looked at her with their hairy eyeballs.

§

Elise's anxiety of being caught dwindled with every step she took further out of town. Just past the cemetery on Main Street she swiftly turned around and stuck out her thumb to the oncoming car. Much to her surprise, the first car was her father's 1960 Chevrolet Impala. It braked and pulled toward the side of the road and Elise felt her knees go weak. She approached the car tentatively and peered in at the man in a white t-shirt as he leaned over to roll down the passenger side window. Her mind played with the features of the man's face and attempted to manipulate them.

"Where ya headed, darlin'?" the man asked.

"North," Elise replied. "Newburyport."

"Well that's easy enough. Get in!"

The man had soft blue eyes and pockmarked skin. His hair was long, like Hippie Sullivan's, but the ink from his tattoos, faded so much so the images were unrecognizable, was an indication of age. Elise debated what to do while observing how the sun danced across the spotless cherry red of the car door. Her father used to wash and wax his car on the weekends when he was home; Elise remembered how he carefully soaped the white-walled tires, how the soap slid lovingly down that cherry red door onto the driveway and toward the drain in the street, a soft ooze of bubbles.

As a child, she believed her father lived a beautiful life somewhere else. She dreamed of finding him in the sliding dimensions of the dream world, in Europe, perhaps, where there were snow-topped mountains and small villages with quaint houses and shuttered windows. He would have another family, girls in pinafores, boys in blue knickers. His new wife, a Julie Andrews look-alike. And Elise would tell him how she was his daughter and that he had a son Nathan and a wife Joan. But her father, always in his uniform, stately, and charming, would tell her it was impossible. She learned to think of him this way, after years of searching for him in the grocery store or the pharmacy, the mall, at the beach; the dream, although heartbreaking, presented an answer.

But when Roger came to the house dressed in khakis and a pullover, Elise thought he looked like something out of a JCPenney catalogue. His cologne filled the house. Nana's dogs continuously sniffed his crotch and barked until they had to be turned out to the yard. Elise was annoyed at the way her father talked to her and her brother as if they were still in grade school. They went to pick apples, as a "family," and she remembered her father on the pay phone afterward, talking to his second wife, entering dime after dime to prolong the call. It seemed ridiculous that he should come, that her mother should make him a meal, that Nana should leave so as to not give into the impulse to run him over with her truck. They sat at the dining room table, and her father tried his best to be cheerful. Both her parents were pathetically cheerful. Her father talked about the weather in Colorado, how it hadn't rained in weeks. He sat in Nana's chair going on and on about nothing and Elise thought about jock itch and hernias, constipation, and the runs—all of the unmentionables Annabelle Bradstreet inflicted on her enemies.

She grabbed the chrome handle and opened the door.

"Well, alright!" the blue-eyed man said and skid the tires, accelerating back onto the road. Elise felt suddenly alive as if she had stepped out of her life and into a film noir. "I'm headed up the coast. Got a cousin in Bangor," the man said.

"Where did you get this car?" Elise asked.

Wind rushed through the car and reverberated like a jackhammer when the man accelerated onto the highway.

"What?" he shouted.

Elise shouted her question over the reverberating wind. The man howled and accelerated up to eighty miles an hour. Elise's hair whipped at her face. She cranked up the window.

"Oh this was my uncle's. He bought it at an auction somewheres in Dallas. He's dead now."

The man told Elise his name was Andy. She told the man her name was Sally. This was something she and Temesia always did, make up false names to tell the drivers.

The man swiped his brow with his right shoulder, stared at Elise's knees through the corners of his eyes. "Well shoot. Look at what I found on the side of the road," he said, smacking the steering wheel. "How old are you, darlin'?"

"How old are *you*?" Elise asked.

"I asked you first."

Elise smiled. Andy smacked the steering wheel again. She glanced at the watch on his arm, gold plated with a diamond chip in the middle and wondered if it was his uncle's as well. Elise interpreted the configuration of the hands as ten thirty. The bell to end Pre-Calculus class was going to ring in two minutes. She sat back and laughed. Andy glanced at her and back at the road. He laughed too, swiped his brow again with his shoulder. Elise stretched out her feet and threw her books onto the backseat where there was a duffel bag and a map book of the states.

"Damn, I like you!" Andy yelled.

"I like you too!" Elise yelled back.

"Listen Sal, if you got no plans, we could drive to Nova Scotia. What do you say?"

Elise thought of her mother, how she made suggestions. *Elise, perhaps you should think about visiting some schools*, or *Elise, perhaps you should throw a sweater over that top*. For the most part, Elise ignored her, but she hated herself for it. Her mother didn't deserve half the shit life threw at her.

"I'll take a rain check," she said.

The motel room smelled of cigarettes and Lysol. Andy took out a bottle of Jack Daniel's and fetched two Dixie Cups from the bathroom. "Mother's milk," he said gulping down a Dixie shot. He went to the bathroom and closed the door. Elise had no interest in the hard liquor; she instead checked every drawer for remnants of patrons past, finding only the Gideon Bible. She sat on the edge of the bed, titillated, wondering how this day would end, what she would tell Temesia. The door of the bathroom opened again and Andy came barreling into the room without his shirt. He flexed his lean muscles for Elise. "Punch me. Right in the pecs. Go ahead."

Elise clenched her fist and socked him one.

"You feel that? Do it again."

Elise hit him harder. He clenched his teeth and Elise laughed at his funny expression. He puffed out his breath and went back to the bathroom and shut the door again. Elise heard the cascade hit the toilet and the toilet flush. He turned on the faucet. She thought of the time she and Temesia locked themselves in the bathroom, stripped themselves of their clothes and pretended to pose nude for one another, like Playboy centerfolds. Temesia was the photographer first and then Elise was the photographer. She clicked an imaginary shutter on Temesia's white, supple body. Afterward, they sat in the tub and Temesia asked Elise if she wanted her to kiss her like a boy. Elise had never been kissed on the mouth by anyone, then. She remembered just how it felt, the weight of Temesia's body pressing down on her in the tub, how their skin touched, the gentle tap of her lips, like the petal to a flower folding. Temesia got up and put on her clothes afterward, as if nothing happened. Elise thought about that kiss for years.

Elise heard the shower run and Andy's whistle rendition of "Band on the Run." She accompanied it with the words in her head, got up and pulled back the cover of the bed exposing two pillows. The blanket was soft, a cranberry color to match the spread, the sheets white, perfectly wrapped around the mattress. Elise took off her jeans, shirt and bra and tucked herself in the tightly fitted sheet and blanket like a letter in an envelope. She closed her eyes and tried not to think of her mother.

Andy came out, a towel around his waist. He walked to the edge of the bed and sat. She looked at him through half-closed eyes. "Well look at you," he said.

"Look at *you*."

He half-smiled, stood up and moved closer to her. He raised his hand to touch her, and picked up the strands of her hair and let them fall. Andy, dripping cool water onto the white, stalled. "You do have such fine hair. Must take you a while to wash all of it." He got up, ran his fingers through his wet hair, let the towel fall to the floor. Elise stared at his naked body as he moved about the room, his scrawny legs, his moon white ass, and half erect penis. "I need a cigarette," he said. "You got one?"

"In my purse. On the chair."

He fumbled with the contents inside, wavering. "Front pocket," Elise said.

"You girls with all your *shit*." He lost his balance for a moment and fell sideways onto the bed. The purse dropped and out came her book of poems crafted from the backs of cards, hole punched and fastened with her mother's yarn. Andy grabbed the book, "What's this, little girl, is this your diary?"

"No, give me that."

"Can I read your diary, little girl," Andy teased.

"It's not a fucking diary."

"Whoa, there must be something good in here. Hot damn!"

"Give it to me, goddamn it," she said, lunging at him. He held the book above her head. Andy dodged Elise and fumbled through the pages, mocking her by reading some of the words. Elise leapt at him, tore the book from his hands, scratching the skin on his hand with her nails.

"You crazy little bitch," Andy sneered. Her aggression brought his penis to a full erection and he pinned her on the bed. "What you gonna do now?" he said, gritting his teeth.

"You dumb hick."

The lids of Andy's eyes lowered. He let her go, and she shimmied from beneath him. He got up, grabbed the towel from the floor, wrapped it around him and sat in the chair at the table with the half empty Jack Daniel's bottle, balancing himself precariously on the back legs. "You hurt my feelings," he said.

"I what?"

"You. Hurt. My. Feelings," he repeated slowly. He pointed to his faded tattoo. "Honorable discharge!" he shouted, wavering and slurring his words, "You," he pointed, "wouldn't know anything 'bout that, 'cause I reckon you ain't honorable."

Elise thought a second about being honorable. Her grandmother was honorable. Her mother was honorable. Her father was not honorable.

"You're right. I am not honorable. So what."

"I know girls like you."

"No you don't. You don't know at all. You don't have the capacity to know. How someone who is not honorable may be a virgin."

Andy came down hard on the four legs. " A what?"

"You heard me."

"You don't act like a virgin," Andy said tentatively.

Elise stood up so that Andy had full view of her waif-like body, her small breasts. She pulled the locks of hair around her, like a shawl. Andy got up and pressed his face into her abdomen; she felt the scratch of his stubbled skin. He lifted her up, took two steps and fumbled with her onto the bed, ran his hand down the curve of her back. Terror shot up her spine like a flare. The cool of the water, she said to herself, the cool droplets of water. The smell of soap, of innocence. He fumbled for her panties, kissed her lips with too hungry a mouth, writhed with deadbeat breath; his sex knocked at her like a blind mole. He collapsed moments later and lay upon her like a dead weight and started to doze. Elise rolled him over, watched his chest rise and fall for nearly an hour.

Elise waited patiently for a change, a signal that life continued even in the altered state, a signal to leave the place and go home. It took the pale diffusion of afternoon light coming through the crack in the curtain to rouse her. She rose, picked up her panties, bra and dusty jeans, her leather-fringed pocketbook and book of poetry, but before she left, she tore a page from her notebook and wrote a message: "No interest in Nova Scotia. How about Mexico?" She wrote her number on the back, folded the note and stuck it in the pocket of Andy's Levi's.

The sun lit up a new world.

Elise took out a perfectly good pen she found on the floor of the train and opened to the last page in her notebook. In it she captured the flock of words orbiting her mind:

> Fresh eyes flash, take in unexceptional items
> every banal thing has a name.
> In the mind, a marble finds its grooved track
> that same pathetic winding.
> I get behind the wheel,
> turn off toward Ferncroft.
> yet, what I want lies beyond this
> where righteous firs flank boreal routes—
>
> and the sun rises.
>
> (I shall dazzle myself with novelty
> *until novelty fades*).

She pondered the use of parentheses. Without them, the poem seemed to end too abruptly. She put her pen down. The man next to her in a three-piece suit had his head on the window pane, his paper collapsed in his lap. He was old, white, and murmured between two fat pink lips as he slept. She pushed herself to think of another verse, but nothing came. The train rocked back and forth and the sleepy, dull-faced passengers jostled and swayed. She was awake, alive. She saw herself, juxtaposed with the dull-faced passengers, with their bodies bobbing and shifting to the train's rhythms. She would be nothing like these people.

Part II

APHRODITE AND THE BOAT BUILDER
Etta, 1984

In the spring of her thirty-fourth year, Etta decided to leave Vermont, spend the summer at her sister's in Gloucester, then head out to California in the fall. In the back of Etta's mind, California was still an out. No matter how unfulfilling her life was at the time, she would think to herself, "I will be living there someday and all of this will be a memory." From her conversations with her friend Patsy, people seemed to have meaningful lives there; they had a progressive mindset and were less apt to worry about making a living, or finding a mate, or getting old.

Patsy had a roommate who was moving out to attend grad school, so Etta had a place to stay in San Francisco. It was just a matter of getting herself out there, but this wasn't an easy thing to do. Etta needed people; it was far easier to jump on a bandwagon than create one.

Before Etta arrived at her sister's doorstep in Gloucester, she was living in a small studio near the campus of the University of Vermont. She found a job cleaning the deans' offices and was approached by an art professor to do some modeling. Kyle Kent was a tall man with big hands who looked more like a basketball player than an artist. He was a technician who could reproduce the masters down to the brushstroke; he knew the composition of paints, the science of color, was obsessive about his brushes and how they were stored. He equipped Etta with a sword and painted his own head for a rendition of *Judith Beheading Holofernes*. But Kyle did not fulfill Etta's romantic expectations of being an artist. Art was an external thing Kyle could mimic, not a means to express the interface between the sensual and internal worlds.

Etta believed she had no God-given talent, but she did like to look at her own face. She never passed on the opportunity to gaze at herself in a mirror and often she was genuinely pleased. If, however, God had asked her what gift she wanted for this life, she would have gladly told Him to give her the gift of creativity. Like California, creativity seemed to be a charm against the drudgeries of existence. She had decided if she could not be an artist, then she would be the art. Etta loved the studios, the half-finished canvases, the still life arrangements of clay bowls, marble busts, delicate glass-blown orbs, and exotic silks falling over sharp edges. She began to model for other professors as well and delighted in watching herself materialize on canvas, or paper, or film. She liked to believe these exterior selves lived more exotic lives without her.

The cerebral inclinations of the professors, however, were a mark against their virility. When one had propositioned her for sex, offering her money should she not find him attractive, she was annoyed. As a muse, she was looking to be seduced, not propositioned.

It was her hankering for virility that brought Etta to Cameron's, a local Gloucester restaurant where the fisherman ordered rounds at the bar, drank to get drunk and rehash their stories of the sea. They were rugged, unshaved men with weathered hands; they smelled of grease, kelp, and bait and gawked at Etta; she was the best thing they'd seen in months. The few women who accompanied them were hard looking, had chemical-dyed hair and gruff voices. They glared at her, "Look at that one," they said. "Where do you suppose she came from?"

Etta clasped her pocketbook, a hand-crocheted bag she bought at a fair, unzipped it, and retrieved her lighter and pack of cigarettes. She crouched to light her cigarette but the late spring gale that blew in with the opening of the door extinguished the flame. She ducked lower into a meaty palm for cover. "Success," said a man dressed in Carhartt overalls. Etta pawed at the ashtray just out of reach, and the man pushed it over toward her; she noticed his neck was beet red and speckled with stubble above his white turtleneck.

"You have the eyes of a Selkie," he told her.

"She's out of your league, Tommy," someone shouted.

"You know what they're thinking by the eyes," Tommy continued, smoothing the stubble over his throat and glancing down at Etta, tentatively. "If you're kind to 'er, the eyes turn soft, but if you're not, you'll know the animal in 'er," he said. Then he chuckled softly and looked down at his large hand grasping his beer. "I'll leave you alone," he said and turned toward away from her.

"Buy me a drink," Etta said.

Tommy ordered Etta a beer and monopolized her attention with stories of lobster fishing, standard traps, how to measure a lobster with a lobster gauge, the largest lobster ever to be caught on Cape Ann etc. Etta feigned interest to have someone anchor her in the cacophony of the overcrowded bar. After a while, Tommy had moved his bulk into the confines of Etta's personal space and Etta became acutely aware of a man leaning on his elbow at the bar watching their interaction.

Etta interrupted Tommy's monologue on lobsters. "Don't you know any Selkie stories?" she asked.

Tommy took a step back and wavered slightly in place. He rubbed his eye and looked up at the ceiling tiles. "I can't say I know of any. I know that if you steal a Selkie's hide, you can keep 'er," he said. "Just like I want to keep you." His eyelids lowered and he reached out to twirl a lock of Etta's hair around his fingers.

The first thing Etta noticed about Daniel was how a tender pink hue resonated in the ebbs and flows of his freckled skin. He was tall, could see eye to eye with Tommy, but he had significantly less girth.

"Get your grubby hands out of the lady's hair," he said.

Tommy swayed a bit. He laughed silently to himself. "Shut up, Danny," he said. "Mind your own damn business."

Etta cowered into her drink.

"The lady is here for a few drinks. She doesn't need the likes of you groping her."

"I wasn't groping her. Was I groping you, Selkie?"

Etta looked at Daniel; she was almost annoyed by him making himself the hero.

Before she could answer, someone splashed a drink in Tommy's face and the bar broke out into a melee. Etta slipped out and went to the ladies room. She stayed there reading the obscenities in the stall until the ruckus had stopped, then went out the back door into a parking lot. A man was crouching at a motorcycle in the shadows. "Hey Selkie," he said softly. "Do you want to see the moon set?"

Daniel started the bike and it popped and spat and roared, tackling the serenity of the dark, empty streets. The sky over Gloucester was now unveiling its stars; the moon was an ember, an afterglow just above the horizon. With the movement of the bike, Etta was chilled but her body vibrated with exhilaration. Above the roaring and spitting engine, she could hear herself laughing.

Daniel pulled into a parking lot and shut off the bike. Etta's mind attempted to decipher the shades of the landscape, the tall firs, the patches of grass, a gravel road, a dark path into the arched boughs of trees. Daniel dismounted and headed up the path. Etta followed. In the distance, the waves pounded the rocks and dogs were barking. The trail opened up and he picked up a rock and hurled it upward toward the stars; a moment later it kerplunked in a body of water below. He walked deeper into the woods and came out into a clearing with low-lying brambles. In the ghastly night, Etta could see the gales swoop down through the shrubbery.

She stumbled a bit. "Watch it here," Daniel said. They walked a narrow path along the granite coast where someone had constructed a dozen or so rock structures, precariously balanced but tolerating the wind. Etta watched the surf shoot up, sprawl and retreat behind them. The wind was blowing hard and she was terribly chilled. "Get down low," Daniel said. He huddled below a tall boulder. Etta sat down next to him and the gales passed neatly over them. Daniel fumbled for something in the brush, a black cauldron, lifted the lid and rustled some papers. He set the cauldron snug in a crevice between the boulders and lit the paper. A flame's tongues lapped upward, illuminating his face, his pressed lips. He settled himself down on the ground and withdrew a joint.

"I know everyone on this island and I don't know you. You're not from around here."

"You're right. I'm not."

"So where are you from?"

"I don't have a place."

"Fuck that. Everybody has a place."

Daniel sucked on the joint and handed it to Etta, holding his toke. He puffed it out in a cloud.

"Why did you take me here?" Etta asked.

"You looked bored. You were tolerating Tommy. I can tell when a woman is tolerating a man."

"And how is that."

"She doesn't say much. Looks at everyone but him."

Etta withdrew and tasted the sharp bite of the joint on the back of her throat. The barking dogs seemed to be getting closer now. Etta regarded Daniel, waited for him to tell her what to do. "Be still," he said. The surf sprung up, toppled, pushed into the crevices of the rock and retreated in a hiss. The dogs started to circle; one had burst through the bush and stopped a few feet in front of them, growling viciously. Etta could see it in full silhouette now, steam coming out its mouth; it looked like a wolf.

"Oh Christ," Daniel said.

Someone whistled in the distance and the dog sniffed the air and disappeared back into the brush. Etta felt her warm blood retreat from her rapidly beating heart.

They sat there silently for a long while, passing the joint back and forth. Etta watched the vaporous bodies of clouds move with haste against the backdrop of stars. Daniel watched the clouds as well. He cleared his throat and she waited for him to speak, but he didn't. Once the fire in the cauldron dwindled, he replaced the lid. He stood up and stuck his hands in his jean pockets. "Let's get the hell out of here," he said. They hiked back to the bike and Daniel took her back to Cameron's where she located Mira's Honda Accord and drove home.

If one thing could deter Etta from California, it would be love.

Etta had waited for Daniel to call. She did not give him her number that night he took her to Halibut Point; she thought he would work at it, try to find her. But he didn't. So Etta went back to Cameron's and got the directions to Daniel's shop from the bartender who wrote them in ink on a napkin. She walked the three or so miles from her sister's house to Lanesville and came upon the gravel road just before the center of town. The shop was in a metal building across from a granite pier; in the small cove lobster boats rocked gently with the waves. She knocked at a door with a sign that said "Machinist" with a drawing of a propeller. When no one answered, she tried it, but it was locked. Etta removed her sweatshirt and tied it about her waist. It was mid May and several trees were in bloom in various shades of pink and white; tulips and forsythia added focal points to the burgeoning green everywhere. She went around the back where there were lobster traps stacked, a pile of buoys, a lobster boat with half its hull painted crimson. Propped up, its belly of a hull was grossly misplaced in plain air.

"Hullo?"someone called. An old man sat in an Adirondack chair at the house next door. "He ain't here," he said. "Went back for suppa. Lives just up the street over Red's. You got a boat that needs fixin'?"

"No," Etta said. "I'm a friend."

"That's what they all say," the old man replied and lifted his oil-stained cap.

Lanesville is a small gathering of storefronts, a post office, a general store, several art studios, and a coffee shop. Etta reached the stairway to the apartment over Red's and heard someone, a woman singing the *Ave Maria*. The singing appeared to be coming from Daniel's apartment. The voice so impressed Etta she stopped a moment and inhaled. She climbed the stairway to the door and knocked three times. Daniel opened the door.

"Holy shit," he said.

He invited her in. Inside was a wooden table with a pale blue plastic cafeteria chair, a mattress on the floor with a crumpled sheet and blanket, and a basket of clothes. Etta looked for a place to sit and eyed the cafeteria chair. "Please," Daniel said.

The singing had stopped. Etta noticed a woman's silver clutch on the kitchenette counter. "Someone was singing," she said.

Daniel leaned against the door and folded his arms. "Yes," he said, trying to keep from smiling. "A friend. She's practicing for a wedding."

Etta bit her lip. Suddenly, a toilet flushed and the bathroom door burst open just beyond the mattress and a beautiful woman dressed in a silver gown shimmered in the middle of the room like a mirage. She was fair and had ivory-colored skin, wore several thin bracelets that tinkled when she walked. On her right shoulder was a tattoo of a treble clef. When she saw Etta her countenance divulged anxiety.

"Who are you?" the woman asked.

"Cassie, this is my friend Etta. Etta, this is my friend Cassie. Cassie was just leaving." Daniel tapped at his watch.

"Where's my purse," Cassie asked, twirling about. Daniel pointed to the clutch on the cabinet top. She grabbed it, then went to the cabinet and retrieved a bottle of rum, unscrewed the cap, and took a few gulps.

"I get nervous," she said.

"You'll be fine," Daniel said.

Cassie glanced at Etta, fetched a lipstick from her clutch and did a once over on her lips. "Nice to meet you," she said, perfunctorily. Before she left, she looked at Daniel; it was a brief communication of sorts.

"Go," he said.

Etta told herself to be cool; if she acted too hastily and left, Daniel would surmise that it wasn't just a friendly visit. They went to the granite pier by his shop and drank beer until the sun set and the sky turned blush and the wind started to pick up. Daniel took her to his shop to see *The Rune*, the wooden sloop he was nearly finished building. The shop was neater than the apartment, with tools meticulously hung on a pegboard, labeled drawers, a shelf of books in alphabetical order by author, a stack of plans under a glass paperweight, and various professional woodcutting machines. *The Rune* was a work of craftsmanship, even to the untrained eye. *She is a seventeen-foot sloop, with cedar strakes and cabin and mast made of spruce*, Daniel told Etta. He sifted through the plans, showing Etta how he built it, using jargon that sent her blurred mind into a tizzy.

Afterward, they bought some day-old sandwiches, potato chips and bottles of Coke at the general store and went upstairs to eat and watch a Red Sox game. Lying on the mattress, Daniel took Etta's hand and held it gently. He stroked the knuckles with his thumb. When he kissed her, he settled the ache that had manifested in the core of her body.

The next day Etta woke up to Daniel's freckled back and the late spring sun streaming into the apartment. Something metallic was sticking out from the pillow reflecting its light. Etta reached under the pillow and withdrew a thin, silver bracelet. She pocketed the thing, dressed, and hitchhiked home.

Imagining Daniel and Cassie making love mere hours before she and Daniel were intimate was titillating to Etta.

Daniel had attempted to downplay his relationship with Cassie after she left for the wedding; they had known each other since junior high, had the same friends, were more like brother and sister. Etta scoffed, "I don't think anyone could be a brother to that woman."

§

Daniel was a boy/man dichotomy. Etta loved the boy part and the man part; she loved his freckled body, his curls, his childlike fascination with things, boats, fish, birds. She had found detailed drawings of swordfish, ospreys, kingfishers, tucked away in books; drawings a boy would create as a study. The man had a keen understanding of mechanics and carpentry; he had helped build a seventy-foot schooner in Tahiti one summer when he was twenty-one, and lived upon it when he was twenty-two; he had reputable stock in General Electric. He wore spectacles to read, paid his bills on time. He was twenty-four years old.

One hot day in early summer, Daniel took Etta swimming in the quarry. He parked the bike under a large elm tree, near a picket fence where a yellow rose bush was cascading in full bloom. The minor keys of Beethoven's "Für Elise" trickled out of a nearby window. They walked down the road past kids on tricycles circling in a driveway and into the woods where there was a well-tread path to the quarry. In the distance, boys' voices were echoing. Etta and Daniel veered off onto a secondary path and passed the rusted frame of a small car and several fire pits of charred wood, burnt glass, and crushed beer cans. They reached an opening and beheld the kingdom of rock and its body of water that mirrored the sky. On a clearing below, bronzed teenage girls were supine and sullen listening to "Jungle Love" by the Steve Miller Band. They shielded their eyes to regard Etta as young girls might regard a woman whose beauty and mystique had matured to fruition—half in adoration, half in envy.

Daniel removed his shirt and headed down into the water, navigating the large granite boulders to get in. He dove in and surfaced near a floating log. Etta removed her jean cutoffs and t-shirt; she wore her niece's bathing suit that was small enough to exhibit the vanilla parts of her and contrast it starkly against her bronzed limbs. She lowered herself thigh high into the water; it was warm and had a slight soft film. Daniel wrestled with the log and then mounted it. He stood up, wobbled, outstretched his arms to balance himself, tripped and fell into the water. There were boys perched on a cliff nearby; one of them clapped. Daniel swam over to the path to the cliff, hoisted himself up. Long-limbed boys, dripping wet, stood around him, joking with him. It was clear Daniel knew them. A few of the boys leapt from the cliff in opposite directions, grabbed ahold of their knees and hit the water in a series of cannonball splashes. Daniel dove off the cliff after them. He swam over to Etta and grabbed ahold of her leg.

"Go try it," he said. "It's fun."

"I don't know. I have a thing with heights."

"OK," Daniel said, laying on his back. Etta observed Daniel's body in the quarry water; it seemed to take on a yellow glow.

Etta decided she should jump. She hoisted herself up the rocks, to the top of the cliff, about twelve feet off the surface of the water. Boys fumbled behind her; the water from their bodies wet the rocks. She stood at the cliff and looked across the quarry at its circumference of stone walls, other cliffs, each with its share of divers. Overhead, crows were squawking in the tall oaks. Etta focused on Daniel below, waving his arms to keep afloat. The boys began to crowd her on the rock. After a while, one of them said to Daniel, "Tell her to do it. We don't have all day."

"Yeah," another one said.

"Who's up there?" another asked.

"The lady."

"Cassie did it," one boy recalled.

"Cassie did it a hundred times."

"Give her some room, assholes!" Daniel called up.

The boys shimmied back. Etta shielded her eyes from the sun and looked at the girls who were now sitting up on their towels, watching her on the cliff.

"OK," Etta said. "OK."

She knew if she stalled, it would be harder, so she hurled herself into the air, quaking and shivering and crashed into the water awkwardly on her left hip and thigh. Beneath the water, she registered how much it smarted, but she was thrilled she had done it and wanted to jump again. When she surfaced, she heard everyone laughing.

"Are you alright?" Daniel asked, smiling.

Etta was embarrassed. "Yes, I'm fine," she said. She surveyed the cliffs for Cassie, but she didn't see her.

Later, they sat on a grassy knoll in the waning afternoon sun. The water of the quarry was now still; the boys and the teenage girls had gone home. Daniel picked a tall reed of grass and brushed it along Etta's thigh.

"I'm older than you," she said to him.

"So."

"Maybe I'm ten years older than you."

"Maybe you are."

"Maybe I'm more than ten years."

"You're perfect," Daniel said. He put the end of the reed of grass to his lips. "Besides, I like dark women. When I was in Tahiti I was enchanted with the dark women there; they were exotic, yet innocent. I don't know if you're innocent, but you certainly are mysterious."

Etta imagined Gauguin's brown, supple natives, the sensual atmosphere of the tropics.

"Was there anyone in particular?" she asked.

"I wasn't available."

"Gauguin left his wife for those women."

"Who?"

"The painter, Gauguin. You must regret it now."

Daniel crunched the grass between his teeth. "Maybe," he said.

It was late July and the wind at 7 knots when Daniel took *The Rune* for her maiden voyage. A small group of men gathered to see her off and were admiring the boat as she sat on a trailer towed by a friend's truck that was idling and filling the pristine sea air with exhaust fumes. The boat ramp plunged into the cold, still water of the harbor; a pair of mallards navigated between the boats, the bland, speckled female following the male's iridescent emerald head. Etta, holding her beach bag with towels, sun tan lotion, and cut-off jeans, observed an iron eyehook protruding from a granite block and wondered who had put it there.

The men with a penchant for craftsmanship smoothed the boat's strakes, commented on her curves. They talked of types of epoxies, how to plane wood the right way, who built what boat on the island and recounted the construction process of *The Rune*, who visited Daniel at what stage, how construction was faring at the time.

"You buy a steam box?" one of the men asked.

"Used Burnham's," said the old-timer, answering for Daniel.

"You know Burnham?"

"Who doesn't know Burnham, you old fool," the old-timer said.

The man who plunged the iron eyehook into the block of granite was dead. The men before her wore pastel Izod shirts and khakis, were shod in leather sandals. They were the appreciators and Etta speculated how they were no different than she in not knowing first hand what the sea could do, how it could wreck things. She thought of waves she had seen on television, a surfer descending the belly of a forty-footer like a fly dashing down a windowpane.

One of them, an older gentleman about sixty, detached himself from the group and approached Etta. "Well she's full to the gunwales, me lady," he said. "Know anything about being a first mate?"

"Nothing at all."

"Dick Durkin," the man said, extending his hand to Etta and she took it; it was as slender as a woman's. Dick told her about the schooner he had docked at Rocky Neck, how Daniel was integral in her upkeep. He knew Daniel because they had both helped build a friend's seventy footer in Tahiti. That friend, he said, went on to sail the world.

Etta's interest in sailing was piqued by the discussion. Sailors, it appeared, were romantics who knew how to bring their dreams to fruition.

Daniel stocked the boat with life preservers, nautical charts, jugs of water, beer, sandwiches, and blankets. He handed Etta a bottle of champagne in a canvas bag, "Will you do the honors?" Ropes clanged against the masts of moored sailboats as the men grew silent, their focus now on Etta holding the canvas bag with the champagne.

"What happened to the blond?" one of them murmured. "They were supposed to get married."

Etta clutched the glass neck of the champagne through the canvas bag and realized Cassie never sailed in the boat; this was a first. She looked at Daniel and he gave her his dimpled smile.

"Hit it hard," he said.

The Rune motored out of the harbor and into open waters where Daniel let up her sails and she heeled toward Rockport. He pointed out the main elements of the boat and attempted to give Etta a lesson in sailing, but Etta was not at all interested in learning the mechanics and mechanisms of *The Rune*. She was there to observe Daniel in his element because that's what turned her on. She was also there to relax. So he told her to be vigilant of the boom, the horizontal cantilevered beam protruding from the mast that could knock her senseless, and left it at that.

   Daniel pulled into Folly Cove and anchored his boat. The cove was cooler and partially shaded, its rocks wet and black with the receding tide. White-breasted gulls perched on the roofs of a few moored trawlers that floated below the dark tide line of the rocks. Cormorants perched nearby on an anchored dory with draped wings spread for drying as Daniel and Etta ate lunch and drank beer. Afterward, they dove into the water and swam to a pebbled beach. Etta hunted for shells and Daniel hunted for mussels in the seaweed beds draped over the wet rocks. Daniel placed the mussels in a netted bag and they swam back to the boat. After dumping the mussels in a bucket of water, Daniel held out his hand for Etta to come below deck. They made love and lay in each other's arms listening to the soft drone of life happening elsewhere.

The land from the vantage point of a boat brought on a new perspective; it was ripe for exploration. They sailed into Bearskin Neck and tied the boat at the dock adjacent to Motif No. 1, a world-renowned fishing shack. Etta had been to Rockport before with Mira and Samantha and thought it typically quaint and uninteresting with its knickknack colonial shops, ice cream stands, and family-fare restaurants. From the perspective of the sea, however, Rockport was both elegant and eclectic in its thin white spires, menagerie of colorful boats, and well-crafted homes of stone and glass built harmoniously into the coastline. As they motored in toward the docks, someone was playing classical guitar perched on a rock in the jetty and the aroma of roasted peanuts wafted through the air.

Daniel took Etta to his favorite places, first, a shop where Tibetan bowls and giant tribal masks were sold; Daniel bought some incense and Etta bought a bracelet of Buddhist prayer beads. They visited an art gallery where canvases of giant red poppy flowers were on display, each one remarkable in capturing the ephemeral, slender and passionate essence of the flower. They perused antique shops, drifting away from one another, back, away, feeling the force of an intimate gravity between them, the excitement of moving in and out of a new lover's personal space in public. Afterward, Daniel knew of a lobster company where you could get takeout and eat out back at a table overlooking the harbor, but when they arrived, the line was out the door and down the street. They tried several restaurants and settled for a table indoors where an elderly waitress with a checkered blue uniform and large bust took their order.

It was the dinner hour and the restaurant was crowded. An obese couple in the next booth ate lobster rolls, the flesh of the woman's thigh spilling over her seat. An elderly woman with an oxygen tank complained to a young waitress that she had forgotten to bring her tea. Daniel stroked Etta's hand with his thumb as he looked around at the patrons, at a family with a young boy rolling a toy truck over his father's arm. The father grabbed the truck and threatened to take it away and the boy began to wail. The chatter stopped. The obese couple continued to eat silently and intently, as the other diners crouched in their booths.

Ugh, Etta thought. Ugh. She shifted in her seat, debated going to the ladies room until the boy stopped. It would have been much worse if she were with Mira and Samantha; not being able to gaze upon Daniel's ruddy-bronzed skin would have made the place intolerable.

The boy stopped and the chatter resumed. She looked out the window for a glimpse of the boat, maybe the top of the mast or the tip of the bow.

"You can't see the boat from here," she said.

"It's behind us," Daniel said pointing in the opposite direction.

Daniel registered Etta's chagrin and leaned back in his chair. He tapped at the napkin with the end of his knife.

"How do I prevent you from leaving me?" he asked.

"Who said I was going to leave you."

"You're fidgeting."

The waitress arrived then with the plated food and Daniel told her to box it up to go.

He leaned in closer. "My plan is this: I will tie an imaginary string to your ankle and when you stray, I will feel it tug on my end."

"That's fair," Etta said. "I think I can handle an imaginary string."

Afterward, they floated aimlessly in the vicinity of Thatcher Island and the Twin Lights. The sky had turned pink and sea ducks oscillated up and down in the soft, teal-colored waves. They huddled under a blanket and Etta stroked Daniel's calf muscle with her big toe. Suddenly a slick head bobbed up from one of the waves; it disappeared and bobbed up again, further away. Etta pointed to it.

"Harbor seal," Daniel said. "Selkie."

Etta probed Daniel for a Selkie story then and he told her the one about the McClosky child who was thrown from the bow of a ferry in rough seas around the Isle of Man. A seal hunter had found him several months later, naked and suckling aside a pup from the teat of a Selkie.

The night pooled into the blush of dusk as they waited for the first pinprick of a star. "Maybe you and I will have a child someday," Daniel said.

Etta did not reply. She thought him bold to say such a thing, but it made her happy. She was beginning to think her time for having a child had passed.

"Tomorrow is another day," Daniel said. "You're not going to believe how delicious those mussels will be sautéed in butter and wine."

Etta lay with her head in Dick Durkin's plush pillow, the name *Lady Artemis* embroidered across its fine cotton sham. Daniel was next to her with his hands behind his head, staring at the planks on the ceiling. It was their last night living in luxury; Dick Durkin was to return from the south of France in a few days and the honeymoon, as Daniel called it, would be over.

"Being inside the ribs of the hull felt sacred, like Jonah inside the whale," Daniel said. He was talking about the boat he helped build in Tahiti, a schooner similar to the *Lady Artemis*.

"There was no wine bar, no espresso machine, no master suite with a down comforter and embroidered sheets," he said, motioning to the sheets crumpled at the foot of the bed and referring to Dick's penchant for fine things. Etta stroked Daniel's freckled hand and noted the boat's slight undulation, the creak of wood, the sound of piano and laughter in the distance. She traced her finger around Daniel's birthmark, just above his navel, and then above that, around a filigree of hair across his chest. When he is older, it will grow dense, she thought to herself.

"It was a great experience," Daniel continued, "but it wasn't real. I suppose I'm more provincial than I'd like to admit. I like a summer that is earned by a hard winter."

"I didn't know a boat could have a room like this. It doesn't feel like a boat."

"It'll feel like a boat in 60 knot winds."

The air got cooler; it was nearly eight in the evening. Etta got up, grabbed a terry cloth robe from a hook behind the door. Daniel reached for her, pulled open the robe, put his face to her soft abdomen. She stroked his curls. "If you were to get pregnant—I'm telling you, I wouldn't mind."

Etta gushed with post-coital emotion. Tears came to her eyes. "Do you mean it? Think of what you are saying."

"I know what I'm saying. It would be a travesty, a woman like you, not having a child."

Etta stared at a framed photograph of the bow of the boat heeling into the spray and thought about the minutiae of domesticity, how a child would demand that; she thought of how living on a boat like this—or any boat for that matter—might remedy it. Anything was possible.

Daniel found a tuxedo and a white chiffon dress in the master bedroom closet and insisted they play dress up. They cooked steak and shrimp with saffron rice; they popped open a bottle of champagne. Etta and Daniel danced barefoot on deck as the people around the piano bar at Rocky Neck sang "Cheeseburger in Paradise" and artists opened their windows to let in the ambiance of a midsummer's night. On the terrace of a fine restaurant, a party of men and women moved about white linen tablecloths and candlelight. A silver-haired man gazed down at Etta and

Daniel and cupped his hands around his mouth, "A man keeps his hand on the small of a woman's back, son!" he shouted.

Daniel acknowledged the man with a nod and moved his hand down.

The silver-haired man raised his glass and the others, in their stiff black bow ties and pale shimmering gowns, followed suit

"That's better, son," the older man shouted. "You lead and she'll fall into place."

"Dickhead," Daniel murmured. He whispered in Etta's ear, "How 'bout we give 'em a show." Daniel got down on one knee.

Etta sobered quickly, noting Daniel's position, the mischievous look in his eyes. The crowd quieted. Someone threw an ice cube across the way and it slid across the deck. Daniel took Etta's hand and brought it to his lips. "Etta," he said, kissing her hand. He cleared his throat.

She balked, looked at the crowd who was now leaning over the railing.

"Say yes," Daniel whispered to Etta. "Say yes."

The silver-haired man leaned in and pulled at his ear.

"Yes," Etta said.

Daniel laughed and Etta could see the white of his back teeth. He was drunk. "Say it louder. Say it real loud."

"Yes!" Etta shouted.

The crowd broke into a festive melee and showered the couple in ice and paper napkins. Daniel stood up and kissed Etta squarely on the mouth. The piano banged out a rendition of "Here Comes the Bride."

After the elegant diners had left the candlelit terrace and joined the drunken singers at the piano, Etta and Daniel lay on the deck wrapped in a blanket drinking champagne and staring at the satellites flickering across the night sky. Ropes were pinging against the masts of moored boats and a saxophone played above the drums and bass of a band in the distance. The moon, an illuminated perambulator, rolled imperceptibly down the slope of the sky.

"You were kidding." Etta said. "I assumed you were kidding."

"Do you want me to be kidding?" Daniel leaned back; his tuxedo tie and top buttons were undone and his eyelids were heavy. There was a dimple in his left cheek.

"You're fooling with me."

"I am not. I am not fooling with you. I am in love with you. Are you in love with me?"

Etta felt the wine warm in her veins. "Yes. I'm in love with you."

"Then let's do it. Why the fuck not? Let's get married."

Just when Cassie's mirage had started to fade in Etta's mind, she reappeared in her life. It was a week after Daniel proposed; he was working late, repairing a trawler in Annisquam. Etta lounged on his mattress painting her toenails listening to the rain hit the roof when she heard someone knock. She opened the door and at first did not recognize Cassie, whose hair was plastered to her round white face.

"Is Daniel here?" she asked.

"No, he's working."

"Is he in the shop?"

"No. He's working on a boat in Annisquam."

"In this weather?" Cassie said and glared at Etta a moment then looked out toward the metal building where Daniel had his shop; the rain splashed from the gutter around her white sneakers.

"Please come in," Etta said. "You're soaking wet."

Etta held the door open and Cassie ducked inside. She took off the army jacket she was wearing and hung it on the doorknob. It was soaked through and her cotton t-shirt was soaked as well. "I'll get you a shirt," Etta said.

"No, I'm fine. You don't have to do that."

"You're going to get sick."

Cassie shrugged her shoulders like a child. Etta fetched one of Daniel's flannel shirts and gave it to her. She folded over, removed her shirt so that Etta could see her bra strap taut against the rolls of her soft flesh and the tattoo of the treble clef on her right shoulder. She was rounder, plumper than Etta remembered. Cassie placed the wet t-shirt on the table, sat down, and angled toward Etta. She propped up her head with her left hand and bounced her right knee, nervously.

"Is something wrong?" Etta asked.

Cassie sucked in air. "He owes me some money. I know he's good for it. But I need it now."

Etta wondered if Cassie knew she and Daniel were getting married. She assumed she knew, but she wasn't going to broach the subject unless

Cassie broached it first. Etta put on a pot of coffee and the coffee maker gurgled and hissed as she stood at the counter waiting for it to finish. Cassie looked around the apartment as if she had never been there; her bouncing knee vibrated the glassware in the cabinet.

"When did he say he was coming back?"

"He didn't."

"Huh. Well I'm not going to wait long."

"I don't mind," Etta said. She set two mugs on the counter and poured the coffee. Its aroma filled the apartment and eradicated some of the dampness. Etta was hopeful; she thought that maybe Cassie would talk to her, that they could be friends; she didn't have any friends in Gloucester. She imagined the two of them going out for a drink, laughing about Daniel's eccentricities, the way he pats the back of his head and feels for his curls when he's contemplating something.

"I take mine black," Cassie said and stopped bouncing her leg. Etta poured the coffee into two mugs from Lobstaland and slid one over to Cassie. She cupped her mug in her hands and sipped. Etta fixed her own coffee and leaned against the counter. She glanced down at her rolled sleeve; she too was wearing one of Daniel's flannel shirts.

Cassie curled up toward her coffee and sipped quietly. The rain pelted the roof hard and they both looked at the ceiling. "He's quite a catch," she said, finally. "But I bet you know that."

Etta looked at Cassie's face and saw that the color had been washed out of it. She was pallid and her eyes had dark shadows under them. Etta didn't know what to say to her.

"I don't regret breaking it off with him, though," she continued. "I mean, he's just so fucking mature. I'm not half as mature as he is. I want to live, for Chrissakes. I have a cousin who has a houseboat in the Keys. I might go visit her." Cassie set the mug down and delicately traced her finger around the rim. "You're older. You probably want what he wants."

Etta was taken aback by Cassie's candor. "I suppose I do," Etta said.

"Yeah," Cassie said. She almost scoffed when she said it. She stared into her coffee cup. "I go to a psychic in Salem, off Essex Street. Last time I went she told me my sister's boyfriend was cheating on her. Even had the name right—Michelle. I went to her to find out about my life and that's the first thing she tells me, 'Your sister's boyfriend is cheating on her.'"

"What did she say about you?"

"She mentioned you. How Daniel would fall in love with you. But it wouldn't be right."

The rain had stopped and it was silent. Etta stewed in her seat. She wanted to tell Cassie to get the fuck out. Cassie peered at Etta over the rim of her cup, surveying her face. "Are you sure he's working late?"

"Of course he's working late."

Cassie got up, peeved. "This is bullshit. I can't wait all night for him." She put on the wet army coat over Daniel's flannel shirt and grabbed her t-shirt off the table. "Just tell him to call me," she said and was out the door.

Etta told Daniel about Cassie's visit, but he didn't call her. She called two days later. Etta could hear her from across the room, sobbing. Daniel hung up the phone and grabbed his coat. "Oh the drama," he said. "I'll be back in a little while."

When he came back, hours later, his nonchalance was replaced with dejection, manifested in his silhouetted, slow body movements. Before he lay down next to Etta on the mattress, he squatted down at the edge and stared blankly at the wall for a moment.

"What is it?" Etta asked.

"I thought you were asleep."

"Is something wrong? Did you give her the money?"

"What money?" Daniel hesitated then. "Yeah, yeah everything's fine," he moved under the covers and turned away from Etta.

"What is it?" Etta asked again, anxiously.

Daniel didn't answer.

"I told you she came to visit," Etta offered.

"I know."

Etta stared up at the darkness. She waited a while for Daniel to say something, but the next thing she heard was the rolling breath of sleep.

Daniel woke the next morning with newfound cheer and Etta dismissed the issue; she wasn't one to deliberate on things, and also, the wedding had momentum now and demanded her attention, especially since her sister Mira had inserted herself into the planning. Etta insisted on something simple, a Justice of the peace in lieu of a priest, a short guest list of only immediate family and close friends, no flowers; she would have her mother's gown altered and save herself the agony of finding a dress. Mira contested Etta's decisions, but Etta was firm; if her sister would not honor her wishes, she and Daniel were going to elope.

The night before the wedding, Etta had an anxiety attack while having dinner at Friendly's with her sister. They had just fetched the gown from the seamstress and Mira was casually nibbling on fries, reminiscing about her own wedding, who was there, what was served for dinner, how she wished she could relive every moment of it because it went so fast, when Etta suddenly experienced a sudden onslaught of lightheadedness. Her heart started to beat wildly and she broke out into a sweat. Etta dismissed herself and went to the bathroom, taking quick, short breaths; she ran warm water over her hands, trying to soothe herself.

The next day, she hurled herself into a marriage with Daniel just as she hurled herself off the quarry cliff.

§

The house had a disease. This is what Etta took from the conversation with the realtor. She had told them that the previous tenant—the house was heretofore a rental—had left suddenly for New York. He was ill. "Perhaps you know him? His name is Julius Laurendent. He is a painter and some of his work is on display at the Rockport Art Association."

"Oh," Etta said.

"I'm not familiar with him," Daniel said.

"It's not important," the realtor said. She had long acrylic nails, was unnaturally tan, wore a black polyester suit with heels one might wear to a cocktail party. When she talked, her tongue clicked between her sentences. "Isn't it cute? I just love the fireplace in the living room. And the wooden floors—to die for." She clutched the listing, sucked at her lower lip. Debra the realtor waltzed across the wooden floors toward a south-facing window and pulled back a white sheer curtain. "And the yard—all perennials—lamb's ear, lilies, bleeding hearts, hostas."

It was a gray day in early September and they had been married two weeks; Daniel had just taken the boat out of the water to coat the hull in another layer of epoxy. They were driving home and saw the Open House sign on a patch of grass in front of a small yellow house. Daniel insisted they go in and just take a peek. Etta was indifferent; she didn't mind living in Daniel's place in Lanesville; she liked the town and was getting to know some of the neighbors, but Daniel was adamant about buying a house. He and his new bride were not going to live like immigrants, sleeping on a mattress in a one-room apartment.

"And the heating system?"

"Oil. The furnace was recently updated."

Etta glanced at the backyard. An assortment of chairs were moldering in a circle around a small makeshift fire pit. Debra smacked her lips. "Shall we go upstairs?"

The carpeting in the stairwell was well tread at the center of each stair. Debra went into the first bedroom and opened the closet. "Decent size," she said. Her voice resonated slightly in the empty room. "Walls are all freshly painted. I like the color—autumn haze."

Daniel looked up at the ceiling fan with one lit bulb. Etta fingered the broken shade at the window. "What illness did he have?"

"Who?"

"The artist."

"Not sure," Debra said.

"What's an average heating bill during the winter?" Daniel asked.

"I have all of that information downstairs," Debra said, snapping her heels across the wooden floor toward the hallway. She flicked on the light in the bathroom. The shower rod had fallen down and was propped up inside the tub; there was a putrid green toilet. It reminded Etta of a gallbladder.

"Ew," Etta said.

"What?" Debra asked.

"No window," Daniel said.

"The seller just added a new ventilation system," Debra offered, flicking a second switch. A fan whirred overhead. "The tub is newly sealed. And the fixtures," she said, stroking the chrome of the sink faucet, "all new."

"Any plumbing problems?"

Debra shook her head.

They visited the two smaller bedrooms, one, according to Debra, could be an office, and the other—she winked at Etta— a nursery.

"Let's see the attic," Daniel said.

"The roof has another ten, fifteen years," Debra exclaimed, pulling down the attic door and staircase. Etta lingered in the bedroom below, restless and irked by a sense of debilitation. Outside, the gray clouds coagulated and formed a padded ceiling over the sky. She thought of the boat, propped up in Daniel's office, prematurely removed from the water when there was still some fine sailing to do. Etta went to the closet and peered inside; there was a rolled piece of paper in the corner. She unfurled a drawing of a nude man with his hands on his hips staring at a space on the floor in front of him. The sketch was done in thick, grasping strokes; the man's scrotum was greatly exaggerated and looked like a punching bag.

Upon hearing Debra's calculated steps down the attic stairs, Etta rolled up the paper and placed it back in the corner. "It's a quiet neighborhood. I just sold a two family down the street. Young couple like yourself. They love it here," Debra said.

They followed Debra down the stairs and out the front door. Etta glanced back at the house—it appeared ashen. "I think this house is perfect for you," Debra said, handing Daniel her card with the listing. Daniel took Debra's card and put it in his wallet. He told Debra he would be in touch and placed his hand on Etta's back to guide her to his car.

"What do you think?" Daniel asked. He started the car then waved to Debra as she passed by in her silver Mercedes.

"It's a house."

"You don't like it."

"It has an unnerving sense of permanence."

"You need to get over it."

"Over what?"

"Your need to drift."

"I've never had the need to drift," Etta said, putting her hand on Daniel's knee as he drove down the street.

Lanesville was ripe for small discoveries. While Daniel was at work, Etta spent many a day walking with a small backpack filled with books, a bottle of Coke, and a towel. She had discovered Plum Cove and went there for a morning swim when it was warm and the water was sultry and speckled with sunlight and white herons sauntered along the rocks looking for fish. Up the hill was a small Catholic church where the sun sprinkled the colored light of stained glass martyrs across a marble altar as a group of elderly women recited the Rosary. Sometimes Etta sat behind them, attempting to meditate. Often she went for a late morning cup of coffee at Red's and ordered a freshly baked blueberry muffin, or for a walk to Halibut Point, or to the cemetery where she would lounge about reading a book under a troop of arborvitaes. Sometimes Daniel would meet her and they would make love in the grass while sailboats tacked between Crane Beach and Halibut Point, squirrels buried their food for the winter, and gulls caught the rising thermals and ascended like souls.

She had made one friend named Edgar, a sculptor who had a studio in a shed in the back of his house. She had seen him out watering his garden several mornings and waved. Once he had her over for a glass of iced tea. Edgar was a man in his seventies and a widower. He wore a white v-neck undershirt and plaid shorts, was kind and soft-spoken. She told him she had done some modeling to which he said, "I bet you have darling." His garden was tiered and impeccably mulched; bronze sculptures of fish, crouching children, globes, mermaids were thoughtfully placed. They sat on a stone bench under a trellis of dangling crystals drinking iced tea, Etta gazing at the strong bones in the old man's hands. "If you seek the sublimated self, you must read Whitman," Edgar advised. She liked his slow, calculated movements, the way he gesticulated as he pontificated, his childlike senility, how he called her Ellen no matter how many times she told him her name was Etta. "As in James?" Yes, yes. He took her into his studio and showed her his current work—a statue of an emaciated pregnant woman supine, the jutting, angular bones contrasting with the soft rounded belly. There were several watercolor paintings on the walls, one of a bowl of pears, another of a pitcher of water and a glass vase with red star-like flowers. Etta commented on them, said they reminded her of Matisse, how she loved Matisse, his use of color, his loose style. Edgar told her his wife had painted them, that he pressed her to do models, but she underestimated herself. She preferred the simple lives of things. Edgar repeated the phrase, *the simple lives of things*, and his mind went somewhere else for a moment.

Later she would walk home recalling what was said in conversation, feeling elated she had found a kindred spirit and wondering what Edgar looked like as a young man, what kind of lover he was.

When Daniel told Etta he had bought the yellow house in downtown Gloucester, she was incredulous. Daniel had walked in whistling a tune, something Etta had never heard him do. He placed the papers he was carrying on the kitchen table and went to Etta, throwing his arms around her and lifting her up. "Debra and I worked out a deal. She said she would take a cut because she didn't have to split her fee with another realtor. The house is ours," he said, planting a kiss at the crux of her neck.

Etta scrambled out of his arms.

"What?" Daniel asked.

"You're kidding."

"I thought you'd be happy."

"I'm surprised."

"Why are you surprised, you knew I liked the house."

"I didn't know you liked it that much."

Daniel touched the curls on the back of his head and waited for Etta to say something. "It might take some getting used to," she said.

That evening Daniel sat at the kitchen table with his spectacles on, calculating different figures. She watched him scribble down numbers, shuffle through opened envelopes of mail kept in a tackle box. Etta observed him while eating a dish of vanilla ice cream, her hip leaning firmly against the counter. "I think the deed should be in both our names. This way we own the house together," Daniel said. Etta glanced at the chest hair that trickled in a thin stream to the button on Daniel's jeans and thought of the last time they made love in the cemetery.

"Stop working. Take me to bed."

"You're not taking this seriously."

"I *am* taking this seriously. This is very serious," she said, laughing.

§

Two years later when Etta lay dying in the guestroom bed at Patrick's house, she paused at this point in her recollections and let herself feel what she should have felt then, how, despite his impetuousness, she was touched by Daniel's determination to make a future for them. It was in his firmly pressed lips, the figures on the paper, numbers, doodles, words; it was in his mussed hair, his inaudible mumblings. She wept then, for what she did and what she did not do.

Mira furnished Etta's house for her. She hauled up Philomena's old dining room table, Pop's rocking chair and other furniture from the basement and Daniel and Mira's husband Paul loaded all of it onto the U-Haul truck. Mira gave Etta a full-size bed, two dressers, a loveseat, a suitcase of linens, and boxes of Philomena's china and stemware including the Venetian glass goblets from Italy. She wrote down several family recipes and offered to show Etta how to cook them. Mira was excited to have her sister living nearby and periodically dropped in unannounced in the late morning before she went food shopping or to the mall. With every visit, Mira was siphoning bits of Etta. After Mira left one morning, Etta sat at the dining room table with images of Mira drifting from room to room; Mira positioned her father's rocking chair, analyzing the light coming through the sheer curtain, "You know what you could do," she began, her voice ripe with anticipation, "you could cozy up this room a bit with Roman shades underneath the sheers." Etta's body followed Mira throughout the house as she gave her suggestions; she appeased her sister, saying sentences like, "I think the trim needs a second coat of white," or "Yes, I believe a sconce would brighten up the stairwell a bit," but the real Etta floated a few inches above her head, wondering when her sister would leave and just how she was going to rectify this new feeling inside her.

The boxes were stacked in the kitchen and the dining room and Etta imagined herself plunging a box knife into each of them and putting away the dishes, the pots and pans. She surmised that unpacking might settle her. Outside a man was beating a rug over a wrought iron fire escape; Etta watched the man drape the rug over the rail and reenter his apartment in the utilitarian building beyond the chain link fence at the back of the yard. The refrigerator in the kitchen chugged on; the backyard next door contained the frame of a rusted swingset and a maple tree losing its leaves; the lawn had grown past a height manageable by a mower. Etta thought perhaps she needed a walk to invigorate her, so she went upstairs to throw on a sweatshirt and jeans and headed out into the blinding light of a November day. She walked away from the yellow house and its banal environs, away from houses with their faded, vinyl facades and the tired cars parked against the curb and followed the road as it snaked around coves toward the backshore where the ocean was uninterrupted and vast. In Etta's mind, the spotlight was on Cassie, singing in a cabaret in the Keys, her hair parted to the side, a slit up her red sequined dress. Etta imagined that Daniel's ex had moved on to a new life, the life of her passions, and she was envious of her.

Etta walked several miles to Good Harbor Beach and crossed the bridge over the inlet. The ocean was a steel blue and there were six surfers in wet suits riding the waves like cowboys on horseback. One surfer rode a wave in and emerged from the froth of the surf. He ran toward shore with the board under his arm, his long blond dreadlocks swaying stiffly in the wind. When he came near her, he looked at her, as if he might like to talk to her.

"Is it cold?" Etta asked. "Is it unbearably cold out there in the water?"

"No, it's not bad. Not with the suit."

He started to walk toward her and she noted the curves of his lean muscles in the slick of the suit, how a strand of his hair fell between his blue eyes. She remembered last week when Daniel took her for Mexican food at Jalapeno's and how he nearly punched a man at the bar for ogling her.

"That's all I wanted to know," she said and turned away from him.

"Hey, what's your name?" the surfer asked.

Etta turned back once and waved at him, then marched rigidly away in the sand.

§

Etta walked to Mira's house, only a few blocks from Good Harbor Beach. She rang the doorbell and Samantha answered; down the hall Mira stood above the dining room table with a casserole dish in her hands. Etta followed her niece into the dining room.

"Is everything alright?" Mira asked. "You look flush."

"I'm fine," Etta said. "I took a walk."

"That's a long walk," Paul said. "A good four or five miles from your place." Mira passed along a dish of cauliflower and pasta, redolent of Philomena's cooking; she made all of Philomena's dishes and she made them well.

"Isn't Daniel home by now?" Mira said to her sister. "Honey go get your aunt a folding chair from the closet," she said to her son.

"Yes, Daniel must be home by now."

"Don't you cook him dinner?" Mira asked.

Etta thought of her brief repertoire of meals, the most prevalent being mac and cheese and hamburgers. "Yes, I cook for him. Not extravagantly, but I cook for him. I just lost track of time."

Etta had every intention of asking her for a ride back, but Mira's raised eyebrows signaled that she knew what her sister wanted and she wasn't about to be inconvenienced.

"You need a ride back? I can take you," Paul interjected.

"No. I'm going to call Daniel," she said moving toward the phone. "He won't mind." As the words left her mouth there was the dangling possibility that Daniel might mind indeed. She picked up the receiver and stalled. She couldn't remember her number.

Mira put down her knife and fork. "You can't remember your number," she said.

Etta laughed nervously. She touched her cheek. Her face was burning up.

"It's in the book on the counter," Mira said and resumed eating. "Under E."

Etta's mind unscrambled itself and she recalled the number. She dialed it while observing Mira's family eat. Outside the wind that whipped her face nearly all day was whistling. The windows were fogged from the cooking; the aroma of the food and the coziness of Mira's family were inviting.

Daniel said she had worried him by not leaving a note. Etta tried to explain that she meant to turn back, but it was such a fine day and with every bend in the road, there was a new sight and she was curious what she might find. She felt ridiculous attempting to explain. Daniel sighed. He told her he would be there in ten minutes.

Mira went to fetch another folding chair from the closet and to the cabinet for additional place settings. She filled a bowl with cauliflower and pasta, placed a roll on top and pushed it toward Etta. "Just eat," she said. Etta devoured the roll. She nibbled away at the rest of the food slowly, while waiting for Daniel and feeling awkward because Mira was not talking to her. She knew she had disappointed her sister somehow in taking the walk and not feeding her husband dinner. So Etta sat quietly at the table, and focused on Samantha who was always enthusiastic when she was around. They talked about books. When Daniel arrived, he sat down and voraciously ate the meal Mira placed in front of him. He complimented Mira on the sauce and turned to Etta. "Did your mother teach you how to make a sauce like this? Damn!"

Mira and Etta both knew that Philomena had tried to teach Etta how to cook, but Etta was not interested. Once she had seared one of her mother's favorite pots because she left the heat on high while she went to read a book. This is the memory that was in Etta's mind when Daniel asked about the sauce.

They stayed a while and then drove home in silence to the yellow house, dark inside with one light in the hall illuminating a stack of boxes. Daniel tossed his keys on the counter next to an opened box—he had started to unpack while waiting for her. He pulled a beer from the fridge, popped it open and went to the living room where Pop's chair was positioned in front of the television. He turned on the Celtic game and sat in the rocking chair. Etta went to the bedroom, exhausted. She undressed and took a hot shower. Daniel came up later, when she was in her blue robe, unpacking her clothes from a valise and placing them into one of Mira's old dressers.

"My sister was annoyed with me," she said. "I suppose you are too."

"Not annoyed. Perplexed," Daniel said. He leaned in the doorway to their bedroom and drank the rest of his beer. "I don't expect you to be here all the time. Waiting for me," he said.

"That's good," Etta said with a tone. She zipped up the empty valise and fit it into the closet. Before she closed the door, she caught sight of the rolled drawing and it jarred her memory. She shut the door. "Perhaps I should find a job. There are a few motels on the backshore. Maybe I could apply for a housekeeping position."

"And the baby?"

"I'm not pregnant yet, and besides I can always quit."

"That's no way to take a job."

Daniel reached out and grabbed Etta's hand when she passed by him. He sat on the bed and patted the space next to him. When she sat down, he started to massage her shoulders.

"It's an adjustment," he said. "For both of us. You knew it would be this way."

"I never thought about it."

"That's ridiculous. Of course you did."

"No. I didn't."

"Well maybe you will think about it now."

Daniel bought a framed map of Cape Ann and several Monet water lily prints for the living room and dining room. Etta inferred he did this because he believed she wouldn't. It had been four months since they moved in and she had yet to buy a decorative item, or any item, for that matter. She thought about it. She wanted real art for the walls but real art was expensive and she could not justify spending money when she did not yet have a job, nor could she bear to ask Daniel especially after he had just paid off her eight hundred dollar credit card bill to maintain their credit. It occurred to her she could frame the drawing in the closet, but she could not bring herself to share the sketch with anyone, not because it may be interpreted as obscene, but because somehow it was privately hers.

Etta was up with Daniel at dawn to share a cup of coffee with him because she could not bear lying in bed in anticipation of hearing the front door close behind him. She dressed and brushed her hair and quietly sat with him sipping her coffee as he ate a bowl of cereal and read the paper and the pale gray light of dawn brightened the windows.

One day while Daniel was reading the paper, Etta told him she wanted to see Edgar, but did not know his last name or phone number. She asked Daniel if he knew.

"Who, the sculptor? The old man? He's no threat," he said under his breath.

Etta was taken aback by Daniel's comment. "What do you mean by that?"

"Just what I said," Daniel said, pushing back his chair. Etta followed him into the kitchen.

"That's very superficial of you," she said.

Daniel grinned, kissed Etta on the forehead. "Dirty old man."

"Just get me his last name," Etta said as he walked out the door.

Etta went that day to borrow a copy of Whitman's *Leaves of Grass* from the library. She sat between the stacks of books and read a few pages, feeling inspired, but the question remained, how could she raise her tepid mind to that kind of consciousness? She needed to ask Edgar what he thought. She took out the copy from the library and went home hoping Daniel had obtained information on Edgar. But when she asked him, he claimed it was a busy day at work and forgot to inquire about the old man.

That night Etta dreamed of Edgar's house. She had only been to his studio and had never actually been inside the house, but her dream was so vivid, she felt as if she had been there. She could, upon waking, recount the red walls in the dining room, the painting of oysters on the half shell above the fireplace, the vase of peonies on the dining room table, the hand-painted bowls that looked like succulent opened mouths. In the living room were whimsical line drawings of old men, their faces only spectacles and bulbous noses. She felt alive in the house. A feeling culminated inside her when she saw Edgar standing in the doorway; it was like a crush. She waked and the euphoria permeated her consciousness for a brief moment, like a sparrow that sat in the hand a moment before fleeing. She remembered how she wanted Edgar to kiss her, passionately, as he did his wife, and what he said when he registered this: "Oh darling, I'm useless. Can't you see? Look at me."

Daniel had the ability to transform other vessels, why not her? She stopped smoking in anticipation of becoming pregnant. She began to buy fresh vegetables, fruits, and whole grain cereals. She waited. With each winter month, she was convinced it had happened; she took on the symptoms—sore breasts, fatigue, morning sickness. "I didn't have symptoms this early," Mira said, "but every woman is different." Etta perused pregnancy magazines in the library and made note of the items she might need; a diaper bag, a lightweight stroller, a bassinet. She looked at paint swatches for the nursery. She knew she was getting ahead of herself but it gave her something to think about: the baby dream had replaced the California dream.

Each time her period came, she became dejected and a fit of lassitude would set it. She tried to keep herself busy. She walked the downtown area, the wharf, and was at first intrigued by certain nooks—an Italian bakery, a bookstore, a consignment shop, but one visit to each of these places seemed enough. She washed the windows, swept and mopped the floors, painted the trim in the hallway. She spent hours at the library reading magazines or perusing books and yet no matter what endeavors had temporarily distracted her from the ennui, she would find herself gazing at the faux paneling of the kitchen cabinets with the edges peeling back, or Daniel's coffee cup and bowl in the drying rack, or the folded paper on the table, or the neighbor's leafless maple tree—a hardened artery without a beating heart—and think about how her life meant nothing; that even a child might not change this.

One Saturday in February the heat went off during the night and the house became terribly cold. In the morning, Daniel went down the basement to look at the furnace and Etta heard him cursing and banging things around. He stopped for a moment and there was silence. Etta sat up anxiously in bed. She heard footsteps on the stairs and then Daniel talking on the phone to someone about the furnace. Etta got up, twisted her hair in a bun and put on a sweatshirt and an extra pair of socks. She went downstairs and found Daniel sitting at the dining room table sifting through literature on the furnace in a manila folder. Next to the manila folder was a pastel drawing of a woman in blue jeans clutching her knees to her chest. She was sitting on a chair at a window; her hair was drawn over her eyes such that Etta could not see her expression. Below the woman was a caption that read, "The Emptiness of Life."

"Where did you get this?" Etta asked Daniel.

"I accidentally dropped the flashlight and saw it under the workbench when I went to pick it up."

"It must be by Julius," Etta said.

She read the caption again and sat down at the table disheartened. It could be that the house was trying to tell her something. "That is an awful drawing," she said.

Daniel stared at her over the rim of his spectacles. "We need a new part. A coil. It's going to cost us three hundred bucks. I thought she said the system was updated. Goddamnit!" Daniel said, slamming his fist on the dining room table. Etta's anxiety was heightened with Daniel's anger. She went to the closet to get her coat and a scarf to stop feeling chilled. The phone rang; it was the furnace company. "Yes? OK. An hour. That's fine. We'll be here." Daniel hung up. He sat down across from Etta at the dining room table. When he finally looked at her, he seemed to notice something.

"What?" Etta asked. "What is it?"

"Your ears. I've never noticed them before. They jut off your head a little."

Etta wanted to laugh because what Daniel said was silly, but he wasn't laughing. He continued to stare blankly at Etta until he flinched, got up, went outside the backdoor to the yard and lit a cigarette; Etta had never seen Daniel smoke when he was sober. He stood outside in the barren yard covered in patches of ice and snow and looked up at the gray clouds. She realized then how separate he was from her, as if he existed in a different sphere entirely.

Daniel's hostile mood remained intact. He swore a lot and mumbled to himself; he kicked the cabinet door off its hinge when it wouldn't close properly and hung up on a woman from the Salvation Army seeking clothing donations. Other times he was aloof and barely said anything to Etta. After dinner one night, Etta sat at the dining room table with him as he drew sketches of birds. She leaned over and observed the birds' long legs and s-shaped necks. "Are they storks?" she asked.

"Egrets."

They sat a while until Etta got up the nerve to broach the subject about Daniel's mood. "The imaginary string between us is tugging and it's not from my end," she said.

Daniel grabbed his beer and took a swig. He put his elbows on the table, looked steadily into Etta's eyes. "I know."

"Is it the furnace? The money?"

Daniel glanced down at his chaffed knuckles aside the drawings then sat back in his chair. "No."

The baby, Etta wanted to say. But there was no baby.

"It's the winter," Daniel said. "The egrets are a harbinger for summer. When they're here, it's here. I can only take so much before I need to get out there. On the water."

Etta was relieved. She reached for Daniel's hand and clasped it. "Good. Good, I know just what you mean."

Etta and Daniel went out to run some errands one Saturday morning; afterward they had time to spare, so Daniel suggested they browse one of the new antique stores on Main Street. Etta had visited the shop before looking for affordable artwork from local artists and was snubbed by the pompous, ornery proprietor who challenged her for a name and upon receiving none, replied haughtily that his prints were the finest *reproductions*. When they entered, the man eyed them and perfunctorily explained should they have any questions to not hesitate to ask. Daniel found some brass candlestick holders and Etta an antique ring with semi-precious stones. While Daniel was paying for his items and listening to the old man's nasally advice on how to clean brass, Etta slipped the ring into her pocket. She joined Daniel at the door and the two walked out of the store and to the car, Etta's heart pumping hot nervous blood to her limbs.

Daniel pulled away from the curb and Etta disclosed the ring letting out a proud laugh. The adrenaline rush made her feel as she did when she first met Daniel— exhilarated.

"What?" Daniel asked, smiling from her infectious laughter. "What? What?"

"I gave the bastard what he deserves," she said.

Daniel glanced down at the ring and stopped smiling; he glanced ahead at the road then down at the ring on Etta's finger. "What? You took that? You stole it. Did you steal it?"

"I stole it because he's a pretentious asshole."

"It doesn't matter if he's an asshole! I can't believe you took that. Have you stolen anything else?"

"What? No, of course not."

"You'll have to give it back. Tell him you forgot it was on your finger."

"Are you kidding?"

"No. I'm not kidding," Daniel said and slowed the car.

"I'm not giving the fucking ring back, Daniel," Etta said. "Get over it."

Daniel pulled over and stopped the car. He looked hard at Etta. Then he shook his head. "You're reckless," he said. "Uncontrollable."

"I'm reckless? You're the one who bought the fucking house without asking me. I hate it there. I hate everything about it."

"You know nothing," Daniel said quietly. He stepped on the gas and promptly merged into traffic. "The house," he murmured. "It figures you would think it's the house."

Etta leaned in front of the bathroom mirror brushing rouge on her cheek. She wore a white v-neck cashmere sweater and jeans; silver hoops dangled from her ears. In the bedroom, Daniel was choosing a shirt for the party. It was mid March and still daylight at six o'clock in the evening. A robin sat in the crabapple tree outside the window amidst the dried fruit from last fall and sang the song of spring. It had been warm that day and some purple crocuses had opened in the backyard along the fence; Etta interpreted these things as a good omen.

The party was Etta's idea; it was an act to reconcile her feelings for the house. Daniel thought it was a creative way of clearing the air; also he was happy to extend the invitation to friends he hadn't seen in a while. So Etta bought flowers and frozen hors d'oeurves and Daniel stocked the fridge with beer. She placed votive candles in dark spaces and spritzed the air with a floral scent. Daniel warmed the hors d'oeurves because she did not trust herself not to burn them.

Etta invited some of her cousins whom she hadn't seen in years: Tilly and his wife Barbara, Jimmy and his wife Charlanne, Camille and her fiance Donny. Mira would be there with Paul and Aunt Jenny talked of taking the ride with Uncle Andy. Daniel invited friends who didn't make the wedding list. About a half hour before the guests were to arrive, Etta became anxious. She regretted the idea of a party; having the house full of people seemed especially daunting.

Mira and Paul arrived first and set Etta's nerves at ease. Mira carried a china tureen that held a beef brisket. She also brought several bottles of merlot and crusty bread with Brie. Daniel took out the hors d'oeurves and placed them on dinner plates. The mini wieners and quiches looked flaccid against Mira's elegant tureen and hefty wheel of Brie.

Mira was dressed fashionably in a silk button-down blouse and scarf. She wore her hair in a French twist and smelled of lilacs. Mira was in a good mood, as she was any time there was a family gathering. Etta was slightly intimidated by this; she felt inadequate for not being excited, herself. But she told herself she had a layer of complexity that Mira did not have. She was always telling herself this.

The guests conversed in two very disparate groups; Etta's family in the kitchen drinking liquor and wine and Daniel's friends who either huddled on the couch drinking beer and watching the Celtics or outside smoking cigarettes (as a courtesy to Etta who had quit). None of Daniel's friends were married and their girlfriends were especially chatty about exclusive subjects, the gossip of friends and acquaintances, mostly. They wore t-shirts and jeans; their bangs were hairsprayed stiffly in place. They talked about their makeup and their pathetic jobs at the mall, their aspirations of becoming beauty consultants. Etta, although hospitable at first, eventually shrugged them off.

Unlike Daniel's friends, Etta's family brought housewarming gifts: a stainless steel coffee pot, a wooden block of knives, a box of delightfully scented tapered candles, potted herbs, and Mira's gift of their mother's Venetian goblets. After a few drinks, they talked about the way things used to be and teased one another and told stories. Their laughter was infectious and Etta slowly relinquished her anxious, avatar self that rambled about aiming to please. Her blood was warm and snug from the wine and she felt lighthearted and proud of the house; having her family bring their history into it was a sort of initiation. Etta was hopeful that she could change.

Aunt Jenny and Uncle Tony were the first to leave. Aunt Jenny told Etta that her parents would be pleased; this nearly brought tears to Etta's eyes. Etta went upstairs to fetch their coats in the spare bedroom, piled up on a lone chair; she glanced at the color swatches taped to the wall when she smelled cigarette smoke wafting up from the backyard. She looked down at the dark forms of the women sharing a cigarette

"Who told her he was getting married?"

"It wasn't me. I didn't know until afterwards."

"Somebody told her."

"But she never even asked him. He didn't know anything about it."

"He did so know."

"That's not the point. The point is she changed her mind. She was going to keep it."

Etta shut the window. Something collapsed into the emptiness inside her. She looked at the swatches taped to the wall, pulled off each one, and tossed it into the garbage.

§

In the still of the gray underworld, Etta sees the hull looming like a ghost and the flecks of the ocean drifting before it. She touches the strakes of the hull's belly thinking of Daniel's hands and how they were here once, smoothing the strakes, setting them in resins. Planks of light filter down from the surface as Etta reaches for the edge of the boat and her ex-husband, the boat builder, sleeps with a beer bottle in his hands.

Etta rises up quietly. She can see the back of his head bobbing with the slight motion of the boat in the water. She swims around to the other side and reaches her hands up to the stern, pulling the boat to her. He opens one eye and surveys the event of his ex-wife pulling herself up. Daniel can't help but grin; since the divorce the trysts on the boat had become almost predictable. With both eyes open now, he steadies himself as she lifts her legs out of the water. She stands there for a moment dripping wet, chilled, wanting to dive back into the warm gray underworld and away. But he fetches her a towel and wraps it around her, giving her shoulder an affectionate squeeze. He tosses her a sweatshirt and a bottle of beer and she sits with him as the sky becomes opalescent, as her black hair falls in tendrils about her face and his races in circles about his temple. He is serene, as natural as air. She likes him this way, without expectations, promises. She likes the freckles on his shoulders. The silence. His stare. It is simple when a man acquiesces to a woman. His big toe caresses her ankle, then her calf. He lays down a blanket on the deck and she crawls closer to him to stroke his hair, to twirl the red curls about her fingers. He traces her body with his calloused hands and kisses her mouth, her bare shoulder, her navel. Together they stare at the firmament, the satellites speeding past the stars, the meteors burning themselves up.

Part III

THE DARK NIGHT OF THE SOUL
Samantha, 1986

In a dream, I met my unborn daughter. We were just two souls without bodies who happened to meet in my subconscious. She told me she would be ready to come in two years. This seemed too soon. My career as a writer had only started to take off, but more than this, I feared if I had a child I would have little time to create. The world of imagination is a sort of underworld, and if you're an artist you get used to living there; in fact, at times, you prefer it to the routine monotony and drudgery of everyday life. And yet, there is an element of the artist in every mother; by the nourishing flesh and bones of her body she creates a new life. By her wisdom, she shapes a new mind. What greater act of creativity could there be? Etta had told me this when she had her son, Andrew. I never was an artist, she said, but I created him and I am proud of it. Patrick captured that sense of pride and serenity in Etta when Etta was dying. He painted the portrait of mother and child now hanging above the fireplace in my living room. You can clearly see Etta's serene face; she had lost that restlessness in the eyes and the tightness of the mouth that comes with the existential angst of youth. I have since learned where that serenity had come from: it was not only the delight in your creation; it was also a strong sense of purpose.

Through that flicker of aberrant sensuality with Patrick in came life, the real thing and I was more than willing to live it. First there was Edward. Winter turned to spring and I watched him exist in different seasons, retiring his blazers with khakis, his red cashmere scarf over a peacoat, for penny loafers and Izod shirts. Edward was a young man pressured to succeed in school to acquire a high paying, prestigious career. This is what I deduced from meeting his mother who knew virtually everything about his school life, checked his homework, his grades, edited his college essays. I was fairly sure, however, she did not know Edward and I went parking down by Eastern Point in his father's Mercedes, stripped down to our underwear, the windows fogged, the heat leaking from the car, the piano music playing, the keys crashing with the waves, the wind, the shadows. I was in love with him then, and only then. I was in love with experience, with sensuality, with the crashing waves, but I was in love, alone. There was no bridge from my heart to Edward's heart. In Edward's burgeoning man-mind, I had a body, a girl-body he liked because it aroused him, but this is all he knew. I was a girl and he knew nothing about the inchoate mind of a woman. I knew nothing about the inchoate mind of a woman.

I met Christian in art class. He was somewhat lanky, but he had the brightest eyes I had ever seen. Life with Christian morphed into splendor. I had found in Christian a similar spirit who saw the world as I had begun to see it, who wanted to paint it, write about it, who suspected what I suspected, that it was a menagerie, a design, a bounty. I watched him paint, noting how he was patient and forgiving, his soft eyes directed toward the work and nothing else, not even me. There was no anxiety in Christian, no ego. He was an art student the way an art student should be, with no preconceived ideas or expectations.

So I broke Edward's heart. It was very peculiar to be the one breaking another heart. You volley back and forth from the aching heart to the brimming heart and ultimately you choose the brimming heart. I awoke in the middle of the night, quaking with mere euphoria, manifested in a touch I remembered, or Christian's kiss.

To put it bluntly, Christian was a Christian, and came from a family that refused to sin. They went to a church that eliminated all forms of possible temptation—movies, dancing, drinking, foul language. Theirs was a religion not of burning passion, but of avoidance. These people didn't believe you learned from your mistakes.

Their church, a Protestant sect, was the focal point of their lives. If I wanted to date Christian, I needed to assimilate, somewhat. On Sundays, I attended mass with my family in the morning and then went to Christian's fellowship service in the evening where there was quirky born again Christian music, people singing ballad rock songs about God. It was irksome to me, to combine rock and Christ, sort of like eating spaghetti with a side order of pickles, but I went along with it. "Catholic," I told Christian, "means having sympathies with all."

Christian's mother was a soft-spoken woman with wide hips. It was her eyes her son inherited, eyes like visible tuning forks that resonated sensibility. But for Christian's mother, that sensibility was fear, mostly. She was terribly afraid of the world. She did not have a job; she rarely left the house, aside from doing necessary chores or going to church. His father stayed within the circle of the church as well, by building more of them. I pictured him maneuvering the spire with the bare, austere cross atop it, lifting it off from the ground, steady, steady, until the cross could be seen for miles.

The fact that I was a Catholic made Christian's parents very nervous. This is why I had to be extra careful around them, show them I was a decent human being, that I would be open-minded about their religion and participate. This eased their fears somewhat, that I participated in their fellowship services and at church picnics, at youth group where kids would play checkers and chess, discuss Bible readings, gloat about their tepid pranks on Catholics, like how they placed a paper bag over the Virgin Mary or stole her from one lawn and carted her to another. In return, Christian's parents were fairly amenable to me and allowed Christian to take me places in his car.

The churches Christian's father built were not unlike the one I attended with Christian and his family. They often had some sort of stage with light blue carpeting. The focus was not gold ornate candles, colorful mosaics of glass, pious saints with sorrowful hearts, the Blessed Mother in her bounty of roses; the focus was that bare, austere cross. During the evening service, people randomly stood up and voiced a testimony, a short ditty of how Christ made a difference in their lives. This was new to me, people standing up and speaking out individually.

The young minister, whom everyone called "Pastor Jim" (always with his equally young, pregnant wife one step behind him) was especially diplomatic to me, which made me slightly wary of him (I was also slightly wary of the older men dressed in pale blue or beige suits, who were incredibly austere, my tapestry-like long floral skirts a direct assault against their austerity). Pastor Jim was on the alert for lost lambs. Being a young minister, he was especially eager to gather his flock, supplement his spiritual resume. We conveniently steered away from any religiously divisive topics. Instead, Pastor Jim told me jokes; it was his way of establishing neutral ground. The jokes were always clean; sometimes they were riddles to stump me or get his flock thinking, if others were listening in. I would pretend to laugh and he would chuckle like Curly from The Three Stooges and do that strange snapping thing with his fingers. At some point he would ask me if I were going to such-and-such a gathering, and I would decline and he would say, most genuinely, "Good to see you."

After fellowship, Christian and I went parking at the quarries; being in the company of those austere, sinless Christians made me long for indulgence. Sometimes we dared ourselves at the rock ledge, to move closer, sometimes we hiked down and skipped stones across the placid water. Other times we made love in the bushes. I was indoctrinating Christian, knocking him off, albeit slightly, from the path of the straight and narrow.

Life went on and the inertia of high school became unbearable, however, despite the brimming heart, despite my choosing a college to go to and a major. High school was a controlled monotony where there was no room for one's own rhythms. I had become restless and withdrawn; nothing excited me, not even Christian. I felt small, insignificant, incapable of expression. I pretended, went through the motions, did my homework, went to class, debated deep within me if there was a God. What did it matter which religion you chose? Life seemed to me, meaningless. I had discovered its empty vault, lying cold and hollow beneath all thoughts.

Then there was the day I was holding Etta's baby and he stopped breathing. We were in my room at the time and I was reading him a story. First I thought it was me, that I was imagining the worst, that everything was coated in death, but then he started to actually turn blue, his cheeks, his hands, blue. I screamed and Etta came running up and took him from me. What happened? she asked. He's blue! He's blue! Then my nose started to gush blood. I panicked, I was dying, the baby was dying. This was finally it; all that evil thinking had come to this, all that skepticism. Etta took him from me, lay him flat on the bed and put an ear to his mouth. She began CPR by blowing in the mouth, but she became flustered, took him off the bed and shook him until he coughed.

Had my darkness tried to pull in the baby as well? Was it the devil or Yahweh? Was I going mad? I felt I was sick and should go to the hospital;

maybe there was a drug they could give me to make my brain normal again. I slipped out of the house late at night and rode my bike across town to Christian's house. The night and its stars and the ride, the wind, my pulsing muscles—I felt alive then. I crept up to his window, tapped at it gently. He opened the shade and then the window and pulled me inside, steadying me as I climbed in. In the light of the room I could see his smooth skin, his blond hair like an aura; he didn't look real.

"I'm afraid I killed the baby," I said. "He's in the hospital."

"What are you talking about?" he said.

"He started to cough and turn blue in my arms because of the bad thoughts in my head."

"I'm sure they're no worse than anyone else's."

"Christian, do you believe in modern day saints?"

"What, you think you are a saint?"

"I don't think I have a future. I'm headlong into the dark night of the soul," I said.

"That's ridiculous."

"You don't even know what the dark night of the soul is. St. John of the Cross said it's when the soul purifies itself for God. I think that's what's going on. God wants something from me."

Christian rolled his eyes. He didn't believe in intercessors. "I think what's going on is you need some sleep." He rested his head on his headboard, started to fall back to sleep, and I climbed back outside to my bike. The night was warm, lovely and serene. I was calmer in it, alone with God and the sky. I peddled a mile or two and then I heard it, a blip from the vault. *Would you go in his place?* it said. I peddled faster. *Wouldyougo Would yougo Wouldyougo Wouldyougo?* I squeezed the brakes, lay the bike down, went under a patch of pines by Thatcher Road. I crouched.

Don't call to me like you called to them, I said. I fingered the dried needles on the ground, smelled the wet earth from the marsh. *I am no saint. No Joan of Arc. No Therese, the Little Flower. I have convictions.*

I held my breath for a second. I was a wimp, I decided; I didn't have what it takes to be a saint, to suffer alone in the black vault for the sake of God. I felt disappointed in myself. No, I argued; that's not the point. No, no, no. I am not a wimp. I have *convictions*. And then I saw it, a bird, perched on the overhead wire. It was past midnight and there was a bird, a dark silhouette above me, silent, waiting. I thought of Joan, how it could be Joan. I thought of how perhaps it was confused and nature was losing its foothold; it should be sleeping, away in its nest. I should be sleeping away in my bed. It was an anomaly. I was an anomaly; we were both awake and troubled.

It flew away and I slowly peddled home.

It turned out the baby had apnea and it was a good thing he turned blue in my arms and not alone in his crib at night. You would think that would settle my mind, but it didn't.

There was one fellowship service when the door of the vault had slammed shut with me inside. I was desperate. Instead of ending with a blessing and a hymn from the small group of religious rock stars on stage, the melodic sounds of the synthesizer radiated throughout the nave. The young bearded minister called people who were experiencing some sort of trouble in their hearts, some darkness they could not name, to come to him at the front of the church. It was uncanny how he could focus on exactly what I was feeling. I watched as more people stood up and went to kneel before Pastor Jim. I stood up. Christian looked at me, his face, incredulous, elated. With shaky knees and head not so high, I went to Pastor Jim who made a beeline right for me. He knelt before me with tears in his eyes, paused and said my name, will you, Samantha, reject all sin and take Christ into your heart?

I thought then, of parking with Edward down by the crashing waves; I thought then of being in love, alone, because this is what was happening to the minister; in his head, he was in love alone, with Christ and the idea of instigating my miraculous salvation.

I had made a big mistake.

But what could I do? Say Sorry I was just looking for the exit? So I lied and tried my best to look redeemed, but the longer I knelt there at the stage with the pale blue carpeting, the more I became enraged that this really wasn't about me.

Pastor Jim scrutinized me for some indication that *it* was happening; he waited. I opened my purse and took out my rosary beads. With the eyes of the austere Christians on me, I started to pray, one by one, a Hail Mary for each bead.

Hail Mary, full of grace, the Lord is with thee, I whispered.

Blessed art thou among women and blessed is the fruit of thy womb, I said, louder.

Holy Mary, Mother of God, pray for our sins, now and at the hour of our death, still louder.

Amen.

"What are you doing?" Christian asked. "What do you think you're doing?"

The synthesizer sent its electric soul song radiating outward as the whispers hissed around me. I started again with a separate bead and with every word of the prayer, Pastor Jim seemed to shrink, until at one point, I couldn't see him at all.

The vault inside me had swallowed him whole.

ABDUCTION
Joan, 1976

Nicolette, a dark girl with braided hair close to her head and perfect teeth, said the old woman had spared herself. She was at peace when they found her, her lips parted delicately enough to fit a rose petal between them, her eyes peering upward, as if to follow the ascent of the soul. Joan was incredulous. "Dead? How could she be dead? She's only been there a week," she said. She had thoughtfully packed Margaret's clothes, including only her favorite and most comfortable outfits and sewed tags at the neckline with her name, as Nicolette, her mother's aid, had told her to do. She packed framed pictures of Margaret's daughters and grandchildren in various stages of their lives and hung them on the wall. She fetched the framed picture of her father looking like Clark Gable with a pencil mustache and angled it appropriately on the night table so her mother could see it while she lay in bed. She had brought her mother fresh flowers every other day— roses, dahlias, hydrangeas, mums because this is what her mother would have done for herself.

Margaret had barely spoken to the other residents and preferred to eat her dinner in her room with the curtains drawn. She had to be there, Joan told herself; Margaret had nearly burned the house down, twice, in the middle of the night cooking eggs and baking muffins for "the children." "The children" were now seventeen and fifteen years old and they could bake their own muffins, Joan had told her. Both Joan's sisters had agreed upon examining the torched wall in the kitchen: something had to be done. They had witnessed Margaret descend the stairs in one of her silk Mother of the Bride gowns during Christmas, insisting it was the day of her daughter's wedding. Which one? She did not know. Always the countenance of confusion. Always the restlessness.

Joan trusted the Jamaican aids with their singsong voices, waddling their robust bodies through the halls; she thought the setting of lawn, rose trellises, and fir trees was idyllic. She had seen Nicolette sitting with a woman in a wheelchair feeding her cut carrots and when the woman had fallen asleep midway through the meal, Nicolette gently patted the woman's hand. It was a kind gesture, humane.

§

The turning point came with the debacle at the church, with Temesia's father Reggie at the door at three in the morning. They drove with Reggie's lobster traps rattling in the cab; Joan noticed his profile in the streetlights, almost the same profile he had as a boy when she sat next to him in English class. Joan wondered about his marriage to Faye Benton, his high school sweetheart; she wondered how one could grow up and grow old with another person. She had thought it was for the shortsighted only, for those without aspirations. And yet people like Reggie and Faye would never know the plight of the prodigal, the one whose aspirations had soured and the wisdom gained from it. Joan prided herself on this.

Reggie asked her if her mother had been acting funny. Joan recalled the Sunday she and her mother took a drive to Essex to browse the antique stores. On the way home, Margaret was convinced Joan was taking the wrong road. She became agitated, demanding Joan let her drive. Margaret stirred anxiously in her seat, peering out the windows for familiar landmarks and yelling at her daughter, but Joan continued to drive, pointing to each road sign and landmark, Rt. 133, Rt. 128, the cemetery in Manchester, the high school, the 76 gas station on the left. Remember? Do you remember?

"Doctor changed her blood pressure medication," she told Reggie.

Reggie shrugged his shoulders. They pulled up to the church and the cops were shining a flashlight into Margaret's face. It was the first time she saw her mother visibly unhinged: Margaret's hair had come loose from her bobby pins; she was flushed, later it would be the eyes—there was something about her eyes. Joan would come to recognize this dullness, as if someone had removed a part of her mother's mind and the eyes just did what they were supposed to do, take in light without emitting that flicker of self.

"I know he's in there," Margaret said. "He's doing this on purpose. Oh here's Jane. Jane would you kindly tell these officers I have a job to do?"

"Mom, it's Joan and there is no one in the church. It is three in the morning."

"Mrs. Bradstreet, your daughter is here to take you home," Tim McCabe said.

Margaret had always wanted to give Tim an earful for "laying down the law" and extricating his wife from the choir because it was getting in the way of her keeping house. And then there was Peter Winslow, Tim's partner, whose brother P.J. was "delicate" and "creative" and it was a shame he was born into *that macho cop family*. In her right mind, she would have given them both an earful, but now Joan could see her mother squint; she had no idea who the officers were.

"Thirty-five years I've been playing for that man! Everyone in this town knows that!"

"We're going with Reggie," Joan said firmly, taking hold of her mother's arm.

"Oh he doesn't know what he's talking about," Margaret said.

Her mother always said that about certain people but after the night at the church she said it out of the blue, out of context, about people she didn't know. It was as if her mind had forsaken all other appropriate and creative retorts and relied strictly on rote sayings. "I may be old, but I'm not crippled!" she said, snatching her wrist from Joan's fingers.

Joan had managed to get her to the truck when Margaret dug in her heels. She spun around with hell fire in her face. "Magistrates!" she sneered.

Both men instinctively went for their guns. Joan jumped in front of Margaret.

"Let's not let this get out of hand, boys," Reggie said.

The cops raised their hands and showed their palms. "Don't like the quick movements, Reg," Tim said.

Joan was relieved she wasn't alone with this situation. She sandwiched her mother between Reggie and herself in the truck and tried to calm herself down by ignoring the sharp rise of panic in her throat and focusing on Reggie's movements, his sure and steady hands, they way they loosened the shift stick, turned the key and the knobs for heat.

Nana's death was having its effects on her granddaughter. This is what Joan was thinking the night her daughter was late for dinner. Joan looked across the kitchen table and noticed that Nathan had started shaving; he had patches of stubble on his chin. This was something Roger never allowed—stubble. He was always clean shaven with a splash of cologne. Fastidious, that's what Roger was. She had mistaken it for gentlemanliness, but it had worn on her. Irritated her. Her son, unlike his father and his sister, was always punctual for dinner. He was courteous. He was responsible. Joan had never once asked to see his studies because she had trusted him. His grades were impeccable. It was Elise, the "free spirit" as Margaret called her, who worried Joan. It was Elise who was now an hour late to dinner, who had yet to apply to college, who was in trouble with the principal for her outrageous outfits, who had skipped school last week. Mr. Peter Hewitt, the tall, slightly overweight man who had Margaret play organ at his wedding and father's funeral, greeted Joan amicably when she arrived at his office for a "conference." He offered his condolences. He knew the family was grieving, but he had to keep order here at Manchester-Essex and it began with clothing. He told Joan Elise must first report to the office before she reports to homeroom. He would rely on his secretary's discretion regarding Elise's outfit whether she would be admitted to school for the day or not.

Joan did not want to stifle her daughter and told Peter this, but ultimately they agreed; she would tell Elise she could wear the jeans, just not to school. She would sit her daughter down and explain that it was imperative not to make waves her senior year in high school.

But Elise was adamant about being able to express herself. Suppression was the beginning of all evil, she said. And maybe she didn't want to go to college. Maybe there were other things she wanted to do. *You sent her away*. Elise said. *You killed her*. Don't be so dramatic, Joan told her. She told herself it was all drama, all of Elise's outbursts. It always was. Two days later Elise made a fool of Joan and skipped school. The mathematics teacher called; Mr. Hewitt called; Elise would be suspended. But Temesia had just gotten engaged; wasn't that punishment enough?

It was seven thirty. Nathan brought his plate to the sink.

"She should have walked in about now," Joan said, making a hill with her mashed potatoes and stealing off the peak. Her mother's dog sat at her feet, waiting for something to drop. Joan placed the rest of her roast beef in Jake's dish. He lifted his old bones off the rug and gulped the pieces down. Only food could get the dog to move now that Margaret was gone.

She would hire a lawyer and sell the house. Her sisters would approve. Now, ironically enough, she felt more the interloper. Her mother may have been physically gone but you could still find her in the baking stains on the potholders, in the tarnished metal of the kettle on the stove, in the crystal candle holders that tossed the morning light onto the dining room wall, in the worn yarns of the rugs. By this time, Margaret would have cut the dead stalks off the dahlias and dug them up. She would have picked up the apples in the orchard and turned them into pies, tortes, cider and sauces. (Joan remembered her sisters calling from those limbs of the trees, contesting as to who climbed higher. When Jane fell and broke her arm, Margaret had argued with the doctor on how to set the bone.)

Nathan headed back up to his room to do his homework. Joan sat alone at the table listening to her mother's dog breathe. Why had she stayed this long? The answer was simple: because of Elise. Nathan could live anywhere, but Elise needed a beacon, someone to set the rhythm. Neither Joan nor Roger could do this for her, but Margaret did.

Joan called Temesia's house and Faye answered. Faye with the perfect potted plants on the porch and the Fourth of July bunting and the wreaths on each window during Christmas. "Haven't seen her today, Joan," said Faye, somewhat shortly. Joan asked for Temesia. "Temesia's asleep," Faye said. "It's a school night," as if Joan didn't know.

Joan hung up the phone, went out to the porch and looked at the moon. This is where she usually sat with her mother, after dinner. "You had a hard lesson marrying that man of yours," her mother told her when she first moved back. It was true; Margaret never liked the dandy (a man who smells as nice as he does couldn't be trusted). "Your father built this place from the ground up. He trolled for his traps in weather cold enough you could lose your toes. And he read Dickens. Now that's a man," she said.

Joan watched and waited for a moment, listening to the hushed waves. She looked out at the night sky, at the rise of Orion over the firs. There was a glow becoming more prominent in the eastern sky and then a sliver of virgin white appeared over the trees. It bloomed into a blood-colored moon, almost full. A cloud swallowed the moon and it lit up its insides.

§

At ten o'clock Joan burst into Nathan's room. "This is ridiculous!" she said. Her son had a circuit board on his desk and he was looking at it with a magnifying glass. She paced Nathan's room. "She's doing this on purpose," she said.

"What did Temesia say?"

"That bitch wouldn't let me speak to her."

"What bitch?"

"Mrs. Fancy Flowers, Happy Bunting," Joan replied.

Joan went downstairs to the table where her mother kept her address book and the phone. She started to dial the neighbors. Gruff, ornery voices answered the phone. No one had seen Elise.

At midnight, Joan and Nathan trolled the empty streets. Joan flicked on the high beams and the night lit up under the trees of the woods.

"Maybe she got lost," Nathan said, "in the woods."

"What the hell would she be doing in the woods in the rain?"

"She's probably staying over someone's house. A new friend maybe."

"She's being spiteful," Joan said.

They had pulled up to the overlook and saw the white caps glow on the incoming waves. Joan shivered; she could feel the waves moving through her, moving through everything, everything was rippling with it, everything was touched with premonition.

Joan gave Tim McCabe all of the information he needed for the missing persons report, hair color, eye color, skin tone. She tried to remember what it was Elise was wearing when she last saw her at 2:30 when she arrived home from school. A bandana around her head? Braids? The X-rated jeans? Tim told Joan to go home and get some sleep. She would probably find her back there anyway and all this grief would be for nothing.

Joan had fallen asleep with her clothes on. When she woke up, her windows were illuminated with the fused light of dawn. She bolted up, ran to Elise's room and opened the door; the lump of the blanket on the bed was hopeful, but on closer scrutiny, she saw that her mind had tricked her with the shapes of Elise's unmade bed. She panicked, called the cops. She called every neighbor again. When Faye answered the phone, she demanded to talk to Temesia. "She's getting ready for school. I don't want her to be late."

"Elise did not come home last night," Joan said. "I need to talk to Temesia. She may know something."

"Why drag Temesia into this, Joan. She's not Elise's keeper. You are. So why don't you start acting like it," Faye said.

"You inconsiderate bitch," Joan retorted and Faye hung up the phone.

Temesia had come from school, she clutched her books to her chest, had a new hairdo now, her long, straggly locks cut and shaped, a designer pocketbook dangling from her wrist. She was engaged. Last week, Elise had told her mother Faye had planned on giving the couple an engagement toast over the weekend. She told her mother she would not go. But now Elise was gone and Joan had not changed her clothes in two days, had not slept, nor eaten. Four sheriff's patrol cars were searching the city limits of Gloucester day and night. Joan had photos of Elise sprawled across the coffee table. Temesia sat for a moment, books still clutched, knees pressed together. "I thought you should know," she began and then stalled.

"Know what?"

"She met someone. A man. Not from around here."

"Who? What man?"

"I don't remember his name."

A dog barked outside and Joan jumped. "Try and remember. Please," she said.

"He picked her up hitchhiking," Temesia said.

"Hitchhiking? Jesus. When?"

"A couple of weeks ago. He had a car like your husband's. Ex-husband's. He took her to Newburyport and then she took the train back. She said something about Mexico."

Joan suddenly felt nauseous. "Did she say what the man looked like?"

"Blond. A tattoo . . . somewhere."

"Where?"

"I don't know!" Temesia said and began to sob. "I've been such a miserable friend." Temesia dropped her books and hung her head in her hands. "I can't get this feeling out of me. There's something wrong. There's something very, very wrong."

Temesia told Joan that Elise wasn't hanging out with the friends they shared. She ate lunch alone, and she didn't talk much to anyone. Temesia rubbed her eyes, then picked up her books and stood up straight. "Lately, I can't help but feel as if she's jealous." Temesia clutched her books to her chest. "She told me she thought Rick wasn't a good match for me. That he was superficial, a conformist. I used to believe her, what she said about people. But now I think it's her. Her values are all wrong. People should have goals; they should have aspirations, like Rick has. It's important."

Joan had no retort to Temesia's comment, because she knew it wasn't Temesia talking now; it was Faye. She watched the girl collect herself and walk toward the door. She stopped. "When she comes home, tell her to call me," she said, and left.

That night Joan and Nathan went to all of the rest areas along the highway within a thirty mile radius. They passed out fliers with descriptions and photos of Elise. They tacked the fliers to trees and taped them to windows. They spoke with waiters and waitresses at several Cracker Barrels, but no one had seen Elise. The next morning a Detective Dalton from Gloucester, the man now in charge of the case, had rapped at the kitchen door. Joan sat with Detective Dalton and answered the same questions Tim had asked the night Elise went missing. Detective Dalton wore a tan suit with no overcoat, despite the rain. When he came in, Joan saw that he had been pelted with several large drops. Dalton smelled like coffee and had dark circles under his eyes. He listened, yes, yes, took no notes, fetched a packet of tobacco and rolling papers from his suit pocket, sprinkled a heap of tobacco on a small white sheet. He licked the length and rolled up the paper, neatly. "Should I write this down for you?" Joan asked. What she wanted to say was, "Shouldn't you be writing this down instead of rolling that fucking cigarette?"

"We will go over it again," he said. He raised the cigarette, "Do you mind?" he asked.

"Please," Joan said. She went to the hutch in the dining room and fetched her mother's ashtray, a large clamshell.

They talked about Elise's friends, her hangouts, where she was last seen. "Drugs," the detective said. "Is she on drugs?"

"What? No. I don't think so," Joan stammered. "No."

"No marks on her arms, rolling papers, vials."

"No."

"Are you on drugs?"

"What kind of question is that, of course I'm not on drugs."

"Do you have any prescriptions that she could have taken?"

"No. Nothing."

Joan thought of her mother. The cornucopia of drugs in the bathroom cabinet. "My mother," she began, "there are still some of her prescription bottles in the bathroom."

Dalton inhaled, held his breath for a second or two, and then exhaled. He waved his hand to dissipate the smoke.

"I don't think she's a drug addict," Joan said. "I know my daughter."

"Do you?" Dalton asked. "Nine times out of ten a parent will have no clue that the son or daughter is a drug user."

Joan wavered a moment with her insecurity.

"Where is your mother? Is she here?"

"She passed away recently."

Dalton spied Joan over the smoke. "My condolences," he said. He leaned forward, tapped at the cigarette, but there was no ash. "Any history of mental illness?"

Joan stalled. Dalton raised his eyebrows. "Yes?"

No, she heard Margaret say. *He doesn't know what he's talking about.*

"Trichotillomania. Once, when she was ten years old."

"Never heard of it."

"She pulled out her hair."

"Hmmm. And nothing since then?"

"She's been in trouble at school."

"For what?"

Joan told the detective about Elise's jeans and skipping school, about what Temesia had said.

"And her father? Where is he?"

"Colorado. We were divorced seven years ago."

"How often does she see her father?"

"Once, maybe twice a year."

"Does he call?"

"Every so often."

"What's every so often?"

"Once every couple of months."

Dalton balanced the cigarette on the ashtray and took out a black book.

"How is your relationship with your ex-husband?"

"Amicable. Relatively speaking."

Dalton's stare lingered. "Is there any reason your ex-husband would have abducted her?"

"Roger? No . . ."

Joan remembered the car.

"What," the detective said. "What is it?"

"Temesia said the car was the same as my ex-husband's. But I'm not even sure he has that car any longer."

"What make and model?"

Dalton stubbed out his cigarette. He made a note of the make and model of the car in his black book and tucked it in his suit pocket. "More often than not it's the estranged parent who abducts the child."

"But he is not estranged. I told you our relationship is . . . amicable."

Dalton raised his left eyebrow. He was suspicious. "May I look in her room?"

Joan rose from the couch. "Yes, yes of course," she ushered the detective up the stairs and opened the door to Elise's room. Elise's clothes—panties, bras—were strewn about the floor. Joan opened the shades and the light betrayed the verses of an Anne Sexton poem, written on the wall:

Man is evil
I say aloud.
Man is a flower
that should be burnt,
I say aloud.

Man
is a bird full of mud,
I say aloud.

Dalton paused to read the wall. "Is anything missing?" he asked.
"Only what she was wearing. Her purse."
"What does it look like?"
"Fringed. Leather."
The detective bent to look at the photos on Elise's bureau, of herself
and Temesia. He picked up the book of poems and flipped through it.
"May I borrow this?" he asked and Joan nodded her head. He slid the
closet door aside and fingered the clothes hanging there. Joan fixated
on the detective's left hand; there was no wedding ring. How would he
know what it would be like to lose a daughter? What does he care? This
is just a job. She watched the detective drive his unmarked car out of
the driveway.

Twilight is the most devastating part of the day. Always Elise is returning
without a care in the world, her fringed purse hanging off her shoulder, a
cigarette dangling from her fingers. Joan positioned herself in the kitchen
to witness this very scenario, shifting the photos of Elise in her hands.
She waited, aware of the change in light and shadows in the kitchen. She
thought that perhaps the photo she used in the fliers was not accurate
enough. She thought for a moment she might get down on her knees
and pray, but she was overwhelmed by the hopelessness of it. Instead
she decided to take a shower. She disrobed, balled up her clothes on the
bathroom floor and let the hot water rain down on her. She had never
really known evil. Suffering, yes, disappointment, yes, but not evil. She
thought perhaps it did not exist, that it was only a deviation in psychology;
people can be wired all wrong. She remembered a young Elise sitting
on the floor of the kitchen drawing a picture, her hair falling in front
of her face. She had always praised her creativity and expressiveness; she
wondered then, if perhaps she had made a mistake by doing this. She
recalled the painting of the impressionistic sunflowers and the man;
she had never framed it because it disturbed her. She remembered how

a four-year-old Elise so desperately wanted to make words, she wrote her childish jibberish between the pages of the novels Joan was reading. When Elise finally did find her voice and started writing poetry, Joan was pleased. She thought it would be a good outlet for her, but all it seemed to do was turn her more inward. Joan thought about what Temesia said, how it's important to have aspirations. Then she thought about what her mother said, how Elise had sensibility. And people who have more than a fair share of sensibility live by different rules.

Joan heard the phone ring. She turned off the water and wrapped a towel around her. "Hello," a man's voice said, "I'm calling about the girl. I saw the posting at a rest area on Route 128."

"Yes, yes," Joan said. "Have you seen her? Have you seen my daughter? She may have been traveling with a blond-haired man. He has a tattoo."

"I saw a girl, about the same height, same hair color. Just a few days ago. Maybe Tuesday."

"Yes, that's when she went missing."

"I usually stop for a donut in the morning. This girl, she had fair skin and long blond hair down her back. Just like you said in the posting."

"Did you see what she was wearing?"

"Well, she was sitting down. She might have been wearing a sweater. Pink."

"Pink?"

"I don't know. Every day I usually get a donut and sit with my coffee. But this girl caught my eye because she seemed to be upset."

"Upset?"

"Yes."

"Why did you think that?"

"She was swearing at the guy she was with. Using the f-word."

"Who, what guy?"

"He wasn't blond. Older. I think she had a mole on her chin because I looked at it and thought of my sister. She had the same mole."

Elise did not have a mole on her chin. But she could have drawn one on her face. She was always drawing on her body, writing on her skin, notes in pen on her palms, phone numbers. Joan's towel dropped to the floor. The phone slipped from hands and bounced on the carpet.

"Hello?" the man's voice said. "The posting talked about a reward.

How much is it?"

There is no mole! Margaret sneered. *Hang up!*

"Was she wearing jeans? Jeans with words written on them?"

"Probably. I don't know."

"Please try and remember."

"I'm pretty sure it was her. She looked just like the posting."

"Did you see the car they drove?" Joan asked.

"They went out the door and I started to read the paper after that. If you need help, I could maybe lend a hand, help you find her. I wouldn't charge much."

Joan's brain jammed. *Hang up the phone!*

Joan hung up the phone.

The cops in Denver obtained a warrant to search Roger's house. Joan had begrudgingly relayed what little information she had on Elise's disappearance to Roger, who called while the police were ransacking his place; he sounded more inconvenienced than worried. Roger reprimanded Joan for being far too lax in raising Elise. Joan hung up the phone. Roger called back twice, but Joan did not pick up.

Several days later Dalton called Joan and said that he had something; it was Elise's purse. It was dark and bitter cold; Joan saw Dalton before he knocked, clutching a Stop and Shop bag in a gloveless hand, a cloud of breath rising up from his mouth into the porch light over the door. Before Joan let him in, he looked at her through the pane of glass; his guard was down then and she saw the pity in his eyes, intermixed with apprehension. He sucked in the night air and Joan opened the door.

Joan tried to speak but the lump in her throat swelled up and became painful. Nathan lingered in the doorway to the kitchen. Detective Dalton reached into the bag and extracted the purse. Joan's vision became blurry. She started to shake.

Nathan stepped forward. "What's going on?" he asked.

"I talked with Temesia," Dalton said. "Got the details to Elise's last . . . excursion. She did take a train from Newburyport. We found a conductor who remembers selling a ticket to a girl with words on her jeans and long blond hair. But that was two weeks ago. We talked to the locals and no one can vouch for seeing Elise after two thirty. She must've been picked up on Rt. 127 sometime afterward and taken out of town. We put out an APB and the police in Portsmouth combed the beaches up the coast and found the purse."

Joan took the purse in her hands. It was cool and damp. She fingered the fringe, traced the name "Elise" etched into the soft leather. She looked inside; there was an empty pack of cigarettes and nothing else.

"It came in with the tide," Dalton said.

Joan shook her head. She clutched the purse in her hands and buried her face in it and wept. Nathan went to her and put his hand on her back. She held on tightly to the purse.

"She may have been with a man. The Portsmouth police questioned some kids in a bar up there who may have seen her. Said they saw a girl with long blond hair with a man with dark hair. There weren't enough accurate details to make a sketch. It seems as if the witnesses were in disagreement about his features."

"She's been seen," Joan muttered. "That's hopeful, isn't it?"

Dalton took a breath; he held it for a moment and then let it out. "I can't say," he said. "There is no way of knowing. Whoever she was with may have taken her out there on the ocean, which means he owns a boat. We've alerted the area harbormasters and the Coast Guard. They're searching the waters from Maine to Gloucester."

Dalton looked at Joan grappling with her composure. "We're doing all that we can do." He cleared his throat and then said softly, "I need the name of her dentist."

Joan looked at Nathan. His face was white.

She couldn't breathe; she thought she might vomit.

"I'm sorry," Dalton exclaimed. "I don't mean to be morbid. It's only protocol. We must have a record of these things."

Detective Dalton waited for Nathan to find the dentist's phone number in his grandmother's phone book. He copied it down onto a piece of paper. Dalton took the paper, rose and grabbed his coat. "You should alert the media. Call the papers; give them her photo and the information we discussed. Call everyone you know and tell them what happened. This is no time to be discreet." He turned to Nathan, "Take care of your mother," he said and showed himself out.

§

Joan wept for hours in her bed, reeling in the shockwaves of supposition and memory that pummeled her brain. Then, near midnight, her mind shifted and began to obsess. She stoically whittled away at the case to one particular item—the empty pack of cigarettes in the purse. She flicked on the light, went to retrieve it, extracted the empty carton and tore out the paper and foil filler. Inside she found a small, folded piece of paper. The ink smeared a little but the writing was still legible:

> Mother, I hear your feet above me
> step softly amongst the straw
>
> your bruised heart, a forgotten fruit
> past ripe for plucking
>
> your eyes have worn your cheek raw.
>
> I have fallen through the cleft
> due west of the cresting waves
>
> where ships carry a cargo of souls
> who bemoan the stone
> of their graves.
>
> Mother, the blood of these seeds
> still stains my lips
>
> and the taste is bitter, like sin
> But I have learned to shine
>
> my own light,
>
> the Blessed feminine.

Joan instinctively looked up upon finishing the poem and Elise was standing at the edge of her bed. She was diaphanous and wore a robe of light. Her countenance was virtually expressionless. Joan was neither afraid nor reassured; she regarded the apparition as she would an elegant heron in the marsh, something she did not want to scare away.

What enveloped her was the whole essence of Elise, her daughter—her creative, disturbed, vulnerable daughter who was a spinoff of the most treacherous parts of herself. She recalled how she used to sit in Elise's room and just watch her sleep, her face soft and innocent, reconciled. She breathed her in then, when it was safe.

And it was in this similar state of placidity, in a place somewhere between the underworld and consciousness that Joan sat with the apparition. As the night went on, parts of Elise slowly began to fade, first the hands, then the neck, then the top of the head, until Elise was gone and Joan, fast asleep.

PERSEPHONE'S APPEAL
Elise and Michaelis, 1976

It started to rain, a cold rain that comes with mid October, and once again she was hitchhiking underdressed, wearing only a t-shirt and jeans. It was the gray of the sky that had provoked her, magnified her angst. It's only weather, Nana used to say. But Elise didn't see it that way; it framed her life, intensified her highs and lows. And in the gray, home was dull, a dead end, a low, so she rushed out, away from it. But now she longed for it, for its warmth, that place she called home, Nana's house, even though Nana was dead.

She thought about stopping at the nearest house, which could be more than a mile away on this part of the road, to call her mother. Then she heard a car behind her and eagerly stuck out her thumb; it hissed by her. Elise wiped her brow. The leaves were coming down with the rain; the yellow and brown leaves filled the sky. Another car came up behind her, a pale blue Cadillac. She could hear the music from inside it. It slowed down and stopped. Elise peered in through the tears of water on the glass. A man motioned her to open the door, and when she did she was pummeled with the smell of the man, a rich, sweet, musky cologne. She recognized the smell. It was her father's cologne.

"Hello!" the man said, cheerfully. "It's raining! Come in!"

The man was a foreigner with an accent she couldn't place. He told her he was headed home to Gloucester. Great, Elise said. You can drop me off at the train station. OK, the man said. He put on his blinker and glided back onto the road.

The man had black hair on his knuckles; his temples were graying. He wore a dress shirt a size too small, slacks with no belt. He kept smiling at her. It rained harder now and the windshield wipers groaned in cadence.

"Why are you out? You're soaked!"

"I didn't think it would rain this hard," Elise said. "Sometimes I just go. I don't think about anything else."

"You go." The man waved his hand. "Ahh, you're young. Strong. What's your name? You live here?"

"I live in Salem. I was visiting a friend in Magnolia."

Elise fingered a trinket hanging from the man's rear view mirror. It was a glass eye. "What's this?" she asked.

"Nazar. For protection," the man said. "You know, the evil eye." He leaned over and pointed to his eye.

Elise was confused, but she didn't want to press the man. The eye swung back and forth slightly, as if to hypnotize her. It was interesting. She looked out through the window, through the dancing streams of water traversing the glass. The music in the car was festive—a mandolin— and exotic, counter to the dismal environs. It lifted her mood.

"Who are you?" the man asked. "What is your name?"

"My name is Persephone," Elise replied.

"Persephone! Really? That's Greek! Are you Greek?"

"No. My mother just liked the name."

"Ahh. Yes. You know, ah, Persephone is a goddess. She's very beautiful. Like you."

Elise smiled, satisfied with herself in charming the man.

"She's the goddess of the underworld," Elise said.

"Yes. Right . . . ah . . ." The man wanted to say more, but his brain seemed to jam, so he started singing to the music. She regarded the wavering glass eye, looked in the backseat that had a few grocery bags.

"I went to the market," the man said, "but I go the long way. I like to look," he motioned to the trees, the marshland. He drove slowly. Elise felt as if she were on a tour.

"Listen, I make fish. I cook for you like we do on my island. It's good. You can dry off. Then I take you to the train and you can go to Salem. We check the schedule. Yes? Good?"

"OK," Elise replied. "Why not?"

The house was just as neat as the car with everything put away in its proper place. The décor was somewhat eclectic with its orange velvet couch and hanging lamps, the stone reliefs of urns on the walls. The man pointed to the black and white photographs of his family in Greece. He named the stocky old men and women, the black-haired goddesses with tiaras in their hair, the men who looked like him, the nieces, nephews dancing or sitting at long tables with food. There were white stone buildings with shafts of vertical light illuminating water.

"Naxos," the man said. "My island. You know, where Theseus left Ariadne."

"Ariadne," Elise said, "the princess who led Theseus through the labyrinth to slay the Minotaur."

"He left her there. And then Dionysus, eh, the god of wine, took her."

The man pointed to a picture of a structure, a rectangular arch. "Portara. It was never built, eh for Apollo. Just the gate."

"Portara," Elise said under her breath, gazing at the picture of the tremendous arch.

"Come, come," the man said, ushering her in. He went to the record player and put on a record. It crackled and hissed and then there was a man's voice singing a ballad accompanied by that quintessential Greek mandolin sound. The music started to pick up and the man raised his hands and snapped his fingers. He started to dance. Elise clapped her hands. "Come, come," the man said, taking her arm. "I give you a dress."

The man took her to what seemed like a guestroom in the back of the house, behind the kitchen. It had blank walls and a made bed, a dresser with a mirror with another glass eye hanging from it. He opened the closet door and took out a white v-neck gown wrapped in plastic. "You wear this for dinner. I dry your clothes." The man removed the plastic covering and gave the gown to Elise. She touched the silk chiffon folds. "For you, Persephone," the man said. "I go and make dinner."

When the man left the room, Elise laid the gown on the bed just to look at it. She took off her clothes and sandals and slipped it over her head. The bodice was somewhat big, and she'd have to lift the folds when she walked, but she'd manage. She twirled and danced and the gown swished and caressed her legs. She piled her hair atop her head and looked in the mirror. She was transformed. Elise waltzed out of the room in her bare feet.

"Eh, Persephone! Look at this girl!" The man took her hand and slowly spun her around. "Wine?"

"Of course."

Something was sizzling in a pan on the stove. It was a silver fish. The man poured her a glass of wine. "Cheers," he said, and they touched glasses. He showed her the lettuce, cucumbers, and tomatoes from his garden. He chopped them up and put them in a bowl. They drank and danced in the living room to the festive Greek music with its Greek mandolin sound and then the tempo became slow. The man went to the kitchen. "Come, come," he said. He plated the food and put it on the table. "Now we eat. *Kali Orexi*!"

Half of the shimmering silver fish lay on its side with a sprig of something across its eye. Elise poked at it, perused its flaky flesh, put it to her mouth. It was salty but good. The man offered her a piece of hot, crispy bread and she took it. He poured more wine from a bottle with ancient lettering. She fingered the stem of her glass. She and her friend Temesia used to pilfer sips from the bottles of liquor stashed in a box in Nana's basement. The liquor burned her throat going down and wasn't at all pleasant, but she felt like she was getting away with something. In the fall, her grandmother made wine from the fruits in the orchard and offered her some at dinner. "Not too much," she always said. The Greek wine was not as sweet, but she knew she could have as much of it as she wanted, and this was exactly what she needed: no limitations, no restrictions.

Conversation with the man was arduous and awkward, so they ate and drank and the man sang to the record. Elise thought of her mother and brother sitting down to eat without her. In the past, she'd gotten an earful when she came in, but that would only last a few minutes. Then she would eat her cold dinner in peace. Tonight, she would be later than she ever was. Her mother might start to call around. She thought of calling her from the man's phone: she could see the yellow rotary by the pale green refrigerator in the kitchen, but her mother might detect that she was drunk. What was better, to hear her daughter's drunken voice, or to not hear her voice at all? Elise sipped her wine again and giggled at the man whose face was contorted in melodrama as he sang. Then he rose and went to the fridge. He brought out a plate of pastry. He gave her a piece.

"Baklava."

Elise picked up the sticky, flaky pastry and took a bite. "So sweet!" she said. "My tongue is drunk with sweetness!"

The man shoved a piece of baklava in his mouth. "Mmmm. Ahhh, wait," the man said, rising from his seat. He fetched a bottle from the fridge, a liqueur, two demitasse glasses from the cabinet. "Citron. You try. It's good for your stomach."

She finished the wine and drank the citron. When the music picked up, they danced some more. Elise began to feel as if she were on a boat with the floor swaying and dipping. The Greek life oozed around her. She was euphoric; for the first time in her life she felt simply delighted by the world, by all it could offer her. She sat on the couch for a moment. The man came to her, tapping his watch, and started asking her questions, but she couldn't understand a word he said. She felt as if the delight and euphoria of the world were pulling her under. She rested her head on the pillow of the couch.

Michaelis waved his hand in front of the girl's face. He called her name: Persephone. Then he carried the girl and laid her on the bed in the guest room. He wasn't sure why he did this; she seemed comfortable on the couch; he could have just left her there. Michaelis sat down next to her and pushed her hair out of her eyes. She was fair and blond, nothing like his family or Melina's family for that matter. Melina's dress was a bit big for her, especially in the bust; the bodice of it shifted and the girl's nipple was exposed. Michaelis stood up. He ran his fingers through his hair. How long had he and Melina been divorced? He knew she wore the dress once more, after the wedding, but he couldn't remember the event. It would have been wrong to wear the white dress to someone else's wedding. It was wrong for Persephone to wear it now, Michaelis thought. And then his mind doubled back: It is Greek custom to clothe and feed the stranger; the divine often appeared in humble ways. This is what Michaelis told himself. He leaned over and tugged the dress over the nipple. He touched the girl's face. Persephone, she called herself.

After Melina left, he went nearly every weekend to his cousin's house in New Castle, New Hampshire. They had a sailing boat. Michaelis would come home tan and drunk, still hearing the echoes of conversations in his ears. They—his cousin and his wife—had tried to set him up with some of the women in their church, but nothing panned out. The women were too—Americanized. He longed for Melina even more, but Melina returned to Naxos. She had packed her things, left a note saying she was lonely and miserable in America. She couldn't take one more day here.

Michaelis sat down next to Persephone and traced a finger down her arm. He could just lay with her and hold her. He missed holding a woman in bed, feeling another person's warmth. He went to the other side of the bed and lay on his side. Outside the rain was patting the windows and the roof. It was a delicate sound. He stroked the girl's arm again. He reached down and pulled the folds of the dress back to stroke the girl's leg. He stopped. This was too much, the girl's thigh exposed like that. He started to become aroused. He could just get it over and done with, surreptitiously, with her lying there asleep. He unzipped his pants. He brushed the dress aside to see more of the inner thigh. He leaned over and put his lips there. She was so drunk, the girl. No one would ever know. And it had been so long. He lifted up the dress and lay against her with his skin to her skin. He slid a finger inside her underwear and tugged at it. He wasn't satisfied. He wanted to lie on top of her. He took down his pants and spread the girl's legs. The girl moved; she lifted up her arms and opened her eyes. He held her arms down. Shhh, he said. She started to squirm, to fight him. He panicked, put his hand over her mouth, shhhh. She pulled it loose. He grabbed the pillow to stifle the scream. Were the windows open? It was still early. She continued to fight. He pushed harder. The scream was muffled by the pillow and then it was silent. The girl stopped fighting. She was asleep again.

Michaelis lifted the pillow; sweat was pouring down his temples. He checked to see if the girl was breathing. Did he kill her? How long did he have the pillow over her face? He buttoned his pants. He pulled the dress down. It was wet. He grabbed her wrist and checked for a pulse. He listened for a heartbeat in her chest, but didn't hear anything. He tugged at the dress and put his ear to her skin. He just couldn't tell if her heart was beating or if she was breathing. Michaelis paced the room. He could call his cousin: he would know what to do. Michaelis started to cry. He went to the phone in the kitchen and dialed his cousin's number. The record had stopped. The rain had stopped. It was unbearably quiet.

His cousin answered hello in a firm voice, as if he were already angry. Michaelis burst into explanation, a torrent of Greek into his cousin's ear. Calm down, his cousin said. Calm down. Slow. Tell me what happened. Michaelis told him exactly what happened, how it was all so innocent. He never intended to touch the girl. Get her out of the house, his cousin said. What about the hospital? Michaelis asked. Should I bring her there? No. You will be arrested. They'll cut your balls off, Michaelis. Are you stupid? You'll rot in an American prison for the rest of your life. His cousin told the story of a friend who was in trouble with the IRS; he's been in prison for years. For nothing! I don't know if she's dead or alive, Michaelis said. What difference does it make, his cousin said. Is she a slut? Is she a whore? She's a whore, the cousin said. You need to think that way. Michaelis, your parents paid for you to come here. They depend on that American job you got. You want to be a disgrace to your family?

The cousin told him what to do: to meet him at the dock in New Castle where he had a dory. Michaelis put the phone down. He looked out the window at the house next door. It had several lights on. There was a middle-aged couple who lived with their youngest son. He just got back from Vietnam. He picked up the phone again, told his cousin he would come at midnight when the neighbor's lights were out.

The leftover food was on the table, the wine, the record silently hissed, the carcass of a fish. He shut off the turntable, threw the food in the trash. He went back to the room, closed the lights and waited for midnight, sitting vigil next to the girl.

At midnight, he fetched his keys and coat and went to open the trunk of the car. He went back for Persephone. He thought of taking the dress off her, but it was soiled, so he left it on. Michaelis struggled with Persephone and nearly dropped her twice, but he got her there, to the trunk. He thought of throwing a blanket over her. He went inside, pulled the spread from the guestroom bed and covered the body. He went back for her purse and clothes.

Michaelis pulled up to the boardwalk where his headlights shown on the small group of dories bobbing in the dark. He shut off his lights and sat for a moment. He was exhausted and he wanted to sleep. He looked out at the flickering lamp over the bobbing dories; his cousin was nowhere to be found. He started to panic again; the thought of being alone with the body was unbearable. He started to cry again, thinking of the girl as she twirled in his living room, how she was happy. How she trusted him. Michaelis rubbed his eyes. When he opened them, he saw the nazar; it was remarkably still. He took it in his hands. Its colors were different now; in fact he could have sworn that there were colors inside the glass that weren't there before, a tinge of orange or maybe red. His eyes could not be trusted, he told himself. He was tired. Then, there was a rapping at the car window. Michaelis jumped. What if it was the police? He leaned over to unlock the door and his cousin opened the door, sat down, and shut the door in one smooth motion. He reeked of Marlboro cigarettes. Michaelis was relieved; he had long associated that stench with his cousin and now he was here and Michaelis was not alone anymore. The dark form that was his cousin did not turn to look at him when he sat down; he looked straight ahead at the ocean. We move quick, to get her on the boat, he said. They sat for a moment in silence. Michaelis wanted to ask his cousin why he was doing this—helping him—but he didn't. He knew his cousin was a man of few words. He was a man who did what he had to do and he was coolheaded. This was something Michaelis always admired in him.

His cousin told him he had been setting traps all summer for lobster and he knew the way out by heart now. It would be better to leave while it was still dark; the buoys would guide them through the channel, he said. He had done it before and was confident. He told Michaelis to pull the car closer to the dock.

When Michaelis opened the trunk, he looked at the lump of blanket as if waiting for it to move. It would be worse if it moved, he thought, but he somehow found himself rooting for her, the girl. Michaelis's cousin sighed, as if he was irritated. Don't just stand there, let's get her out, he barked. They shimmied across the deck with the body and then Michaelis nearly tripped and his back gave out. He let out a small yelp and dropped the girl. His cousin cursed him in Greek. Then he picked up the body and went the rest of the way with her, stumbling across the dock, until he came to his dory where he heaved the body onto it and it pushed backward then jerked forward by the rope tied to the dock. Michaelis was bowled over in pain. Come! sneered his cousin. Get in! Michaelis didn't move. I can't, he said. My leg. There's pain down my leg. His cousin spat and then swore at him again. Do I have to carry you too? Michaelis was scared now, scared of the dark waves moving with the wind, the clouds moving across the moon like phantoms, scared of his cousin. He was cold, chilled down to his bones. His cousin helped him into the boat. He started the motor.

They motored in the moonlight to a place off the Isle of Shoals. Michaelis's cousin shut off the motor and the boat coasted, then gently bobbed in the waves. The full moon lit a path through the water; Michaelis looked over at this cousin and thought he could almost see his face. They sat there for a moment as the boat rocked under the light of the moon and an elegant arc of stars and the wind had become soft; Michaelis almost felt as if something grand and behind the scenes was complicit in what they were doing.

His cousin removed the blanket and regarded the girl. From what Michaelis could see the eyes were still closed. Don't worry, the cousin said. This sort of thing happens all the time to girls like this. It's sad. Michaelis nodded his head. You need to be more careful, Michaelis. Don't do stupid things. Then the cousin tossed the clothes overboard and the purse too. Michaelis watched as his cousin sent Persephone back to the underworld, her ethereal white gown matching the ethereal white moon as it billowed down. They sat there a few minutes as the pale ocean took on a curious glow. Then Michaelis's cousin turned the boat around and motored home.

WOMAN IN THE SHAPE OF A CROSS
Mira and Etta, 1986

It was early evening and Mira was at the sink doing the dishes, fixing dinner and staring at the now fern-covered ledge just beyond the yard. The ferns were flourishing in fiddleheads and fronds. Perhaps the ferns had found places where the rock was vulnerable and plunged in. Perhaps a storm had taken down a tree and cleared a space for light and water and this water cleaved the rock and the sustenance vitalized the ferns. Mira's wonderment over the ferns rumbled below her consciousness as she washed her last dish and placed it on the drying rack. She was thinking about her sister, Etta, and her diagnosis. Etta called to tell her a few weeks ago a strange black growth had developed *down there*. The doctor said it looked like melanoma and she was going for a biopsy in two days. She told her sister this thing was going to do her in; it was a monster, a black hole right in the middle of her, and Mira knew in her gut that her sister was right.

Years ago, Mira stood at this same spot staring at the ledge, thinking about her mother, how this was the time of day she would call; Mira would grab the phone on its second ring to hear her mother speak her name tenderly and with a twinge of hope. *Mirabelle?* She would ask, and Mira would say, *Hi Ma.* They would talk about the family, current events. Sometimes her mother would give her advice. Sometimes they would laugh. And then her mother died and Mira stared out at the ledge, thinking of her.

Weeks later, after she had buried her mother, ordered a tombstone, planted daisies in the fresh mound of dirt, Mirabelle went to Mass with her family and discovered the holy water receptacles still dry. Fans whirred above a crowded church where bodies swayed with boredom and restlessness as Father Olsen introduced a visiting priest, a Father Scott who would give the homily. Mirabelle was enticed by the dark stranger; it was the first time she felt engaged since her mother had died.

Father Scott did not stand behind the podium as the more perfunctory Father Olsen; he walked among the people. He was animated, kind, his jet black hair and features, and dark skin made him exotic, as if he were from India or the Middle East. He talked about how compassionate acts create a certain "lightness," how Christ's compassionate acts can be divided into two types, those we can understand—role modeling, and those we cannot understand—miracles. Father Scott believed Christ's capacity for compassion was so intense, it had reached a mystical level and this level of lightness enabled Him to walk on water, to turn five fishes into five thousand, to resurrect the dead.

Mirabelle was intrigued with this philosophy and at the end of the Mass, she approached Father Scott and introduced herself. His hand was warm, as if it had a strong lifeblood running through it. She asked if she could make an appointment to speak with him about grief. Father Scott's countenance immediately changed with the word from hospitable to concerned. They stood just outside the shadow of the roof in the glorious Sunday heat, and she noticed how he had beads of sweat clinging to the curls at his temples. She thought of the layers of clothing he wore, the clergy shirt and pants, the outer vestments, cope, stole—all that cloth—she felt guilty for keeping him. They agreed upon a time and Father Scott housed her hand in both of his when he said goodbye.

Home was the sacristy Philomena built. It was her mother who prepared the meals, ironed the sheets, grew the sweet basil on the windowsill. Mirabelle eventually followed suit and had her own children, made her own home, but she could always go back to the home Philomena made, and her mother would butter her toast, poach an egg, make a pot of coffee and talk of family. Like Philomena, family was the mechanism that kept Mira intact.

She knew her tribe—they ate under her mother's crystal chandelier after Mass and gossiped and reminisced and laughed and smoked. Mira liked to sit and listen to their stories of the old days when they all lived in an apartment building in the North End and knew each other's business. Pop sat at the head of the table crushing walnuts in his palms, listening to the gossip and current events being filtered through the old folks. He would chuckle softly in his seat or solemnly shake his head and Mira would then know what to think.

Philomena made fun of all of them. She had the uncanny ability to imitate people; she took on their facial expressions, their voices. A cup of coffee with her mother on a Saturday afternoon meant a cup of coffee with Mickey, or Ida, or Rita, and their respective neuroses. It was funny. She and her mother would laugh and laugh and her mother would pound the table with her palm. Mirabelle missed these comedic interpretations; she missed her mother's infectious laugh, its effervescence-like quality infused the world with levity.

The only person not up for discussion was Mirabelle's sister Etta, who left with a group of hippies for California. It was no secret Philomena was worried and disappointed in Etta, whom she referred to as a *puttana* and a vagabond. Mirabelle felt the primal filial pride that her sister was bad in her mother's mind and that she was good. Etta wasn't there to say the rosary with Philomena or sit quietly watching the evening news while nurses padded around the bed. Etta wasn't there to honor her mother's last wishes to have her nails and hair colored so she would look like a lady and not a corpse. Mirabelle was the one who brought her mother joy during her last days, and it didn't go unnoticed. "Don't kid yourself," Aunt Jenny said. "She's eating this up."

While Philomena was on her deathbed, Mirabelle went to morning Mass. It had been a while since she had attended a weekday Mass, and she felt like an interloper. She went through the imposing wooden doors and stuck her hand in the receptacle of holy water, but it was dry. She sat in the back of the church, behind the regulars, and fidgeted, thinking her mother could already be dead. After Father Olsen served communion, she left, headed out to the car and sped over the bridge down Rt. 128, where the water had retreated so far out, the boats in the bay were lying on their hulls in mud.

Philomena was asleep when Mirabelle arrived. She sat next to her mother and waited, watching her breathe for most of the afternoon. Aunt Jenny came unannounced and sat by Mirabelle's side and they prayed the rosary. When Aunt Jenny went out for a cigarette, Mirabelle leaned in close to her mother. "Ma," she said. "Ma, it's me, Mirabelle." Philomena moved her mouth and Mirabelle moved in closer. She was waiting for a glimpse of the master plan, something her mother, now in-between worlds, could say to soothe all of her worries, something that could give her solace and insight when times got inconceivable and dark. Philomena opened her eyes; they were covered in a film. She murmured something. Mirabelle asked her to repeat it. "Goodnight Etta," her mother said, "wherever you are," and she died. That was it. Death was very anticlimactic and simple. Mirabelle left the room in a stupor; there was no miraculous event to take with her, no closure, no burst of love, only a valediction meant for someone else.

Upon meeting Father Scott, Mirabelle's grief was now peppered with thoughts of him. She imagined walking up to the rectory door, knocking on it softly. Father Scott would usher her to his room. In his room there would be a wooden table with a wooden bowl. The bowl would be clean. There would also be a ceramic cup and a wooden chair. Mirabelle imagined a fire in a fireplace, tended well with ample wood stowed at its hearth. There would be books written by the mystics and Christian philosophers, a single bed with a pressed white sheet and pillow, blankets folded over the end. Father Scott's life would be that of an ascetic and a scholar and Mirabelle longed to be near it, occupy that room herself, eat from the bowl, drink from the cup, pray fireside in the evening when the sky's firmament was silent and vast.

When the morning of the meeting arrived, Mirabelle was nervous. She thought perhaps her makeup was overdone and spent an extra ten minutes touching up her face. She made sure to choose a floral skirt, remembering what priests in her day thought of shorts, also, to use the bathroom; her nervousness weakened her bladder. She ran out of the house, late, hearing the toilet run and cursing her husband for not fixing the problem that had plagued her for weeks.

She waited on the porch of the rectory where there was a potted basil plant, limp from the late June heat; the leaves hung down like folded wings. Father Scott called her name from the side of the porch. He wore a short-sleeved clergy shirt; there was a rectangular bulge in the breast pocket. He suggested they take a ride to Rocky Neck and sit under a tree in the park by the water; it might be cooler there. Mirabelle agreed and Father Scott followed her to her car. She had never met with a priest before, outside of a confessional, and it was awkward to have one in her car. Father Scott, seemed to be relaxed. He rolled down the window and patted at the rushing air with his hand.

Mirabelle parked the car in a freshly paved parking lot. It was ten thirty in the morning and the heat engine of day was beginning to rev; she could feel the hotness from the pavement rising up to her calves. Out in the bay, a flock of seagulls were picking through the oyster beds at low tide. Some gathered at a fish carcass to jab at its loose flesh.

They chose a bench under a shade tree. She sat next to him, allowing for adequate bench space between them. Father Scott rested his left foot over his right knee and Mirabelle noticed how he wore leather sandals instead of shoes. She tried to remember if that sort of thing was allowed in her day as a catechumen.

Father Scott withdrew a pack of Marlboro Lights from his clergy shirt pocket. "Do you smoke?" he asked. She shook her head. "Mind if I do?"

Father Scott cupped his hands about the lighter the way he took her hand in his the day she approached him, gently, with great intention. He drew in the smoke and exhaled to the sky. "I like to come to the piano bar here," he said. "You know, sometimes, on weeknights when it's not too crowded. There's a man who plays Billy Joel songs."

Mirabelle thought the piano bar was for the artists, or the locals to get drunk and sing sea shanties. She pressed her knees together for good posture, as she was taught to do in elementary school, and thought of Etta, how Father Scott, despite being a priest, was a man her sister might have liked.

Father Scott asked about her mother. He focused his compassionate gaze upon her. Mirabelle felt the sting of his cigarette smoke in her eyes; she pressed her knees tighter and began the story of her mother's death. The more she spoke of it, the more she felt it trite. Grief had dwindled; it slithered away, under the bushes of the China roses, now in bloom at the edge of the grass. Everyone's mother dies at some point, she told herself. And then it was not trite; it was not the grief that was trite, it was her words. She felt as if she had betrayed her love for her mother by using inadequate words. "I wanted something from her. I think I wanted something," she told Father Scott.

Father Scott agreed. "We grow up wanting, expecting, taking from our parents our whole lives. At their death beds, it's no different."

"It seems wrong to want and take from a parent when they are suffering and vulnerable."

"Maybe she was not as vulnerable as you thought; perhaps she was capable and you didn't know it."

"Capable of what?"

"Of giving you what you needed."

"What was it that I needed?" Mirabelle asked.

"Only you know that," Father Scott said.

He finished his cigarette, stifled the ash, twisted the stub between his fingers and placed it on the bench space between them.

A cool breeze rustled the leaves in the tree and Father Scott closed his eyes to succumb to it. Mirabelle closed her eyes too. For a moment the heat dissipated; she saw her mother sitting in a secret room inside her. She was waiting.

They had an amicable lunch at the clam shack at the end of the road. Father Scott was personable and kind and Mira felt more relaxed talking to him, but he provided no great insight to her predicament. Afterward, she dropped him off at the rectory and told him she would have him over for dinner while he was still in town, but she knew after she said it that this would not happen.

As she drove the windy road up the coast, grief slithered back in. In her mind, she visited the room inside herself where her mother sat. It looked similar to the ascetic room the fictitious Father Scott lived in. She could not, however, see her mother's face clearly and she found this disconcerting. She saw the outline of her body, her thick arms, the curls in her hair, the floral pattern on her house dress. Was her face filled with light now and not discernible? She saw Aunt Jenny's face and Etta's face. She saw Father's Scott's face, but she could not see her mother's face. In fact, she wasn't particularly sure if the person in the room was indeed her mother.

In a dream, Mirabelle went to Father Scott's imaginary ascetic room and knocked on the door. He received her in his ceremonial vestments, cloth upon consecrated cloth. She embraced him, felt the form of his lean body. Mirabelle traced her hands gently down his neck and along his shoulders to where the stole rested. It was purple, embroidered with gold symbols she did not recognize. She lifted it from him. She lifted the white cope, pulled the starched collar from his neck, unbuttoned his clergy shirt. She touched his bare chest and then a scar under his ribs. She reached inside the gash but it too was dry.

Mirabelle awoke to the sound of the toilet running; the sound seemed to accentuate her restless sleep. She turned to look at her husband as if he might do something about it, but Paul lay flat on his back fast asleep. It was three in the morning, and the moonlight illuminated the sheet crumpled at the foot of the bed. She remembered how her husband told her he saw a figure, once, standing over her as she slept. He could not make out the features, but the silhouette depicted a human form. This was shortly after her father had died, and Paul said the presence in the room had awakened him; he tried to nudge Mirabelle and wake her to not be alone with it. But then the figure faded. Mirabelle thought of checking each room in the house to see if her mother was there. It was a ridiculous thought, but she got out of bed, went to the bathroom to jiggle the toilet's handle, and then downstairs to the kitchen where she could fetch a glass of water. If her mother was in the house, she would be there. Before she flicked on the light, she imagined her mother standing at the kitchen table with an apron over her church clothes. Upon seeing her daughter, she would give her a directive, to set the table or arrange the antipasto on a presentable dish. Mirabelle switched on the light and saw her empty kitchen as she had always known it at night, quiet, imperturbable.

The next morning, Paul gave a short lesson on toilet mechanics to their daughter, Samantha. Her husband, the engineer, knew the intimate workings of every appliance in the house as well as the cars in the garage. He was reluctant to replace appliances or parts of appliances if certain adjustments could be made.

"Why can't we just fix it so that it doesn't run?" Samantha asked.

"It's just a minor adjustment, Sam. It won't take up too much of your time," Paul replied.

Her husband lectured them on how a running toilet could waste up to two gallons per minute; with the water ban on now because of the drought, this was unacceptable. They could come and put him in jail. Would she like that, if her father went to jail for a running toilet? Samantha smirked. "They can't put you in jail for a running toilet, Dad."

"You never know," Paul said. "They put people in jail for all sorts of things these days."

Later that day, Mirabelle had it in her mind to make a pot of sauce, despite the heat. She was missing a few things for dinner—olives and lettuce for the salad, a loaf of Italian bread, eggs for making the meatballs so she decided to take a trip to the supermarket. Once in the car, Mirabelle turned the air conditioner on high. This was something her husband told her to never do, maximize the demand on the air conditioner when the car was only running for a minute or so. She pulled out of the driveway with hot air blasting at her face and crossed the bridge over the marsh hoping the car would soon cool. The tide was out again, not one blade of grass in the sedge, nor one leaf on the bordering oaks moved; the landscape around her was tolerant and unwavering.

The automatic doors of the supermarket were propped open for airflow; there was a sign in the window: the air conditioner was broken and the manager was sorry about the inconvenience. Mirabelle perused the aisles of the supermarket, hoping that she would run into Father Scott. He would be buying a loaf of bread or perhaps some tea. He would tell her that he hoped she was doing well, that he had thought of something recently when he was contemplating her situation she might like to know. He would ask her if she would like to meet again. Mirabelle ventured down each of the aisles, passing lethargic patrons going about their business. She reached the checkout, paid for her items and with a small pang of disappointment, left.

When she arrived home, the toilet was running again, only this time the churning sound was louder and more imperative. She went to the bathroom to find the water streaming down the sides of the tank and panicked, lifted the cover and witnessed the water shoot up with a mystical force like a genie from a lamp. It doused her head, her clothes, immediately eradicating all oppressive heat. Mirabelle stood among the fountain of cool water as it soaked her and for a moment she was certain she heard it—the familiar sound of laughing.

§

They cut it out. The doctor said they got all of it but it was twice as big as they thought it would be. Etta was more restless than ever. She called Mira up on the phone and asked her to accompany her to California.

"Why don't you come with me?" Etta asked suddenly, almost cheerfully.

"You want to travel the country *now*?"

"I need to," Etta said. "But you won't come, will you. You can't leave your home. You're a homebody," she said.

This was such an Etta thing to do, to try and get Mira to do something by insulting her.

"That's not true."

"Have you or have you not gone anywhere in the past couple of years? You're afraid to leave your house, your husband, your family. You're afraid it will all go to shit without you. Hell, your husband can't boil an egg for himself without your help. You trained him to be that way."

"He can so boil an egg. That's not the point. The point is you always want to run away somewhere when you have something difficult to deal with."

"That sounds very cliché. I am not cliché," Etta said.

"We're all cliché! I'm the can't-go-on-vacation cliché and you are the runaway-from-critical-issues cliché! What's wrong with that?"

"Cliché implies an inability to change one's ways. That's not me," Etta replied. "I spent my life changing."

Mira cleared her throat.

"I'll go to make sure you don't get sick out there."

"I'm already sick."

"Sick*er*."

"So you are only going to make sure I'll be OK. Well, that's not how I want you to go. So don't go."

"Jesus Christ, Etta," Mira said, "How do you want me to want to go?"

"It's very simple Mira. It has been very simple all of our lives. I want you to come with me because you want to be with me. That's it."

Mira was silent for a moment. She held her breath and closed her eyes. She wanted to cry, but she stopped herself. It was easier to play the game.

"You want me to be with you. Really."

"Yes."

"Didn't you spend enough time out there?" Mira asked.

"I've never been to California," Etta said.

"What are you talking about?"

"I never went. I went to Vermont instead."

Mira thought of her sister's luxurious mane of hair, how she might transform with the treatments.

"I can't do this alone," Etta said.

"OK," Mira said. "I'll go."

§

Once, when Etta was twelve, she stole a communion wafer from church, slipped it from her mouth and into her pocket when no one was looking. Later, she sat on Mira's bed and held it in her hands like a small bird, watching it as if it were about to fly away. When Etta showed Mira the wrinkled wafer in the palm of her hand, Mira gasped.

"I wondered what might happen if I didn't eat it. I wondered if it would disappear by itself."

Mira fretted about what to do; should she take it back to the priest? He would think she stole it. She snatched the wafer from Etta's palm and swallowed it. Then she made the sign of the cross and slapped her sister across the face.

Etta was wild; this is how Mira remembered her sister as a child. Philomena was always scrubbing her feet and neck, brushing the tangles out of her hair. Mira, focused on becoming a "lady" (the "little lady" Pop called her), wanted nothing to do with Etta most of the time. But Etta was fearless; she did whatever she wanted.

Mira befriended Etta only when she had no one else, like when Pop took them to the gardens he tended to in Newton. The friendship in the gardens was secretive, delicate. Etta inspired Mira to dance in the grass barefoot, play hide-and-go-seek amidst the arches of wisteria and regal topiary shrubs. They spied through windows at the elegantly decorated homes with marble busts of historic people, chintz curtains, and Oriental rugs, and eavesdropped on mundane conversations between the maids while crouching in the bushes with their hands over their mouths.

Mira remembered the white cat that used to lick the dew off the flower petals; they would find it there at the edge of the path suckling the marigolds in the morning. Then Etta touched her tongue to the dew on the dahlias as the humidity of July reverberated sweetly in the air and the lush blooms toppled over into the path. Mira tasted a cool bead on the petal of a rose that reminded her of a banana cream pie. Then Etta put a petal in her mouth, one, then two; she started devouring an entire rose. She gave one to Mira to eat; the petal was moist and soft; it slipped down her throat as inconspicuously as air.

When Pop saw this he swore at them in Italian. "Don't I feed you enough! Stop eating the flowers!" Mira often wondered if Etta thought of that place, where things were different.

§

It was poor decision-making, impulsiveness that brought Etta pain and as much as she tried, Mira lacked sympathy. More than this, she was intimidated by Etta's dark mystery and was hesitant to delve into it. On some level, she knew Etta knew this. Mira learned to appreciate the humility of her life. She learned to be satisfied with moments. There was renewal in these moments; she happened upon them as she might happen upon a perfectly formed conch shell. This *Gift from the Sea*, humble approach toward life was contrary to the arrogance and selfishness inherent when one pursued an elevated connection to life, as Etta had.

But she didn't have to die for it.

In the middle of the night Mira awoke to the sound of her daughter grinding her teeth. Unable to get back to sleep, she moved from the bed to the window and peered out to see if dawn was coming. But this was the West and the sky and the ocean were still congealed in a darkness. Etta stirred, pulling at the covers and shifting in the bed next to Mira's. *She is awake*, Mira thought to herself. *She is looking at me.* "What are you doing standing there?" Etta asked.

"I'm watching the night. Samantha woke me up with her teeth grinding."

"I used to worry she was going to hurt herself," Etta said. "So I rubbed her back. That usually worked."

"Did she wake you too?"

"No, I need to take a pill. That's the only way I'll sleep," Etta said. She fumbled toward the bathroom. Mira felt pain when she did this, a clenched pain right in the middle of her throat, as if something was stuck there and she couldn't swallow it. Her sister, there, diagnosed with cancer, stumbling past her sleeping child in his portable crib to get a pill because she was afraid. The light to the bathroom spilled across the room floor. Mira saw Etta looking at her face in the mirror. Does she see what I see, a face, slightly gaunt, the dark circles under her eyes, the exhaustion that comes with perpetual anxiety? Etta fumbled with her pills, shut off the light, and went back to bed.

They lay awake in silence. Etta thought about the boats rocking in the mists of Fisherman's Wharf, their masts tolling like bells. The mists had come in to San Francisco surreptitiously, like ghosts; they engulfed the islands, the water, stole the tops off buildings. The bone chilling mists were out there now hiding the moon and the stars. Etta thought of the redwoods in Muir woods, the sunlight spattered through the canopy. They had seen one felled, counted its rings. They had taken pictures of themselves inside the cave of a trunk. Etta had an affinity for those old tree souls. But the mists, unlike the redwood trees, were restless spirits; they were the restless spirits of everyone Etta had known and not known. Patsy, Hank, Vincent, Jack Kerouac, Allen Ginsberg. She had looked up Vincent, dialed a few numbers, hung up. What was the point? She was fifteen years too late and she was dying.

The hills of California were covered in mustard blossoms. The land was lovely and that old song, "This Land is Your Land" came to Etta's mind. Gloucester is a nook, a slight wrinkle on the coast, but the land in California seemed to go on forever, like a giant supine body with curvaceous gold skin. Etta was anxious. She came here to know what she had missed; she came here to find a new hope, because in her mind, California not only had expanse of land and sea, but expanse of mind. She sensed some of the ripples, the way people dressed in vibrant colors and were carefree, out playing frisbee on park lawns or contorting themselves on mats or playing guitars on park benches; she saw them laughing aloud at cafe tables, or huddled with their noses in books. But she would not grasp the full meaning of this mindset from a vacation that lasted five days. It was all a waste of time, she had concluded, walking along with others, cameras dangling from their necks, tiresome images of the Golden Gate on everything from magnets to towels.

It was her preoccupation with her son's accoutrements that eased her nerves, surprisingly, the stroller, the diapers, the baby food, the clothes, the toys. Etta liked to travel light and she worried, before she gave birth, that all the *stuff* that came with a baby was going to be burdensome, that it would turn into more minutiae, and it would wear her down. Now that she was dying, everything associated with her son was precious. He was that new epicenter and she quaked and quivered with life just thinking about him, how he was hers, created by her body. She had noticed boys, teenagers, young men who had her son's features. Yes, she said to herself, in time, he would have that boy's lean frame, long limbs, his curls, the shape of that young man's brow and jaw, or that man's gait.

Then there was Mira, her belief that Etta could beat the cancer. They had walked in the park at Fisherman's Wharf and came across a statue of St. Francis with his arms spread out. Mira had remarked that he looked like a woman and Etta had thought the same thing. So in our minds, it's a woman, she said. Woman in the shape of a cross. Etta wanted to reach out and clutch Mira's hand when she said this.

Life was going on all around, waiters taking orders, pigeons pecking at sidewalk crumbs, people walking, talking, drinking, laughing, being alive. Etta did not begrudge Union Square its vivacity. They sat drinking wine at a cafe, while the afternoon bustle eased into evening. Mira looked at her sister, how she shielded her face from the sun.

"I want to talk to you about something," Etta said.

Mira swallowed her wine and it stung her throat. She knew what was coming.

"I want you to take him when I'm gone."

"Why are you talking like gloom and doom again? You're going to be around for a long time," Mira said, waving her hand at her sister.

"He'll need a family."

"I don't like talking about this."

"We have to talk about this!"

"What about Patrick, what about his father?"

Etta sat back and fingered the thin stem of her wine glass. "This is the thing," she said, "he's not the father."

Mira had resisted the statement and watched the pigeons at her feet peck at crumbs of bread. The more they pecked the more the bread evaded them. They went in circles, with their necks highlighted in a dirty haze of color.

"Do you get some sort of joy out of doing this? Don't you know that what you do has ramifications in other people's lives? What about the father, does he know? What about Patrick? What about me? You're playing with people's lives here."

"Patrick is sterile, Mira. I told him my situation from the beginning. Look," Etta said, "I was ready for a baby. It's the dying thing, well, that was entirely un-fucking planned."

Etta sipped her wine and withdrew a cigarette from the pack stashed in her purse. Mira grabbed Etta's glass and poured its contents into her own.

"Who is the father?"

"Daniel."

Mira downed the wine. "You're sure," she said.

Etta looked at her sister and said nothing. She sipped her wine and put the glass back down. Mira was still looking at her, holding the glass above the concrete of the patio. She could have let it go, the fragile glass with its delicate neck, and have it crash below them on the patio, and have the wine stain the stone, permanently. But Etta's eyes were wide, like a wild animal's when the sun goes down, all pupil, all vacuous space.

"Yes, I'm sure."

"Etta, Etta, Etta," Mira said, starting to laugh maniacally. "This is all crazy." She waved her hand at her sister and changed the subject. She swallowed more wine. "You moved to get away from us."

"What?"

"You heard me."

"Don't change the subject."

Mira laughed.

The waitress came around and Etta ordered fried calamari. Mira was going to need something in her stomach. She watched Samantha making her way through the crowded street with the stroller. She didn't have much time.

"This is a mess. You have to tell Daniel. You have to set things straight."

"When the time is right."

Mira swirled the glass of wine, watching the liquid grab at the glass.

"Stop it!" Etta said. "Can't you see this important to me? Can't you see this is everything to me? You need to promise me Mira, that you will give him a family. You know how to do that. Better than anyone I know."

They sat there in the cool night and Mira started to turn inward. She drank more wine in silence while Etta smoked and Samantha approached. Then she heard it come from her own mouth, a cry, louder than the casual conversations at the street cafe. "No! No! No!" She slammed her finger on the table and the empty glasses wobbled. People turned to look at her. "You're not going to fucking die on me. I'm not promising anything."

Mira could see the lines on her sister's face. She was not a wild girl anymore. She looked old. She looked like her mother and father at the same time. Mira turned away, saw her daughter maneuvering the stroller through the crowded streets, her determined face to get to them. It disappeared in a wash of strangers. It reappeared. Mira quieted herself and sat back, thinking about the ways of the world, thinking about the woman in the shape of a cross trying to embrace the world. There was something wrong with her. There was something missing. There should have been holes in her palms.

CHARON
Michaelis, 1976

Michaelis held onto the hope that Persephone had survived, that after he and his cousin motored away, she floated peacefully to the surface, fully conscious, and the waves gently carried her to shore in the hopeful light of the moon. Someone, some kind soul would find her on the side of the road, dripping wet, just as he had, and take her home. Beautiful Persephone would get to live out her life, get married, have children, be happy. This is what Michaelis wanted more than anything.

When Michaelis saw on the evening news that Persephone was a girl named Elise Vanderhost, that she was seventeen-years old, that she had a mother and a brother and an estranged father, he grabbed a bottle of vodka and went to his garage. He shut the windows and the garage door. He sat in the car and wept, drinking the vodka. He wept for Persephone and he wept for himself, because he did not want to die. He drank the vodka, trying to sink his conscious mind, drown it so that he would get the nerve to turn the key. He saw his cousin's face, heard him cursing him, disgusted by his weakness. He thought of his parents in Greece, how they were supposed to call, how they would be worried about him when he did not answer. He closed his eyes and saw the girl's curtain of hair over her face, rippling like a river over the pillow. He had used the pillow to hush the girl. This is what he remembered: the pillow. He turned the key and heard the car hiccup a few times before the engine took hold.

In the dark dream, he returned to the boat; he could hear someone maneuvering oars. When he looked behind him, a man was there in a hooded cloak. He called out to him, but the man said nothing. Across the water were ships with sails that were illuminated. Michaelis could smell a sweet fragrance waft across the water. He heard the ships creak, as they rocked slowly on their keels, saw the silhouettes of men juxtaposed among the masts. He looked over the edge of the boat and saw forms in the water. He wondered if they were Sirens. He saw how the forms shifted and billowed; they twisted and unfurled, danced and wavered. But they were silent. When he looked closer, he saw that the forms were not sirens, but discarded clothing, skirts, pants, coats, shirts floating in the waves.

He asked the man if he was dead and the man said nothing. They floated peacefully for a while and then the boat drifted to shore, to a sandy beach. The man in the hood motioned for him to get out. Michaelis looked around him. The mountains of Naxos were veiled silhouettes. There in the sand were footprints and the hooded man motioned to them. Michaelis got out of the boat and followed the footprints to a path through the brush and up into the cliffs of the mountainside. He walked the path and came to a place overlooking the ocean where there were whitewashed chapels and the dwellings of the hillside. He came to an opening where there was a bench under a walnut tree with half-eroded statues of ancient bodies adorned in arrays of bougainvillea. There was a woman sitting there, next to a line of small bowls.

Michaelis knew the woman was Melina. This was the place where he spied on her, watched her dance, feed her cats salted fish, let down her hair. He eavesdropped on her private conversations with herself and watched her disrobe and go skinny-dipping in the tidal pool below. Melina, who roamed the beach and the verdant valleys looking for herbs and flowers; the same girl whose mother had suddenly died and was forced to take her place at home as caretaker of her brothers and sisters. Melina, with her black shoulder-length hair now braided and pinned, her limbs a pale white; Melina the town beauty who turned down all of his friends when they asked to take her to the movies, who dozed with her cats under the Cycladican sun only to be rudely awakened by her father beckoning her.

It was amusing, something to do, observe the tender private world of a girl, until Michaelis fell from the olive tree and Melina cursed at him in a torrent of words that made him blush. He was intrigued by her sudden fiery manner, he begged her to allow him to make it up to her. She reluctantly acquiesced, and he built a cedar bench for her to sit on and gaze out at the sea. Her hideaway became their hideaway where she learned to trust him, where they shared tyropita from her father's bakery and wine and talked and gossiped and made love.

The woman on the bench did not turn around when he called out to her. It was almost as if she were in a trance watching the sun weave its first thin rays through the mountains. The sky let out a long sigh and it was dawn; the sea swished and hushed and coveted all of its ancient secrets below. He said her name again and she stood up; she looked at him as she did the day he married her at the small chapel carved into the rock and the light poured in the door, and the family danced barefoot around and around them in the sand, holding hands, singing as the musicians played their music and the sun went down in a glorious blaze. It was a look of concern.

"Melina," he said. "I have missed you."

In the darkness he could not see her eyes and her voice was barely audible.

"It will soon pass," she said. A white cat had come then and rubbed itself against Melina's leg. She reached down and picked it up, cradling it in her arms. It started to purr and this made her smile. He felt a hollow pang inside him: how he missed her nurturing ways.

"We made promises, Melina. You and I, we made vows to one another."

"What is the value of a vow, these days, Michaelis?"

Michaelis looked down at the sea and the boat with the hooded man was waiting for him. It rocked gently off shore.

Melina let the cat down to hunt in the grass. She reached into her pocket for seed and a sparrow landed in her hand. She stroked its feathers as the tiny being circled, pecking gently at her palm. "Do you see this bird, Michaelis? It is a simple creature, the way I am a simple woman."

"I am not sure any woman can be regarded as simple, Melina."

"You are wrong, Michaelis. You overcomplicate things. You make life more complicated than it needs to be."

Michaelis sat down on the bench. Dawn diffused into a pale purple and pink over the mountain. It was serene. The ships were now blips on the horizon. "This island here . . . it is a pleasant dream," he said. "It lulls you into thinking you can only be so much, do so much. I wanted more. To be more."

"You are vain."

The bird flew out of Melina's hand and into a branch. Other birds around it started to chirp; the grove was waking up.

"Why did you have to leave that way, Melina. I had no idea. It was a terrible thing to do."

"Is there a proper way to leave a person? I can't spare you the pain, Michaelis. But I can tell you that I learned from you. A dose of vanity isn't necessarily a bad thing."

A bell rang from down below and Melina disappeared. Michaelis backed away. The bell rang again. Disheartened, he took the path down the rocks and stopped. Melina looked down at him like a Madonna in a grotto.

Michaelis got in the boat with the hooded man and sat quietly as the man rowed out to sea. The man was rowing faster and faster back into the darkness, chasing the night as it dwindled. "Where are we going?" he asked the man. The man turned to him and pulled down his hood and Michaelis saw his own face staring back at him.

He awoke in a feverish sweat. He shut the car off and sat there, shaking, as the car was silent and the smell of the engine filled the air. He grabbed the bottle, exited the car, went to the kitchen sink and poured out rest of the vodka. Then he went to bed.

Michaelis decided that if he couldn't kill himself, he should go to confession. He opened the door to the church and saw Father Boutros sitting in front of the icon of Christ. Michaelis was anxious. He put one hand on a pew to steady himself and then went toward the priest. Father Boutros stood up and told him he was happy to see him. He told him to sit down in one of the two chairs positioned before the icon. Michaelis sat down and regarded the icon of Christ. He had never seen it up close before, how the brow was crinkled, how there were Greek symbols that were half-disappeared floating in a haze of gold paint, how Christ had a discerning face and looked like his cousin. Michaelis began the prayer for confession. He spoke it in Greek and Father Boutros gently corrected him when he made a mistake. After the prayer, Father Boutros sat quietly next to him. He was a large man and he had a full beard. Michaelis had never seen him without the prodigious silver cross that he wore on a rope around his neck.

Father Boutros put his hand on Michaelis's back. "Let's begin," he said.

Michaelis put his hands to his face. Father Boutros spoke in a whisper that it was OK. He went down his list of innocuous sins, speaking in English even though Father Boutros was fluent in Greek. It was a means of disguising his terrible sin, to use broken English. Michaelis looked at the discerning face of Christ. He closed his eyes. "This stain," he said. "This stain cannot ever be washed." Michaelis looked into the priest's eyes.

There was a look of concern on the priest's face. "It is not your place to determine whether your sin cannot be cleansed," Father Boutros said.

Michaelis stood up. He was shaking. Father Boutros stood up as well. He put his arm around Michaelis. "It's good that you've come, Michaelis. I am here to tell you that you have done the right thing by coming here. Does it ease your mind to hear me tell you that?"

Michaelis nodded his head.

"You must believe me that by coming here the stain will be cleansed. Your mind will not believe it. It does not forget. Think of something you could do, some compassionate act to help your mind let go of the sin. Because it is your mind that is holding onto the sin, Michaelis, not God. God has already made you clean."

Michaelis shut his eyes and thought of Melina. As Father Boutros comforted him, he thought of how Melina's melancholy permeated everything in the house, how she had become withdrawn and he would come home and find her in bed, or in her robe. How she had become a weight, a stone about his neck, pulling him under and that he was somewhat relieved when he read the note. Michaelis looked down at the blue stain of tears on his shirt. He touched the wet. In a few minutes the stain would be gone; it would be dry. Above him the windows were letting in the last light of the day, the clouds were parting. The icons around him became radiant.

Father Boutros asked him to kneel and he draped his stole over him. In the shelter of the stole, Michaelis felt his breathing become easier. He would have to work to attain Persephone's honor. There were things that must be done.

SUSTENANCE

Mira and Joan, 1986

Joan awakened to the light and felt grace. She watched her daughter shift with the shadows in the room and after a while, saw her make a motion with her hand. Joan couldn't make it out at first, what Elise was doing. Then she saw it; Elise was wagging her finger at her in anger. Grace turned to anxiety and anxiety to despondency. Why in the world would Elise be upset with her? What did she do wrong? Elise faded into the sunlight and Joan wracked her brain for reasons. She waited for Elise to return, but she did not come.

When Joan learned that Etta was sick, she baked a wheat loaf to bring over to Mira's house because it was the right thing to do.

It seemed as if it were only a short time ago Mira grieved for her mother. Soon it would be Etta. How many people would Mira need to lose before the accumulation of her losses was equivalent to that of a daughter? Mira went to Joan for solace, to her kitchen, with the dried herbs hanging from the ceiling and the smell of soda bread and the whistle of the teakettle and the soft songs and crackle of the record player. Mira cried for her dead mother; she cried for her dead father, she cried for estranged sister, and she cried especially for herself. Joan had no profound words of advice, despite living through loss herself; she provided a safe place for Mira's grief to exist and that was enough.

Could Joan ever confide in her about her loss? Joan regarded the dark spaces of the woods, how vegetation disappeared in shadows; below her the surf crashed and hissed and became silent; it retreated, oscillated back. The earth would be soft enough now that it's spring, Joan thought. They—she and Mira—could work it until it opened up and received her daughter, permanently. With Mira's confidence, she would abandon the myth. Joan reached Mira's door and rang the bell.

When Paul moved his family to Gloucester for an engineering job, Mira regarded the house perched atop the knoll overlooking Good Harbor as the end of the Earth. She beat the path through the woods to Joan's small cape in hopes she would find a friend. Mira knew very little about

Joan because Joan was not the one who needed the confidant; Mira was younger, lonelier, more dependent upon people, and less settled with her mind. Mira sensed that Joan had the compassionate heart of a survivor. She had lived through a divorce, the loss of both her parents, and bore the pain of an empty nest. Also, Mira revered Joan for her independence, how she owned her own house and had a career as a professor at the local community college. And yet, Mira and Joan's relationship was not consistent; there were intimate moments in conversation when Mira felt as if she were a good friend and then months would go by and she would not see her. Or she would see her in the supermarket and Joan would be aloof and their conversation trite and disjointed.

During the summer months, Mira and Joan went to yard sales on Saturday mornings. Joan bought items like a portable record player, a stack of old postcards, a rusty pre-war balloon tire bicycle. Mira would not consider buying these things, but Joan saw the potential, the inherent value. The beauty. She replaced the bike's tires and the chain, painted the frame, added a wicker basket. This is what Mira learned from Joan, how beauty isn't immediately apparent and must, at times, be coaxed into existence. The stack of old postcards offered short glimpses into bygone lives; Joan and Mira would have a Friday night tête-à-tête over tea and create scenarios from the short notes on the back of the cards while listening to Joni Mitchell on the record player. It was a distraction of sorts, from the monotony of one's life, to indulge in the nostalgia of a stranger. It was something to talk about.

Mira opened the door; she was pallid with emotional exhaustion. "What's this?" she asked.

"I baked something for you," Joan said, handing Mira the bread.

"Come in."

"I don't want to trouble you," Joan said.

Mira was irked by Joan's refusal to intrude. "I could use a friend."

Mira made Joan a cup of tea. It was five o'clock on a Tuesday in April. The daytrippers walking the beach had gone home. Mira was frustrated again; she wanted Joan to be Etta; she thought of the two of them as children coming back from church or the North End, laughing;

she thought about what it meant being close to someone warm, close to the laughter, to the voice as it came from a mouth; Mira wanted to feel the life there. The two women stared at the dark slate of night rolling in over the water. Mira put her hands to her face to rub her eyes. "The doctor isn't hopeful. It isn't good."

Joan did not probe into what the doctor said; she would not try to point out something hopeful from the technicalities. She looked down at her friend's hand, at the sprinkled light, at the tiny spectrums scattered over her skin. The descending sun had caught Mira's wedding ring and separated itself into a smattering of tiny spectrums over Joan's wrist. It was subtle and soft; it was a serene display. It made Joan feel safe. Mira placed her hand on the table and Joan took it.

Mira's countenance grew soft when Joan took her hand. "At least you have reconciliation," Joan said. Mira stared at the wash of Joan's hand through her tears. It was a warm, kind hand with freckles over the knuckles. It was a good, firm grasp.

Joan regarded the shadow of her teacup on the table. "I'm sorry, Mira. I'm so sorry about this. About Etta. I know it's been difficult, but I know you love her. You've always loved her."

"I thought it would all be different when she moved here. She had a house and a husband. I thought I could finally share my life with her. Then she divorced Daniel and I just wanted to throttle her. But she eventually found what she wanted. She did it her way; I was at peace with that. With letting her be herself, no matter how screwed up it was, so long as she was *here*. I finally accepted her for being her and now she's going to die and not be here anymore."

Joan thought of Elise wagging her finger at her in anger as she glanced at the shadow the teacup cast onto the table; the length of the shadow began to grow before her eyes. In that moment, the sun had passed behind a cloud and the wind whistled in the eaves of the house. Why did she come here? Joan's mind oscillated back and she panicked; was she too old to change? What would change do to her? Would it make things worse? She was of staunch New England stock; such people survived in heartless conditions; she had done so thus far and perhaps that was good enough. Joan took her hand away. Mira was somewhat taken aback that she had removed it so quickly.

They sat for a while in silence and finished their tea. Joan brought both cup and saucer to the sink.

"You never told me about your daughter," Mira said.

Joan stopped. She stared at the faucet of the sink and its small amorphous stains of water.

"Your daughter Elise," Mira continued. "For years we lived next to each other and you never said a word."

"What was I supposed to tell you about her," Joan said coolly.

"Joan," Mira said, staring down at the teacup in front of her. "It's the tenth anniversary of her death. They had it in the newspaper. Her friend Temesia is creating a scholarship in her name at Manchester-Essex High School."

"I didn't know that."

Mira turned to look at Joan, but Joan didn't move.

"I can't imagine..."

"No, you can't. Of course you can't." Joan hung her head and breathed.

"It's OK. You don't have to tell me anything. I just wanted you to know that I know."

Mira succeeded in ensnarling Joan in her pain. Joan didn't know whether it was out of frustration or spite that Mira did so, but she didn't necessarily care either. She felt relieved.

Mira watched Joan nod her head. She rose and fetched Joan's coat from the chair and Joan went home.

CLOUDS OF FIRE

Samantha and Michaelis, 1986

Etta claimed, most adamantly, that the man next door was a voyeur; he was a fucking pervert getting his jollies off her skin and bones. This is what we discussed in lieu of the results of the MRI, which showed that the tumors in her brain, lungs, and liver were all bigger despite the chemo. Etta rushed to the windows in the kitchen to pull the shades down. She threatened to call the cops. My mother stood with her back to the sink looking at the leg of the kitchen table.

"You're getting yourself all worked up," she said.

Patrick pulled back the shade to glance at the neighbor's house. "Please Etta," he said. "He's not looking at you. He's been our neighbor for ten years!"

The baby started to cry and I went to him, picked him up off the floor. He jutted away from me, looked at his mother pacing the room, stretched his arms toward her and cried. She stared at him long and hard. "You can't do that, boy," she said.

Etta slumped down in a chair at the kitchen table. The velour jogging suit she wore was a size too big but softened her hardened edges. "He's waiting," she said. "He'll come for me like he came for her. Sick bastard."

She slammed her fist on the table, leaned toward us, and spoke in a hushed tone how the neighbor was always out there shirtless, weeding in his garden, his dark tan contrasting with his white hair. When he saw her getting out of her car, he came brandishing phallic zucchini and squash. Sometimes he would be on the porch, slumped over having fallen asleep in a chair, and she would feel relief then, that she could get up the driveway and into the house without enduring the awkward dance through heavily accented and abused English. He was just a child when it came to the English language, she said; after so many years of living here he still had the vocabulary of a four-year-old. In his own language, however, she sensed he was someone else, someone with adult problems and concerns and sometimes, at night, when the evening was still and warm and the windows were open, she would eavesdrop, attempting to decipher his adult code in the vast array of complex consonants and vowels of the Greek language. She thought about how the complexity of sounds may have matched a matrix of feelings in that language—rage, depression, sorrow, boredom. But in English, it was just one thing: lust.

"Etta, please," we said.

She brought up the missing panties. She reasoned how could panties be taken so far by the wind, they disappeared? "Remember?" she turned to Patrick, "remember how he was stealing my panties? We laughed about it; it was funny back then. Now it's not so funny is it. None of this is fucking funny." She slammed her fist on the table again. "Fuck it," she said. "I'm going to bed."

Later, when I went to check on her to see if she needed anything, I found her folding her negligees in a gift box. She fetched floral wrapping paper and tied the box with a white satin bow. "Samantha," she said, "you are going to do me a little favor. You are going to take this box to the man next door."

She handed me the box.

"I'm not sure this is a good idea."

"It is an excellent idea."

Etta's anger burned through her dark eyes.

"Go on," she said. "Just do what I tell you. And don't tell Patrick. Or your mother." She made a motion for me to shoo. "Leave it on the doorstep if you are too afraid to deliver it to his door."

I went out the front door, looked up at Etta looming in the window. She shooed me again. I left the box on the porch. Later, I noticed the box was gone and the blinds drawn.

My mother and I went to Etta's house every day after school. We cleaned, cooked, took care of the baby and gave Etta her drugs. She had moved into the guest room permanently to have a better view of the man's house. She spent most of her time sitting in a chair staring out the guest room window. Sometimes I would find her leaning on the windowpane, asleep. I would gently wake her then and help her to the bed despite my being afraid to touch her, feel her ribs, her prominent bones. "I'm cold," she would say. And I would wrap the bed cover around her. Once she was in bed, she would sit up, touch her head; she was always touching her head where the mane of hair used to be.

"I scraped, swept, scrubbed to rid the house of the foulness of death," she said. "But it came back for me."

"You need to rest."

She grabbed my arm. "I gathered up her things, piled them up in that room—doilies, artificial flowers, moth-eaten curtains, broken lamps—and closed the door. Now that door has flung open; the souls of the old coot's belongings coagulate in my brain like a troop of insects." She clutched my arm, waited for my response; I wracked my brain for something hopeful.

"Maybe you should pray," I said.

"Pray? You think a God who hung His son on a cross is going to listen to me?" Then she laughed, pulled up the covers to her chin. "No. This is retribution. I don't know what I did, but I must have done something."

Days passed and Etta remained in bed. Most of the time she slept soundly and we tiptoed around her, removing plates full of food, saucers with dried tea bags. Sometimes she would sit up, awake, but with her eyes closed. The bed covers were piled and spilling over the end of the bed; opened books were strewn across the floor. Some of the books I knew, *Siddhartha* by Herman Hesse, *The Razor's Edge* by William Somerset Maugham. She touched her head. Once when she spoke, it rattled me. Her voice was that of a little girl, demure. She told me that night was serene and delicate and separate from her. It was safe and in that safety she heard it, God's name. She spoke God's name in the silence and the dark. She said that was all that she needed to do because God ached, as she ached, just looking at the soft pout in her son's lips or the pink of his tiny fingernail.

I sat with her a while until she was asleep, then I went to the window; it was staying light into the evening and the air was getting warmer. There were crocuses coming up along the walkway and footprints in the soft mud leading to the driveway. Down the street the neighborhood boys were playing catch with a baseball; I could hear the ball slap at the leather of their gloves. I knew what Etta meant about the night then, how it was serene and delicate and safe and separate from the doom awaiting us.

§

Paintings of Etta were now found everywhere in the house. Patrick painted her with gold leaves in her hair, in a draped sheet. He painted her Vermeer style, as a handmaiden with a bowl of fruit. During her last days, he worked feverishly in his studio on a Madonna and child painting of Etta and the baby. This is what I told my mother: it was one of Maslow's highest of needs, the need to express a sorrow, a longing, a love in the form of art.

While Patrick was in his studio painting Etta-as-Madonna, we snuck Daniel in.

"Is he hers?" Daniel asked my mother. The baby tried to pull himself up onto Etta's bed while she slept. It was morning and the spring light was pouring in through the window.

My mother opened her mouth to speak, but she was interrupted by a groan. It came from Etta, and we all turned to watch her as she blinked her eyes. The life was rushing back into her and we rushed toward it.

I placed the baby at her side. She moved her lips but made no sound. Daniel looked at the baby.

"Da!" the baby said, looking at Daniel.

The baby curled up against his mother. Daniel touched Etta's face. She kissed the backs of his fingers.

Esther Greenwood wedged herself somewhere in the foundation of her mother's house; she needed a safe, close place. When I saw the neighbor's basement door open, I went in, thinking I needed the same thing. The light from the window exposed a place between the washer and dryer; I wanted to know what it might feel like to be interred. I squatted down, lowered myself in sideways, my palm flat against the cold floor. I set my cheek there, over the palm and regarded the black hoses of the washer, the crumbling cement of the foundation, the wispy, weightless spiders, curled up dead in their own traps. The dryer was still warm; it had just finished its cycle. Above me the floorboards squeaked. I shivered; the floor was unbearably damp. I curled up closer to the dryer and waited; I knew he would come, but I didn't care.

It was nearly an hour and the door opened and the light shone down the stairs. The neighbor descended, then stopped at the last stair. "Hello," he said. "Hello? Hello? Who is there? Who is that?" A light went on and the basement joists became visible.

I shimmied out of my place and sat on the cold floor staring up at the man, whose face, now in shadow, was quite severe. The man had black hair on his knuckles, but his hair was white, slicked back.

"I'm hiding," I said.

"Hiding? In my house?"

"Yeah."

"From whom?"

"From death," I said.

"Eh, no one can do that," he said.

Outside the naked locust trees scraped at the darkening sky.

"How is she?" he asked, timidly, nodding his head toward Patrick's house.

"Worse," I said.

The man nodded his head, paused a moment, trying to find the right words. "Eh, Aphrodite," he said. "She is immortal. Do you know what I mean?" and he banged on his heart.

I nodded my head, traced the rim of the dryer with my index finger.

"Do you want something to eat?" he asked.

"No," I said. I let out a long rush of air and went to the door.

The man said, "Wait."

Outside, there were still some old piles of dirty snow and ice along the path. Spring had turned raw and bitter and started spitting rain. The man went to a dark place behind the stairway. He came back and handed me a warped umbrella for the walk home.

"You let me know, yes, when the time comes?"

"The time is now," I said and went out.

I walked home under the broken umbrella, thinking of what a fool I was. The wind blew the umbrella backward breaking the last of its ribs, and I was thrown off balance. I regained my footing and looked east where there were light-filled clouds that shot up from the sea like flames. Then, only a few feet above my head, a gull appeared; I could see the whole of its body, its tucked legs. It dipped, flew higher, dipped again, its slender wings tapping at the air. I started to run with it, the closed umbrella flapping in my hand. I ran faster and faster underneath the waving wings of the gull until she surpassed me, heading toward the progression of clouds and curtains of light. I stopped and watched her take the air currents up and up until she had left me behind.

Michaelis knocked at the side door of his neighbor's house. He was carrying daffodils and a vial of water blessed by Father Boutros. No one answered and he knocked harder and the door squeaked open.

Michaelis remembered the last time he was in the house, how he thought the awful smell was the garbage that his neighbor didn't put out. The son usually came home on weekends and put out the barrels, but he hadn't seen his car in weeks. He opened the door to the foyer and saw no bags of garbage, but the smell was so powerful, he had to breathe out of his handkerchief. Somewhere a record was skipping. He went through a second door and saw the woman, or what was left of her, lying on the floor. That vision was something that stayed with him for months.

He had sat with the dying, prayed with them, read to them; he believed he was an integral part of the emotional and spiritual process, that his service was warranted. But to see that body as it was, he doubted the entire process. He thought perhaps he was kidding himself, and that he was just trying to make himself feel better, deal with the deep-seated guilt that he carried.

The extent of his relationship with the old woman was wishing one another a good day. Once he tried to bring her zucchini and green beans, a head of lettuce and she told him the food would be wasted on her. He believed her, from the looks of her, despite being somewhat offended that she would not take his offerings. He had come to learn that some Americans had no idea the bounty life could provide. She was a woman who simply did not indulge.

The second woman to come and live in the house was different. She had a beauty that resembled the women of Naxos. And her passion and desire for the bounty of life was something he immediately sensed and was drawn to.

He watched her in the yard planting flowers. He told her which plants preferred sun and which shade. He spied on her when she took off her bikini top to sunbathe. He heard her singing to the radio; she had a terrible voice and this made him smile. She was friendly when he talked to her, but aloof, as most beautiful women are. This enticed him more. He wondered what she was doing with an invalid—how could the old woman's son possibly please a woman like that? He was an intellectual, a sensitive artist type. Women *think* this kind of man understands them. They don't know, Michaelis thought to himself, what a healthy, virile man is capable of—. Michaelis gave Etta bouquets of his best zinnias and roses to win her over. He picked his biggest vegetables for her, because he saw her eyeing his garden from over the fence. It felt good to give her things. It felt right, despite her reluctance in taking them. He cannot deny; he had taken some of her things. They secured her image in his mind.

When he noticed the woman was pregnant, he backed off. She became virtuous then. She walked around the yard with her hand on her belly muttering to her babe and he thought of Melina and all of his failed dreams.

Hello? Michaelis called out. He walked in through a second open door and went to the kitchen where there was classical music playing on a portable stereo. He passed into the living room and saw the woman in a hospital bed. She was moaning in her sleep, grabbing fistfuls of blanket. Michaelis was taken aback by the transformation; the beautiful woman with raven hair was just a wisp now, a husk of a body wrestling with its soul for control.

He went to the woman's bedside and placed the daffodils on an end table. He sat down and waited for the woman to open her eyes. When she did, she let out a long howl and this startled Michaelis. *Shhh*, he said. *No, no, no.* He told her what he came to do. But the woman's eyes were filled with terror. She howled again, a long, low-pitched, primordial howl that sounded unworldly. She pulled at her blankets and sheets and Michaelis stood up. Then her lover came down the stairs. He wore a black turtleneck sweater and hobbled with a cane. He had dark circles under his eyes and was surprised to see Michaelis. Michaelis was surprised the son remembered his name. He asked him if he would like something to drink; he was hospitable. "You brought flowers," he said. "Etta, Michaelis brought flowers for you."

Etta glanced anxiously at the table beside her. The daffodils were in full bloom and emanated a cheery yellow. She wondered if he had cut them from around his mailbox. She had thought about it, cutting a few for herself, but she knew that was not likely. If she could speak, she would say, "Leave the daffodils and get out," but this was impossible, so instead, when Michaelis knelt before her, she spat on his head.

Michaelis wiped the saliva off his head with his sleeve. He had seen this before; some were hostile to dying. He tried to explain that he came to give Etta water; he and the people of his church used it to anoint the dying. He was certain that the holy water would bring the woman peace. He had seen it work on so many people, how it soothed them of their restless fits. He reached into his coat pocket and brought forth a small glass vial. He placed it in Patrick's hand.

"You can do it," Michaelis said.

He made a motion toward Etta's forehead. Etta's eyes grew wide. She moaned a little. Michaelis handed Patrick a white cloth from his pocket. Patrick poured out some of the water onto the cloth and dabbed Etta's forehead. Etta relaxed and closed her eyes. Michaelis moved closer to her, spoke softly. He spoke in Greek. The sound of the man's foreign words was welcoming to Etta. She took in his words. She had lain in the bed for days while people tiptoed around her. She was burdened by the loneliness and alienation of dying and the two men anointing her with water and words settled her. She drifted off to sleep and dreamt the dream of the dying.

Patrick handed the vial back to Michaelis and Michaelis put it in his pocket. He walked Michaelis to the door, put out his hand, and Michaelis took it. "Thank you," he said. Michaelis looked at the man in front of him. He seemed much older than his age might dictate.

What this life does to us, he thought and went back home.

EPILOGUE

One week after Etta died, Mira had dreams of searching for her in the North Shore Mall. In one dream, she had been waiting for her sister in the shoe department at Macy's for sometime, and she never showed. She wandered over to the Clinique counter where women with penciled-in eyebrows were painting the lips of old ladies and scented tissues were flittering about like birds. When a bomb went off, the impersonal souls reacted to it as if it were an everyday event. People went about their business despite the fact that a hole was blown right through the middle of the mall and metal beams and concrete and electrical wiring jutted out here and there.

Mira could feel her blood pulse with the pity she had for herself. She wanted to be loved. She wanted to shout out to the world how incredibly lonely she was, but she wouldn't allow herself to do this even in a dream. Instead, she contemplated taking antidepressants.

The metal beams in the gaping hole yawned; children dangled from wires like ornaments. Mira reached the end of the mall, a dull, obscure place with angular shadows, and exited the glass doors into the falling snow. She was anxious and alone. Then she saw the girl with the Magdalene hair under the light of a street lamp, smoking a cigarette. The girl seemed familiar, but she could not place her.

At this point, Mira was kicked awake by her husband's spastic leg.

In the second part of the dream she searched for Etta in a garden in Newton. Mira walked the path under the wisteria trellis to a fountain—a majestic cement urn with a pool of water spilling over its brim. Mira found Etta's sneakers floating in the water. Etta had danced here. But in the dream, the mansion was now an abandoned building with boarded doors and broken windows. Mira went to the urn. She first saw her face warped by the motion of the water. Then the water became still and she saw a form floating. The form twisted itself like the smoke of a cigarette. Its tendrils of hair became evident; its white dress buoyed up like a plume. Mira thought perhaps the twisting image was an angel, but then she realized it was the girl. The girl extended her hand and Mira took it and plunged in headfirst.

In the dark space of the underworld, she identified the timeless part of her. She identified each shade as it came forward and whispered a name. She felt ecstasy—a glorious love that buoyed her up. Mira breathed easy now. New spaces opened up between her bones, if only for a moment, as she retired her earthly density and ascended into the air above the bed.

I can only wish such a thing for my mother.

What did happen was this: two weeks after Etta died, Mrs. Cassidy called from the main office at the high school to tell me the custodians found my sculpture in the basement. She asked me if I still wanted it. I came to believe it was Etta's doing, a message of sorts that perhaps she was found too, wherever she had gone to.

I keep the statue on my desk, for inspiration. I've written a lot about Etta, trying to recreate her through memories. I noticed however, that the Etta in the stories was different than the Etta I knew and loved; her mystery had remained intact. The Etta in my writing had more of me in her. In this way she was a catalyst, a means for me to find names for all the unnamed sensibilities going on inside me, which I suppose was her intention in the first place when she gave me the notebook.

I guess this makes me found as well.

Sometimes, when I look out at Salt Island I think I can see her walking the place where the sea parts over the sand. She is the goddess we've left behind. And yet it is she who rises when we feel the divine presence of love, and when we nurse our broken hearts and learn ultimately that these are less sorrows than they are threads, leading us from one place to the next.

ACKNOWLEDGMENTS

Many thanks to the following journals for publishing excerpts, including Ovunque Siamo ("Thirst"), pacificReview at San Diego State University ("The Death of Aphrodite"), Madcap Review ("Mermaid," nominated for Best of the Net), Fickle Muses ("Dark Night of the Soul"), and So to Speak at George Mason University ("Novelty Fades").

Thanks also to Doug Glover, Abby Frucht, and Diane Lefer, my advisers at Vermont College who read primordial drafts of the novel. A special thanks to Erin Miller for reading an earlier draft and for making me laugh when I needed to about the vicissitudes of writing, publishing, and life in general. A second special thanks goes out to Nic Grosso, for formatting, reformatting, and reformatting again, and to Catherine Parnell for her impeccable eye.

I am grateful for the support of my fellow unicorns Jennifer Martelli and Olivia Kate Cerrone, my pen pal Vincent Panella, and all of the literary paisans at Bordighera Press and IAM Books, including Nicola Orichuia and Julia Lisella. I am grateful also to my sister Andrea and my mother Camella for shielding me in love when I most needed it; to Jane Mosco for making me feel human; to Cynthia Boyd for challenging me; to Diana Lynch for her knowledge, support, and delicious artisan dinners; to my husband Richard Folk, whose love keeps me balanced and sane; to my children Stephen and Marielle, who give joy and meaning to my life; and finally to my dog Josie who keeps me company during long walks in the woods when I contemplate my imaginary worlds.

ABOUT THE AUTHOR

LAURETTE FOLK's fiction, essays, and poems have been published in *upstreet*, *Waxwing*, *Gravel*, *Flash Fiction Magazine*, *Mom Egg Review*, *pacificREVIEW*, *Boston Globe Magazine*, and *Best Small Fictions 2019*. Her novel, *A Portal to Vibrancy*, was published by Big Table in June 2014 and won the Independent Press Award for New Adult Fiction. *Totem Beasts*, her collection of poetry and flash fiction, was published by Big Table in May 2017. She is a graduate of the Vermont College MFA in Writing program. Her website is www.laurettefolk.com.

VIA FOLIOS

A refereed book series dedicated to the culture of Italians and Italian Americans.

LEWIS TURCO. *The Hero Enkidu*. Vol 107. Poetry. $14

AL TACCONELLI. *Perhaps Fly*. Vol 106. Poetry. $14

RACHEL GUIDO DEVRIES. *A Woman Unknown in Her Bones*. Vol 105. Poetry. $11

BERNARD BRUNO. *A Tear and a Tear in My Heart*. Vol 104. Non-fiction. $20

FELIX STEFANILE. *Songs of the Sparrow*. Vol 103. Poetry. $30

FRANK POLIZZI. *A New Life with Bianca*. Vol 102. Poetry. $10

GIL FAGIANI. *Stone Walls*. Vol 101. Poetry. $14

LOUISE DESALVO. *Casting Off*. Vol 100. Fiction. $22

MARY JO BONA. *I Stop Waiting for You*. Vol 99. Poetry. $12

RACHEL GUIDO DEVRIES. *Stati zitt, Josie*. Vol 98. Children's Literature. $8

GRACE CAVALIERI. *The Mandate of Heaven*. Vol 97. Poetry. $14

MARISA FRASCA. *Via incanto*. Vol 96. Poetry. $12

DOUGLAS GLADSTONE. *Carving a Niche for Himself*. Vol 95. History. $12

MARIA TERRONE. *Eye to Eye*. Vol 94. Poetry. $14

CONSTANCE SANCETTA. *Here in Cerchio*. Vol 93. Local History. $15

MARIA MAZZIOTTI GILLAN. *Ancestors' Song*. Vol 92. Poetry. $14

MICHAEL PARENTI. *Waiting for Yesterday: Pages from a Street Kid's Life*. Vol 90. Memoir. $15

ANNIE LANZILLOTTO. *Schistsong*. Vol 89. Poetry. $15

EMANUEL DI PASQUALE. *Love Lines*. Vol 88. Poetry. $10

CAROSONE & LOGIUDICE. *Our Naked Lives*. Vol 87. Essays. $15

JAMES PERICONI. *Strangers in a Strange Land: A Survey of Italian-Language American Books*.Vol 86. Book History. $24

DANIELA GIOSEFFI. *Escaping La Vita Della Cucina*. Vol 85. Essays. $22

MARIA FAMÀ. *Mystics in the Family*. Vol 84. Poetry. $10

ROSSANA DEL ZIO. *From Bread and Tomatoes to Zuppa di Pesce "Ciambotto"*.Vol. 83. $15

LORENZO DELBOCA. *Polentoni*. Vol 82. Italian Studies. $15

SAMUEL GHELLI. *A Reference Grammar*. Vol 81. Italian Language. $36

ROSS TALARICO. *Sled Run*. Vol 80. Fiction. $15

FRED MISURELLA. *Only Sons*. Vol 79. Fiction. $14

FRANK LENTRICCHIA. *The Portable Lentricchia*. Vol 78. Fiction. $16

RICHARD VETERE. *The Other Colors in a Snow Storm*. Vol 77. Poetry. $10

GARIBALDI LAPOLLA. *Fire in the Flesh*. Vol 76 Fiction & Criticism. $25

GEORGE GUIDA. *The Pope Stories*. Vol 75 Prose. $15

ROBERT VISCUSI. *Ellis Island*. Vol 74. Poetry. $28

ELENA GIANINI BELOTTI. *The Bitter Taste of Strangers Bread*. Vol 73. Fiction. $24

PINO APRILE. *Terroni*. Vol 72. Italian Studies. $20

EMANUEL DI PASQUALE. *Harvest*. Vol 71. Poetry. $10

ROBERT ZWEIG. *Return to Naples*. Vol 70. Memoir. $16

AIROS & CAPPELLI. *Guido*. Vol 69. Italian/American Studies. $12

FRED GARDAPHÉ. *Moustache Pete is Dead! Long Live Moustache Pete!*. Vol 67. Literature/Oral History. $12

PAOLO RUFFILLI. *Dark Room/Camera oscura*. Vol 66. Poetry. $11

HELEN BAROLINI. *Crossing the Alps*. Vol 65. Fiction. $14

COSMO FERRARA. *Profiles of Italian Americans*. Vol 64. Italian Americana. $16

GIL FAGIANI. *Chianti in Connecticut*. Vol 63. Poetry. $10

BASSETTI & D'ACQUINO. *Italic Lessons*. Vol 62. Italian/American Studies. $10

CAVALIERI & PASCARELLI, Eds. *The Poet's Cookbook*. Vol 61. Poetry/Recipes. $12

EMANUEL DI PASQUALE. *Siciliana*. Vol 60. Poetry. $8

NATALIA COSTA, Ed. *Bufalini*. Vol 59. Poetry. $18.

RICHARD VETERE. *Baroque*. Vol 58. Fiction. $18.

LEWIS TURCO. *La Famiglia/The Family*. Vol 57. Memoir. $15

NICK JAMES MILETI. *The Unscrupulous*. Vol 56. Humanities. $20

BASSETTI. ACCOLLA. D'AQUINO. *Italici: An Encounter with Piero Bassetti*. Vol 55. Italian Studies. $8

GIOSE RIMANELLI. *The Three-legged One*. Vol 54. Fiction. $15

CHARLES KLOPP. *Bele Antiche Stòrie*. Vol 53. Criticism. $25

JOSEPH RICAPITO. *Second Wave*. Vol 52. Poetry. $12

GARY MORMINO. *Italians in Florida*. Vol 51. History. $15

GIANFRANCO ANGELUCCI. *Federico F.* Vol 50. Fiction. $15

ANTHONY VALERIO. *The Little Sailor*. Vol 49. Memoir. $9

ROSS TALARICO. *The Reptilian Interludes*. Vol 48. Poetry. $15

RACHEL GUIDO DE VRIES. *Teeny Tiny Tino's Fishing Story*. Vol 47. Children's Literature. $6

EMANUEL DI PASQUALE. *Writing Anew*. Vol 46. Poetry. $15

MARIA FAMÀ. *Looking For Cover*. Vol 45. Poetry. $12

ANTHONY VALERIO. *Toni Cade Bambara's One Sicilian Night*. Vol 44. Poetry. $10

EMANUEL CARNEVALI. *Furnished Rooms*. Vol 43. Poetry. $14

BRENT ADKINS. et al., Ed. *Shifting Borders. Negotiating Places*. Vol 42. Conference. $18

GEORGE GUIDA. *Low Italian*. Vol 41. Poetry. $11

GARDAPHÈ, GIORDANO, TAMBURRI. *Introducing Italian Americana*. Vol 40. Italian/American Studies. $10

DANIELA GIOSEFFI. *Blood Autumn/Autunno di sangue*. Vol 39. Poetry. $15/$25

FRED MISURELLA. *Lies to Live By*. Vol 38. Stories. $15

STEVEN BELLUSCIO. *Constructing a Bibliography*. Vol 37. Italian Americana. $15

ANTHONY JULIAN TAMBURRI, Ed. *Italian Cultural Studies 2002*. Vol 36. Essays. $18

BEA TUSIANI. *con amore*. Vol 35. Memoir. $19

FLAVIA BRIZIO-SKOV, Ed. *Reconstructing Societies in the Aftermath of War*. Vol 34. History. $30

TAMBURRI. et al., Eds. *Italian Cultural Studies 2001*. Vol 33. Essays. $18

ELIZABETH G. MESSINA, Ed. *In Our Own Voices*. Vol 32. Italian/
American Studies. $25

STANISLAO G. PUGLIESE. *Desperate Inscriptions*. Vol 31. History. $12

HOSTERT & TAMBURRI, Eds. *Screening Ethnicity*. Vol 30. Italian/
American Culture. $25

G. PARATI & B. LAWTON, Eds. *Italian Cultural Studies*. Vol 29. Essays. $18

HELEN BAROLINI. *More Italian Hours*. Vol 28. Fiction. $16

FRANCO NASI, Ed. *Intorno alla Via Emilia*. Vol 27. Culture. $16

ARTHUR L. CLEMENTS. *The Book of Madness & Love*. Vol 26. Poetry. $10

JOHN CASEY, et al. *Imagining Humanity*. Vol 25. Interdisciplinary Studies. $18

ROBERT LIMA. *Sardinia/Sardegna*. Vol 24. Poetry. $10

DANIELA GIOSEFFI. *Going On*. Vol 23. Poetry. $10

ROSS TALARICO. *The Journey Home*. Vol 22. Poetry. $12

EMANUEL DI PASQUALE. *The Silver Lake Love Poems*. Vol 21. Poetry. $7

JOSEPH TUSIANI. *Ethnicity*. Vol 20. Poetry. $12

JENNIFER LAGIER. *Second Class Citizen*. Vol 19. Poetry. $8

FELIX STEFANILE. *The Country of Absence*. Vol 18. Poetry. $9

PHILIP CANNISTRARO. *Blackshirts*. Vol 17. History. $12

LUIGI RUSTICHELLI, Ed. *Seminario sul racconto*. Vol 16. Narrative. $10

LEWIS TURCO. *Shaking the Family Tree*. Vol 15. Memoirs. $9

LUIGI RUSTICHELLI, Ed. *Seminario sulla drammaturgia*. Vol 14. Theater/
Essays. $10

FRED GARDAPHÈ. *Moustache Pete is Dead! Long Live Moustache Pete!*. Vol
13. Oral Literature. $10

JONE GAILLARD CORSI. *Il libretto d'autore. 1860 – 1930*. Vol 12. Criticism. $17

HELEN BAROLINI. *Chiaroscuro: Essays of Identity*. Vol 11. Essays. $15

PICARAZZI & FEINSTEIN, Eds. *An African Harlequin in Milan*. Vol 10.
Theater/Essays. $15

JOSEPH RICAPITO. *Florentine Streets & Other Poems*. Vol 9. Poetry. $9

FRED MISURELLA. *Short Time*. Vol 8. Novella. $7

NED CONDINI. *Quartettsatz*. Vol 7. Poetry. $7

ANTHONY JULIAN TAMBURRI, Ed. *Fuori: Essays by Italian/American
Lesbiansand Gays*. Vol 6. Essays. $10

ANTONIO GRAMSCI. P. Verdicchio. Trans. & Intro. *The Southern Question*.
Vol 5.Social Criticism. $5

DANIELA GIOSEFFI. *Word Wounds & Water Flowers*. Vol 4. Poetry. $8

WILEY FEINSTEIN. *Humility's Deceit: Calvino Reading Ariosto Reading
Calvino*. Vol 3. Criticism. $10

PAOLO A. GIORDANO, Ed. *Joseph Tusiani: Poet. Translator. Humanist*. Vol 2.
Criticism. $25

ROBERT VISCUSI. *Oration Upon the Most Recent Death of Christopher
Columbus*. Vol 1. Poetry.